When All Is Said and Prayed:

Book One of the Forever Divas Series

When All Is Said and Prayed:

Book One of the Forever Divas Series

E.N. Joy

www.urbanbooks.net

Urban Books, LLC
97 N18th Street
Wyandanch, NY 11798

When All Is Said and Prayed: Book One of the Forever
Divas Series Copyright © 2015 E.N. Joy

ISBN 13: 978-1-62286-723-3
ISBN 10: 1-62286-723-8

First Mass Market Printing March 2016
First Trade Paperback Printing October 2015
Printed in the United States of America

10 9 8 7 6 5 4 3 2 1

*This is a work of fiction. Any references or similar-
ities to actual events, real people, living or dead, or
to real locales are intended to give the novel a sense
of reality. Any similarity in other names, characters,
places, and incidents is entirely coincidental.*

Distributed by Kensington Publishing Corp.
Submit Orders to:
Customer Service
400 Hahn Road
Westminster, MD 21157-4627
Phone: 1-800-733-3000
Fax: 1-800-659-2436

When All Is Said and Prayed:

Book One of the Forever Divas Series

E.N. Joy

OTHER BOOKS BY E.N. JOY:

Me, Myself and Him
She Who Finds a Husband
Been There, Prayed That
Love, Honor or Stray
Trying to Stay Saved
I Can Do Better All By Myself
And You Call Yourself a Christian
The Perfect Christian
The Sunday Only Christian
Ordained by the Streets
"*A Woman's Revenge*"
(Anthology: *Best Served Cold*)
I Ain't Me No More
More Than I Can Bear
You Get What You Pray For
Behind Every Good Woman (eBook only)
She's No Angel (eBook series)
Angel on the Front Pew (eBook series)
California Angel (eBook series)
Flower in My Hair
The Secret Olivia Told Me (N. Joy)
Operation Get Rid of Mom's New Boyfriend
(N. Joy)
Sabella and the Castle Belonging to the Troll
(N. Joy)

Dedication

This book is dedicated to my sisters, Jawan, I'na, Wakeelah, and Samari. We are family. I got all my sisters with me!

Acknowledgments

God, you never, ever cease to amaze me. The way you allow your message for your children to flow through me is so humbling. On my own, I could never come up with the words to help deliver your people. On my own, I can do nothing. With you, I can do all you call me to. You called me to be a writer. I write, not to become a famous author, but to make you famous with my words. The goal is not that when I enter a room, everyone knows who I am, but that through my work, everyone gets to know you.

Chapter 1

"You may be older than me, but I'm prettier," said four-year-old Norma to her older sister, Adele. Even though she was a few inches shorter than Adele, she stood there with her hands on her hips, leaning in as if she were towering over Adele, instead of looking up to her.

"How you gon' be prettier than me?" replied Adele, who was almost six years old, with her hands on her hips, looking down at her little sister, who mirrored her stance. "We look just alike."

"Yeah, but I'm light." Norma rubbed the skin on her arm. "Your arm is dark, so I'm prettier."

"Stop it right now!" Paige shouted from the doorway of the den, where, the last time she'd checked on them, her two daughters had been sitting on the rug in front of the television, watching it. She threw the dish towel she had been drying her hands with on the floor and marched over to her girls. "I have the dishwater running, the microwave going, and Tamar Braxton playing on my phone. And I can still hear you two arguing over all that."

Paige didn't realize she had assumed the exact same stance as her Mini-mes. Her fists were planted on her hips, and she had a plaid apron tied around her thick waist. She'd been finishing up dinner. She hadn't clearly heard the words that had been coming out of her girls' mouths that past few moments during their argument. It was an argument that had started with one of them wanting to turn the channel rather than watch the program they had both initially agreed on. But Paige knew by their tones and how loud they were that they were not having a friendly conversation.

"Now turn off this television, and both of you, go to your rooms now." Paige pointed to the thirty-two-inch flat-screen television that was mounted on one of the mustard-colored walls.

"But she started it." Adele pointed to her younger sister. "Why am I in trouble?"

Wobbling her head, Norma replied, "And I finished it too, ugly."

"I'm not ugly. If I'm ugly, then Mommy is ugly, because she's dark too."

The girls continued to go back and forth. Paige was in a temporary state of shock. Had her younger daughter just told her older daughter that she was ugly? And why had her older daughter assumed that she was ugly because she had dark skin?

Norma's words had knocked Paige back in time, to a childhood during which she was teased for having dark skin. *Oreo. Charcoal. Black monkey. Darky. Blacky. Midnight. Tar baby.* Paige could hear the voices of her tormentors on the playground. As she got older and society gave celebrities like Wesley Snipes and Denzel Washington credit for making darker black skin beautiful, sexy, and attractive, Paige had become comfortable with and accepting of the skin God had given her. She no longer looked at it as a flaw. After all, these celebrities had brought dark skin "into style."

El DeBarge and dem were on a time-out until actors like Michael Ealy and Terrence Howard brought light skin back into style again . . . according to only some members of society, of course. Not all, and certainly not Paige. When all had been said and whispered, Paige had determined that society's opinion about what was considered beautiful really hadn't played a role in how she felt about her complexion. She had just matured, and she liked to think that so had her generation as a whole. She assumed that such opinions about dark skin and light skin had vanished, along with her generation's immaturity and ignorance, leaving no traces behind for the next generation to dip and dabble in. She had honestly thought this whole "light skin, dark skin" thing had died out. Clearly, it had not. Otherwise, where in the world would her child have gotten this crazy idea from, and how could she have allowed it to come out of her mouth?

"You just mad because you're black," Norma said, adding insult to injury. "And I'm pretty, light, and almost white." She rubbed her arm. "Just like Daddy's side of the family."

Paige saw her past self in the hurtful expression on Adele's face. The child's little brown face had dropped to the floor, along with bits and pieces of her self-esteem.

"Who told you that?" Paige stormed. Norma's last statement had snapped Paige out of her thoughts from the past and into the present. The pain on Adele's face made her want to seek revenge for her daughter—for her younger self. At that moment she didn't even see young Norma as her offspring. Instead, she was just another kid on the playground, taunting and throwing jabs. Paige bent down and grabbed her youngest daughter by both her arms and squeezed. "Who told you that, Norma? You tell me right now!" Paige shook Norma's bony little shoulders. "Who told you that white was better than black?"

"Nobody, Mommy," Norma said, her eyes full of fear and at the same time filling with tears.

"Then why are you saying it?" Paige asked. "You had to have gotten it from somewhere, or else you wouldn't be saying it."

"I don't know." Norma shrugged, and a tear slid down her cheek.

Realizing her actions had frightened her daughter, Paige released Norma and stood up straight. Norma began bawling.

"It's okay, Norma," Adele said as she put her arm around her sister's shoulders. "Let's go to our rooms."

Norma sniffed and wiped tears as her older sister escorted her out of the den. Adele shot Paige a look over her shoulder that said, "Bad mommy," and the two girls disappeared down the hall. Paige could hear them trekking up the stairs. Just a couple minutes ago the siblings had been at each other's throats. Paige had interfered only with the intent of shutting down the argument, sending the girls to their rooms to take a break, and then making them apologize to each other. She had had no idea she'd end up being the sworn enemy. But from her daughters' reactions, she was just that.

Paige stood in the den, taking deep breaths. Although the room was a fairly nice size, furnished with nothing but a television, a couch, a rug, and a bookshelf, plus a couple pictures on the wall, she began to feel claustrophobic. What was happening here?

She was starting to feel engulfed, never thinking in a million years that skin color would be an issue she would have to address with her girls. Yes, her two children did have different fathers. Yes, Adele's father was African American, while Norma's father was Caucasian. But both her daughters were the spitting image of her . . . with the exception of their complexion. Adele was dark skinned. Being biracial, Norma had inherited the complexion of her father's side of the family, which was fair. The girls had similar hair, which they'd inherited from Paige, so at least Paige wouldn't have to deal with the whole "good hair, bad hair" issue between the girls. She hoped not, anyway. But then again, she'd much rather be dealing with good hair versus bad hair than with good skin versus bad skin.

Paige had suspected that later on in her children's lives, there would be talks about the birds and the bees, good secrets and bad secrets, good touches and bad touches. What she had not anticipated in her wildest dreams was that she'd ever have to have a talk with her children about the differences in their complexion. One might think it would be a pretty easy conversation to have with the girls. Paige could just simply explain that because they had different fathers of a different race, their skin was different. The thing was, though, that the girls had no idea that they had different fathers. As far as both girls knew, Norman was their father. In fact, his name was listed on both their birth certificates. And all three of them, Paige and her daughters, bore Norman's last name, Vanderdale.

This whole "two children with two different baby daddies" situation was never something Paige had wanted for herself, nor had she planned for it to happen. Everything had just happened so quickly, though. The same day Paige found out she was pregnant with Adele was the same day her divorce from Adele's father, Blake, was finalized. Divorced and pregnant all on the same day, Paige, who was a member of New Day Temple of Faith, was not about to subject herself to the ridicule and scrutiny of her Christian family. Not only that, but Paige's ex-husband was incarcerated at the time for his physical and sexual abuse of Paige. As a matter of fact, the pregnancy was a result of nonconsensual sex between Blake and Paige. No way could Paige bear that monster's child. No way could the first child she gave birth to be the product of rape—any child, for that matter. Paige couldn't do it.

At the time she'd felt that she wasn't strong enough to handle something like that. After all, she was still trying to put the pieces together after the trial against Blake and the end of the friendship with Tamarra, Paige's best friend once upon a time. It had devastated Paige to no end to find out that her best friend, her sister in Christ, had slept with her husband. Roll it all up together, and it had been just too much for Paige to bear.

God had brought Paige through it all, though. Everything she felt she had lost through the process, He had restored. He'd placed another best friend in her life. He'd placed a new husband in her life as well. It was a blessing on top of a blessing that her best friend and her husband were one and the same. Norman and Paige had started off as coworkers. Over the years of working together, the two had become confidants and friends. Norman had been there for Paige during her divorce from her best friend and then from her husband. He'd been there for her the day she found out she was pregnant. He'd been the one to talk her out of the abortion, thanks to the bright idea he'd come up with that prevented Paige from bearing the guilt and shame of being an unwed, divorced, single mom, and a so-called Christian woman. He'd offered to marry Paige to keep her from being assigned any of those titles. At first Paige had laughed in his face, but a week later she'd found herself saying, "I do."

First came friendship, then came marriage, and then came Paige with a baby carriage. Last, but not least, came love. Given their shotgun wedding and their shared experience of the birth of Adele, it was inevitable that the bond the couple shared would only strengthen. Paige and Norman eventually fell deeply in love. The very day Paige shared with Norman that she'd fallen in love with him, which was after they'd consummated their marriage, was the first time she'd gotten up the nerve to tell him just how in love with him she was. Only thing was, it had been communicated via text. He'd just left their place, on his way to work. Upon receiving the text, Norman had attempted to send Paige a text back while he was still behind the wheel, to let her know that he was in love with her too. Unfortunately, trying to text while driving had been fatal for Norman.

Suffering the loss of her second husband had

been the worst of the worst for Paige. Finding out, though, that consummating their marriage had led to the creation of Norma had filled a void for both Paige and Norman's family. The Vanderdales had treated Adele like she was one of their own, and then with Norma, they really had been blessed with one of their own. Never once had the Vanderdales made a distinction between the two girls. At least not under Paige's watch. But what about when she wasn't watching? This thought now penetrated Paige's mind.

"No, she wouldn't have," Paige said under her breath. She walked over to the icy-gray-colored couch and sat down, feeling sort of faint. She recalled the reaction of Mrs. Vanderdale, Norman's mother and her children's grandmother, when she first found out that Norman had married a black woman. Mrs. Vanderdale had stereotyped African Americans, especially African American women, in the worst way possible. She'd done it based on all the reality shows with predominantly African American casts. One conversation she and Norman had had with Mrs. Vanderdale entered Paige's mind.

"My mother doesn't care about what color you are," Norman said to Paige and then turned to face his mother. *"Do you, Mother?"*

Mrs. Vanderdale couldn't speak, but with her

pupils dilated, she silently begged her son to realize that he'd hit the nail on the head.

"Mother, is that what has you acting this way? The fact that Paige is black?"

The only words she could manage to force out were, "Who on earth names their African American daughter Paige?"

"Mom!" Norman said, embarrassment apparent in his tone.

"Well, I'm sorry, son, but I thought I raised you better than that," Mrs. Vanderdale spat.

"What?" Paige had held her tongue long enough.

"Oh, my, and I see she even has the attitude that comes along with it," Mrs. Vanderdale said, grabbing her chest.

"That comes along with what?" Paige asked with words, while Norman asked with his eyes.

"With . . ." His mother moved her index finger up and down the length of Paige's body. "With that."

Paige took a step toward her mother-in-law.

"Hold on just a minute." Norman put his arm out, stopping Paige from getting any closer to his dear mother. "Mother, I'm not clear on what you're trying to say here, but if it's what I think it is, disappointment in you would be describing how I feel without crossing the line of respect."

"*Norman, it's totally clear what your mother is implying,*" Paige said. "*But just in case you really don't understand, let me break it down for you.*"

"*Oh, gosh, and there she goes, ready to start breaking things,*" Mrs. Vanderdale said, panicking. "*Put away all the china and crystal. I've caught glimpses of those reality shows and know how they like to throw glasses and stuff at each other.*"

Paige's mouth fell to the floor.

And now, after hearing her daughters argue, her mouth fell to the floor once again. What Norma had said truly did sound like something Paige wouldn't put past her former mother-in-law saying . . . back then. But this was now. Mrs. Vanderdale had apologized to Paige for her actions. The two had made amends and now shared a much different relationship than they had at first. They'd ultimately ended up forging a mother and daughter-in-law relationship to be envied.

But had Mrs. Vanderdale's old ways of thinking resurfaced? And even worse, had she imparted them to Paige's youngest child, who was biracial, turning her against her older, 100 percent African American sibling?

Anything was possible. And even if this whole thing between her daughters wasn't about black versus white per se, Mrs. Vanderdale had also had some thoughts on African American women, period.

"She looks like those women on the television," Mrs. Vanderdale had told Norman in a private conversation they'd had, one that Norman had ultimately shared with Paige. "I don't want to have to worry every night that that's what my son is dealing with. Those women are damaged goods. They carry so much baggage with them. They are hurt and are full of pain and misery. Lots of them don't have fathers who stuck around, and some of them have never even laid eyes on their fathers. Wouldn't know him if he was standing in front of them in the grocery store. Then there is their health. They deal with that sugar diabetes, high blood pressure, and all that weight they tend to end up carrying. Have you noticed how thick most of 'em are? Or just outright overweight? I don't want that for you, not my son. Maybe somebody else's, but not mine."

Paige shook her head and covered her ears, as if her former mother-in-law was standing over her, repeating those exact words again. If Mrs. Vanderdale had made such statements with someone listening, God only knew what she kept to herself about black people. But technically, wasn't Norma considered black? Paige had honestly never categorized her children. It didn't matter to God, so why should it matter to Paige? No way was heaven segregated, and Paige just refused to believe that it was.

"Oh, God!" Paige said, standing up, rubbing her temples to try to massage away her oncoming headache. She began pacing. "But she's a saved woman now," Paige said to herself, mumbling about Mrs. Vanderdale. When Paige had first met her mother-in-law, she had not been a churchgoing woman, but between Paige and the Vanderdale housekeeper, Miss Nettie, she had ended up a saved woman in love with Christ. Both Paige and Mrs. Vanderdale even attended the same church. Even after Norman's death, Paige had remained very much a part of the Vanderdale family. She'd seen no signs of Mrs. Vanderdale falling back into her old ways of thinking when it came to African Americans. But could something she'd been keeping in the dark now be coming to light?

"You know what they say," Paige said to herself. "Once a cheat always a cheat. Once a liar always a liar. Once a thief always a thief." Paige let out a harrumph. "Well, could the same be said to be true about a bigot?"

Not able to let this slide, Paige would have to find out if, in fact, the children's grandmother was behind this pending strife between light-skinned sister and dark-skinned sister. She began biting her nails in both nervousness and worry. She was nervous about having to confront her former mother-in-law. She was worried about finding out the answer.

Chapter 2

"Paige, honey, how are you?" Miss Nettie greeted as she opened the door of the Vanderdales' luxurious home.

It was close to eight thousand square feet, and when Norman first drove Paige there to meet his parents, she felt like she was entering a mansion. It sat on three acres, which was more than enough land for them to ride the horses they owned. The land was well manicured, and the house had a private drive that was about as long as Paige's neighborhood street.

"Well, hello, Miss Nettie," Paige greeted with a hug before stepping into the house. "I had just missed you last Sunday, when I came here for dinner." It didn't matter how many times Paige had been to the Vanderdale home or even that she'd once lived there. Entering it always made her feel like Belle in *Beauty and the Beast*. It was just so much for one to take in, but once one did, it just felt like home.

"I know, I know, child." Miss Nettie made a shooing motion with her hand and closed the huge, custom-made oak door. "But I heard that soul food spread I cooked before I left went over well. Wasn't hardly a spoonful of nothing to put away." Miss Nettie laughed.

"Well, you already know I like to eat." Paige ran her hands down her voluptuous curves.

"And you know Mrs. Vanderdale treats my soul food spreads like it's a foreign delicacy."

Both women laughed in agreement. Paige's laughter faded out much quicker than Miss Nettie's, which didn't go unnoticed by the older woman, who seemed to have a sixth sense.

"Oh, Lord. Come and sit down." Miss Nettie headed over to the couch in the parlor.

The parlor had recently been redecorated. To Paige, the style looked like something out of the movie *Gone with the Wind*. The end tables had drapery-like covers on them with lace trim. Doilies covered the coffee table. The couch, love seat, and chair had a tight-seamed yellow pattern. One word to describe the room was *sunshine*. Paige was about to cover the sun up with a dark cloud, though.

"I can tell something is wrong, so don't even try to deny it," Miss Nettie said as she sat down on the couch and then patted the spot next to her for Paige to do the same. When Paige showed hesitance, Miss Nettie hit the spot again. "Come on now, child. I got laundry still to do yet. Bring it on over here and tell Miss Nettie what is wrong."

Paige exhaled and then slowly walked over toward the couch. The entire time she contemplated whether to bring up her concerns about Mrs. Vanderdale and the whole skin color thing to Miss Nettie or to just wait and confront Mrs. Vanderdale first. Paige sat down and then looked down at her twiddling thumbs while she continued to contemplate what to do. If the tables were turned and someone had a problem with her, she would want them to bring it to her first rather than discuss the situation behind her back.

Paige looked up. "Is Mrs. Vanderdale home?" she asked the housekeeper, who had been much more like family to both her and the Vanderdales.

"No. She's out getting her hair done. She should be back shortly, because she's been gone a minute now."

Paige exhaled. Perhaps Mrs. Vanderdale not being home was a sign that maybe she should run things by Miss Nettie first. After all, Miss Nettie was always so full of wisdom and had never led Paige wrong with any of her advice. Besides, it was more than likely that Mrs. Vanderdale would discuss the situation with Miss Nettie, anyway. Those two talked about everything. What difference did it make if Paige told Miss Nettie first?

"The girls were arguing last evening," Paige told Miss Nettie.

Miss Nettie let out a laugh that made her belly jiggle. "When ain't those two gals arguing? They remind me of how Sam and Norman used to go at it when they were youngins." Sam was short for Samantha. She was Norman's younger sister.

Paige sat there with a stoic face.

Miss Nettie stopped laughing and, with a serious tone, said, "That can't be all that's got you bothered. What else is it?" Concern laced Miss Nettie's voice.

"Well, it's not them arguing. I know it's normal for siblings to argue and have disagreements. It's what they were arguing about." Paige paused.

Miss Nettie waited patiently for Paige to continue. Clearly, the subject of the girls' tiff had cut bone deep for Paige, as she was having a hard time even speaking about it. Miss Nettie put her hand on Paige's shoulder to encourage her to gather the strength to continue.

"Norma told Adele that she was ugly because she's dark skin," Paige said.

Miss Nettie's eyes bucked. A brown-skinned woman herself, she wasn't ignorant about the torment some darker-skinned black folks had to deal with within their own race.

"It broke my heart to hear my little one say that." Paige shook her head and began to wring her fingers. "You have no idea how many times I felt that way about myself growing up, that I was ugly because I was dark skinned. I mean, dark-skinned girls never got featured in commercials. The black girls and the other women who did all had fair skin and either bone-straight or natural curly hair. Blue or gray eyes," Paige said and then stood. She squeezed her fists together and began walking back toward the door, in thought. "It just brought back so much pain. And I recognized that same pain on poor Adele's face after those words cut her like a knife."

"I can imagine how bad that made you feel," Miss Nettie said. "No one wants to see their child hurting."

"That's not even the half of it. I mean, the first questions that popped into my mind were, 'Where on earth did Norma get that from? Who taught her that?'" Paige exhaled and turned back to face Miss Nettie. "That's why I want to talk to Mrs. Vanderdale."

Miss Nettie looked a little puzzled. "You want to ask her if she knows where Norma got it from?"

"Yes . . . well, not exactly." Paige looked down at her hands again. "I want to ask if she's the one Norma got it from." Paige looked up to find that Miss Nettie had jumped to her feet.

"Paige Vanderdale, how can you even think that Naomi would do such a thing?" Miss Nettie asked, referencing her boss by her first name. Miss Nettie and Paige interchangeably addressed the woman formally as Mrs. Vanderdale and casually as Naomi.

"Well, I . . . I . . ." Paige stammered. She then got defensive. "Well, you know just as well as I do that she's very capable of planting such poison in the girls' heads. You do remember how she treated me when she first met me. It was as if black people were the gum on the bottom of the white man's shoe." Once again Paige had allowed her mind to go back into the past, revisiting Mrs. Vanderdale's attitudes about having a black daughter-in-law, her belief that the color black was tainting their lily-white family.

"You know good and well she got delivered from that kind of stinkin' thinkin'," Miss Nettie shot, pointing a finger at Paige as she walked over to her. "And you know like I know that when God delivers somebody from something, it is done. Ain't nobody and no thing more powerful than God Almighty. And nothing can reverse anything He's set into place."

"I'm not questioning the power of God," Paige said. "Just the weakness of man."

Miss Nettie went to open her mouth, but no words came out. She huffed. "I guess you've got a point there." Being wrong did not sit too well with Miss Nettie, who was usually right, and she went and sat back down on the couch. Disappointment was etched on her face.

Paige, with a fretful look on her face, joined Miss Nettie on the couch. "I know. It breaks my heart too." Paige placed her hand on Miss Nettie's knee. "As much as I hate to, I have to confront her about this."

Miss Nettie nodded. "I know that as a mother, you have to do what you have to do."

"I just can't let anybody poison my babies' minds."

The two women sat in silence a few seconds, contemplating the entire situation, until they heard a singsongy voice coming from the dining room area of the house.

"I saw Paige's car out front when I drove up into the garage." Mrs. Vanderdale's voice could be heard clearly even before she stepped from the dining room into the parlor area. "That means my grandbabies must be here." Mrs. Vanderdale burst through the swinging door with her arms spread wide, anticipating that her only two grandchildren would come running into her embrace. When there was no pitter-patter of little feet, she stood straight up and looked over at Miss Nettie and Paige, who were sitting on the couch, wearing melancholy expressions. "What's wrong? Is something wrong with my babies?" There was worry and fear in her tone.

Paige looked at Miss Nettie. Miss Nettie nodded at Paige, beckoning her to stand up and say what she had to say. Finding the courage deep down inside to do so, Paige stood. "Yes, Naomi, something is wrong."

Mrs. Vanderdale began shaking her head back and forth. "Oh, no, not again."

Before Paige could say a word, her former mother-in-law's body fell limp to the floor.

Chapter 3

Stuart, the Vanderdales' butler, rushed through the dining room door. "Is everything okay in here?" he asked. "I thought I heard a loud thud or something fall."

"It's Naomi," Miss Nettie said as she and Paige helped a weak Mrs. Vanderdale to her feet. "She had another one of her fainting spells."

Stuart sighed. Helping tend to Mrs. Vanderdale after one of her episodes might as well have been officially added to his job description. She always seemed to manage to get herself worked up to the point where she had a fainting spell or an anxiety attack. The true severity of any of them was still up in the air. "Let me help get her over to the couch," he said.

Stuart, an older black man in his late sixties, went to help the women. He wasn't shocked to see Mrs. Vanderdale looking as though she was recovering from a fainting spell. Since this type of thing was routine with his boss, Stuart wasn't worried that Mrs. Vanderdale was facing a life-threatening issue. He just didn't want to see Paige and Miss Nettie struggle with getting her situated.

Finding Mrs. Vanderdale passed out or in the midst of a phony oncoming heart attack wasn't anything unusual for the Vanderdale household. Whenever Mrs. Vanderdale got overly excited, wanted to divert a situation, or just wanted to be plain old dramatic, she'd put on theatrics that could give Fred Sanford from the old sitcom *Sanford and Son* a run for his money. Despite the fact that she had had over two hundred fainting spells and one hundred near heart attacks, never had a phone call to 911 been required. The usual glass of water always managed to suffice.

"That's all right, honey. We got her," Miss Nettie said. "You just go fetch her a glass of water." She looked at the salt-and-pepper-haired man, who was a year her junior. "You know the drill." She rolled her eyes in her head.

"Indeed I do," Stuart replied all too knowingly.

While Stuart went to retrieve a glass of water, Paige and Miss Nettie led a dazed Mrs. Vanderdale over to the couch.

"Prop that pillow up right there," Miss Nettie ordered Paige.

Paige propped up the orange throw pillow that sat in the corner of the couch. They laid Mrs. Vanderdale across the couch. By then Stuart had returned with a glass of water.

"Here you go." Stuart handed it to Miss Nettie.

"Thank you, Stuart," Miss Nettie said, looking into Stuart's eyes momentarily.

"My pleasure." He nodded and then excused himself.

With her rosy cheeks evident on her thick brown skin, Miss Nettie commenced placing the glass to Mrs. Vanderdale's lips. "Here you are."

Paige's full attention was on Mrs. Vanderdale.

Mrs. Vanderdale lifted her head slightly, just enough so that she could take a sip of the water without it running down her chin. "That's enough," she said, gurgling and turning her head away from the glass.

Miss Nettie placed the glass on the table. Both she and Paige looked at Mrs. Vanderdale, waiting for her to regain her composure. Several seconds went by. Tired and feeling awkward with the two women staring at her, Mrs. Vanderdale finally sat up.

"Okay, give it to me. I can take it," she said, her eyes tearing up. "My poor babies. I can't believe something has happened to them. When I walked into this room and saw that look on

your faces . . ." Her eyes darted from Paige to
Miss Nettie. "I recognized that look of despair.
It was the same look on everybody's faces that
day our Norman . . . left us." Mrs. Vanderdale
burst into tears. "Oh, God! Now what? What has
happened to my grandchildren?"

Paige looked at Miss Nettie in horror. Had
she insinuated to Mrs. Vanderdale that something bad had happened to Adele and Norma?
That certainly hadn't been her intention. But
Paige should have known to just spit it out. Mrs.
Vanderdale was good at jumping the gun and
then running all the way to the finish line.

All Miss Nettie could do was shrug and then
raise her hands in a "Go figure" manner.

"Naomi, nothing is physically wrong with
the girls," Paige said. She sat down next to Mrs.
Vanderdale.

"You mean the girls are just fine?" She seemed
to have found her strength, as she straightened
her shoulders up.

"They are as healthy as the horses out there in
the stable," Paige said.

Mrs. Vanderdale looked at Miss Nettie. Miss
Nettie nodded, indicating that she knew it to be
true.

Mrs. Vanderdale frowned and began to pat
her hair. "Do you mean I messed up my hair

for nothing?" She stood up and walked to the fireplace. She looked in the mirror that hung over it. She turned her head from side to side, putting any loose strands of hair back in place.

"I'm sorry, Naomi. I didn't mean to get you all stirred up like that," Paige said.

"Oh, now, now." Mrs. Vanderdale turned around and smiled as she made a shooing motion with her hand. "You know how I am. I just get excited sometimes." She took in a deep breath and then blew it out. "Now, you said that something is wrong. What is it?"

"Well . . ." Paige stood up. She twisted her lips as she tried to think of the right words to say. Not wanting to cause another mix-up, she decided to just come right out and say what she'd come over to address. "Someone told Norma that light skin is prettier than dark skin. So she called Adele ugly, since Adele has darker skin."

Mrs. Vanderdale gasped, allowing her hand to fly to her mouth and cover it. "My God! Where could she have gotten such a thought from?"

Paige and Miss Nettie shot one another a look. This didn't go unnoticed by Mrs. Vanderdale.

"What?" Mrs. Vanderdale asked suspiciously. "I see the way you two are looking at one another. Just say it."

Paige looked at Miss Nettie, willing her with her eyes to speak up on her behalf.

"Mrs. Vanderdale, I think I'm going to leave you two alone to talk," Miss Nettie said. She then looked at Paige. "Let me know if you need me."

"Coward," was what Paige's eyes said to the back of Miss Nettie's head as Miss Nettie exited the room. When Paige looked back at Mrs. Vanderdale, she was standing there, waiting patiently for Paige to spill the beans. "Well, uh, like I, uh, was saying," Paige stammered. "Norma seems to think—"

"That light skin is better than dark skin," Mrs. Vanderdale said, finishing Paige's sentence. "Yeah, I got all that." She sounded perturbed as she tightened her lips.

"And I had some ideas about where she might have gotten it from," Paige said.

Mrs. Vanderdale took a couple steps toward Paige. "And just who do you think she might have gotten it from?" She crossed her arms and waited, foot tapping, for the next words to come out of Paige's mouth.

"I couldn't help but think back to some of the comments you made back when Norman and I first got married, when you found out I was African American."

Mrs. Vanderdale nodded. "Yes. And I've both apologized and repented for those things."

"Well, even though a person might apologize for something they said, and repent for something they said, that doesn't necessarily mean that they didn't mean what they said."

"Paige Vanderdale," Mrs. Vanderdale said in an accusing tone. "Are you trying to insinuate that I'm the one who planted that thought in my own granddaughter's head?"

Paige remained silent.

"Well." Mrs. Vanderdale stood there, fluttering her eyelids as her eyes filled with tears. "I've changed, and I honestly thought I had shown and proven to everyone just how much I've changed." She shrugged her shoulders. "I'm sorry that I failed, with you at least." She walked over to the huge picture window that offered a view of the front lawn. She stared outside.

"Naomi, I'm sorry," Paige said. "I didn't mean to offend you. I love you. I think you are a beautiful woman. But we all have flaws, and sometimes we do and say things that we don't realized can have an effect on someone else, especially kids."

Mrs. Vanderdale whipped around. "Don't insult my intelligence, Paige. I've always been aware of the things I've said and done. I've always womaned up and assumed accountability. So for you to try to insinuate that I'm some dumb blonde who doesn't filter her mouth and is clueless . . . I'm truly offended. And if that is the case, maybe you're not the person I thought you were."

"Me?" Paige questioned, pointing to her chest. "Are you really going to try to turn this around on me?" Paige walked over to Mrs. Vanderdale.

"The fact that you come to my home, smile in my face, all the while thinking I could be capable of doing . . . of saying such a thing . . . That means that you are a fake and a phony."

Paige could feel her blood begin to boil. If someone had called the old Paige fake and phony, she would have been all up in their face, finger-pointing and neck snapping. But over the years Paige had learned something called a little self-control. But boy, oh, boy, did her flesh just want to rise up right about now and do some name-calling of its own. "Ooh, just let me at her. Let me at her," Paige's inner woman pleaded. But thank God for her spirit woman, who managed to whip and kick her flesh's butt.

"Mrs. Vanderdale, let's not do any name-calling here," Paige said. She addressed the woman in such a way as to show her she had the utmost respect for her. "We are both grown women here. I'm sure we can get to the bottom of this without losing our integrity or saying something we won't be able to take back."

"You started it," Mrs. Vanderdale said, sounding more like Norma and Adele during a fight than a woman on the other side of sixty. "You called me a name first."

Paige thought for a moment, trying to recall the words she'd spoken to Mrs. Vanderdale. She was certain she had not stood in this woman's home and called her a name. "I did not call you a name," she insisted.

"Well, you might not have outright said it, but in so many words you are calling me a prejudiced person and a liar."

"I said no such thing," Paige declared.

"Oh, but you did." Mrs. Vanderdale pointed in Paige's face. "For you to accuse me of telling Norma that she's better than Adele because her skin is lighter is basically calling me prejudiced. It's saying that I have a prejudice against dark skin. I said some awful things about black people in the past, but that was all out of pure ignorance. I said I was wrong about both saying it and what I said. So for you to say that perhaps deep inside those feelings—those thoughts—still exist is calling me a liar. I got delivered from those ways. God delivered me. I asked Him to, He said He would, and He did." Mrs. Vanderdale was good and up in Paige's face with her pointed finger now. "So I guess that means you're calling God a liar too!"

Paige stared down at Mrs. Vanderdale's finger. She then looked up at Mrs. Vanderdale. "You might wanna move that thing. I'm saved, but I ain't that saved."

Mrs. Vanderdale looked down at her finger. She then sucked her teeth and stormed off, mumbling, "You people," under her breath.

Chapter 4

"You people!" Paige snapped. She couldn't believe Mrs. Vanderdale had just said that, but then again, perhaps she could. After all, that was the reason why she was there to confront her in the first place. She had suspected that like an alcoholic who had been clean for years, Mrs. Vanderdale had fallen off the wagon. Her last comment was evidence that she had. No one liked to be wrong, but in this instance, Paige wished to God that she had made an error.

Her daughters loved their grandma Vanderdale. They loved spending time at the Vanderdale home with the Vanderdale family. It would be a shame if Paige had to keep her girls away, but she would if it meant protecting their impressionable minds.

"You people," Paige repeated, shaking her head.

Mrs. Vanderdale stopped in her tracks, turned around to face Paige, and then paused. She'd noted the tone of voice with which Paige had just repeated her words, and now she read the expression on Paige's face. Mrs. Vanderdale instantly started shaking her head and walking back toward Paige.

"I know what you are thinking, and that's not what I meant," she protested. "When I said the words 'you people,' I meant you people, as in your kind of Christians," Mrs. Vanderdale explained. "Christians who choose when they want to act holy and then justify their actions when they don't. Making up excuses and blaming their reactions based on someone else's actions." Mrs. Vanderdale was now back up in Paige's face. "But I see your mind is so hell-bent on this whole race thing that you can't allow yourself to go anywhere else but to the race card. Shame on you, Paige Vanderdale. Shame on you!" Mrs. Vanderdale hollered, wagging an accusing finger in Paige's face.

Reading Mrs. Vanderdale's expression and seeing how hurt she looked, for a split second Paige thought that there was a possibility that Mrs. Vanderdale was telling the truth.

"You are pointing your finger at the wrong person," Mrs. Vanderdale said.

"Well, right now you're the only one pointing fingers here, and I'd appreciate it if you'd kindly step out of my space." Paige looked down. "You and your finger."

Mrs. Vanderdale respected Paige's space and her wish and stepped back, placing both hands down at her sides.

"Now look, Naomi," Paige began in an apologetic voice. "I'm sorry if I offended you or came at you wrong, but someone has been feeding my child poison. As a mother bear, my instinct is to hunt down the guilty party and put an end to it. As a mother, you must understand how I feel."

"I understand a mother protecting her child," Mrs. Vanderdale said in a trembling voice, on the verge of tears. "But I did not put the idea of white being better than black, light being better than dark, or any other form of that nonsense in either of my grandchildren's minds."

Paige stood there, taking in everything about Mrs. Vanderdale. Her expression, her tone, the look in her eyes. She was convinced that her former mother-in-law was telling the truth. "I believe you, Naomi, and I'm sorry about offending you. But the question still remains, if you didn't tell Norma that light skin was prettier than dark, then who could have?"

"It was me."

Both Paige and Naomi turned to see to whom the voice they had just heard belonged. Neither of them would have imagined in a million years that the person claiming to be the culprit behind all this mess was really the guilty party.

"Samantha," Mrs. Vanderdale said. That her own flesh and blood was responsible for these teachings hurt her to the core. Like any mother, she felt responsible. Parents were their children's first teacher. Had Mrs. Vanderdale's actions and what she'd thought about black people for years rubbed off on her daughter? And had they been passed down to her grandchildren? Where would the curse stop? Mrs. Vanderdale bit down on her knuckles in agony at the thought that she was, in fact, indirectly responsible for the words that had come out of little Norma's mouth.

Paige walked over to Samantha in disbelief. "Sam?" she said. "I don't know what to say." Paige would have never pegged Sam as one likely to pass on such foolishness to the girls. She had been Paige's biggest cheerleader when she became a part of the family. Color had never been an issue with Samantha, not even when little chocolate Adele was born and her brother signed the birth certificate as Adele's father. Samantha had accepted that child, had cared for her, had loved on her, and had babysat whenever she was called upon, just like a good auntie would. She'd done the same with Norma, never once making a distinction between the two girls. At least not as far as Paige could tell. But the words right out of her own mouth indicated that she had been treating her nieces differently.

"Dad and I were out riding," Samantha began. "When we came in, we could hear you and Mom in here arguing. Miss Nettie told us what was going on." Samantha looked down and began to wring her fingers. "I told them I had to get in here quick and straighten everything out." She found the courage to look back up at Paige. "When Katie and I were scrolling through my Instagram news feed, we were discussing some of the posts. I was sitting for the girls that day, I believe."

Both Paige and Mrs. Vanderdale listened intently.

Samantha continued. "We kept seeing all these 'Keep calm' posts."

"Keep calm?" Mrs. Vanderdale questioned.

"Yeah. That thing people do on social media," Samantha informed her and then proceeded to give her some examples. "Keep calm. It's Friday. Keep calm. It's my birthday."

"Oh, I see." Mrs. Vanderdale nodded in understanding.

"I was reading the post out loud to Katie." Katie was Samantha's life partner.

For years Mr. and Mrs. Vanderdale had thought that Norman was gay because he never brought women home or mentioned having a girlfriend. That was why when Norman married Paige without them having ever even meeting her, Mrs. Vanderdale wasn't the least bit upset. She was just glad her only son wasn't gay, increasing her chances of having a boatload of grandchildren. But once she met Paige and saw that she was a black woman, she had to determine exactly which was the worst of the two evils.

But, of course, she'd gotten past that, and she'd gotten saved. And thank God for Samantha that she had. The old Mrs. Vanderdale probably would have shunned Samantha, kept her away from the family, or had a real heart attack. But God had touched her heart. God had touched her mind. She was able to love and accept her daughter with the love of Christ. But that didn't mean she didn't use every opportunity she could to preach the gospel to Samantha and Katie, tell them about what God said about their relationship. She always spoke with a loving spirit versus a condemning one.

"I kept coming across all these posts that said, 'Keep calm. I'm on team light skin,'" Samantha said. "Then we'd see a post that would say, 'Keep calm. I'm on team dark skin.' Katie and I, both being white girls, didn't understand the posts. I asked a couple people to explain, and they did. It was just crazy to us. How could a single race basically have prejudices among itself? I was actually going back and forth with some of the people posting that type of ignorance, trying to get an understanding of it all. For most people, it was just a joke, and they didn't mean anything by it, but I didn't get the punch line. I thought it was just stupid and weird that a race would be hating on each other because of the shade of their skin."

Paige spoke up. "I think it's stupid too. I was a victim of the stupidity while I was growing up. But I guess I don't know what this has to do with Norma and Adele. How they would know about all of this."

"They were sitting right there, watching television." Samantha put her head down in shame. "At least I thought they were watching television. But clearly, they heard us and were paying attention to everything we were discussing, everything I read, and all the back-and-forth posts I was repeating to Katie. Things like 'Dark-skinned women are mad and bitter because they are dark' and 'Light-skinned women are just happy and positive because they have the light, pretty skin.' I mean, it was sickening what some of them were saying." She looked up at Paige with pleading eyes. "I'm sorry, sis." She took Paige's hands in hers. "I should have been more careful."

"You should have never been having that kind of discussion while the girls were in earshot, period," Mrs. Vanderdale told her daughter.

"I know," Samantha agreed. "I see that now. But I swear I didn't mean any harm, and I absolutely did not mirror or side with the whole team light skin, team dark skin thing. I was just so shocked and appalled that I really almost forgot the girls were even there."

"Well, they were paying attention to what was going on, all right, and now little Norma, apparently, is on team light skin." Paige sighed. She went and sat down on the couch. "Guess I'm going to have to have a talk with her."

"Allow me to as well," Samantha said. "As a matter of fact, perhaps it would be a great idea if both sides of the girls' family talk with them, and they can hear how we all feel about the situation. We can reaffirm that skin color, race don't matter. That we are all family."

Paige thought about it for a minute. Having both sides of the family come together to discuss the issue was a good idea. The room would be full of different races and complexions, all under one roof. All on the same team, so to speak. "Sure. Sounds nice," Paige agreed. She let out a deep breath. She'd come to the Vanderdales' home to get to the bottom of things, and she had. All was well.

Paige stood to prepare to go. Her eyes locked with Mrs. Vanderdale's. The other woman stood there with tears falling from her eyes. Perhaps all was not well, after all. She walked over to comfort Mrs. Vanderdale. Apparently, old wounds from the past had come back to haunt the woman. Paige had learned a lot about that, and unbeknownst to Paige, she was about to get another crash course in it.

Chapter 5

"Thank you so much for having us," Paige's mother said as Mr. and Mrs. Vanderdale walked her and her husband to the front door.

Norma and Adele were in the downstairs television room with Samantha and Katie. Paige was seeing her parents out as well.

"It was our pleasure," Mrs. Vanderdale said. "I'm just glad we were able to get together and accomplish what we set out to do."

"Yes, indeed," Paige agreed.

They had been successful at discussing with Norma and Adele the whole skin color issue. They were all comfortable with having put the issue to rest. Could the subject matter perhaps come up again in dealing with other children and the outside world? Absolutely. But at least they'd planted the seed for how the girls should react to it. The lesson was that at the end of the day, they were all, plain and simply put, human beings.

"Both sides of the girls' family are going to have to get together for dinner more often," said Mr. Robinson, Paige's father, as he shook Mr. Vanderdale's hand. "My wife can burn in the kitchen."

Mrs. Robinson smiled.

Leaning into Mr. Vanderdale, Mr. Robinson whispered, "But that Miss Nettie's cooking . . . ump, ump, ump." He shook his head and licked his lips.

Mrs. Robinson play punched her husband in the arm.

"Oh, don't worry," Mrs. Vanderdale said to Mrs. Robinson, smiling. "I get that all the time from my own husband."

"Yes, that Miss Nettie can throw down," Paige said, rubbing her stomach. She looked around. "By the way, where is she? I haven't seen her in a minute."

Mrs. Vanderdale made a shooing motion with her hand. "Probably off somewhere with Stuart."

"Yeah," Mr. Vanderdale said with furrowed eyebrows. "I've noticed those two have been spending quite a bit of time together. Anything I need to know about, like a budding relationship of sorts?" He looked at his wife.

Mrs. Vanderdale shook her head and raised her arms. "Not that I know of. The two have worked here together for years. I imagine they've forged some sort of bond over time."

Mr. Vanderdale shrugged. "Yeah, maybe you're right."

"Anyway," Mr. Robinson said, "the food was delicious and the company impeccable."

"Hear! Hear!" Mr. Vanderdale agreed, opening the front door.

"Be careful getting home, Mom and Dad," Paige said after giving her parents a hug and a kiss good-bye.

Mr. Vanderdale closed and locked up the door after the Robinsons exited. "Well, I think I'm going to go start getting ready to turn in for the night," Mr. Vanderdale said, then looked at his watch. "It's after seven p.m. Way past my bed curfew."

Both Mrs. Vanderdale and Paige chuckled.

"I'll be up in a bit, honey," Mrs. Vanderdale said. She smiled, then kissed her husband on the lips.

"Good evening, Paige." Mr. Vanderdale patted Paige on the shoulder before he headed up the steps.

"Good night." Paige watched Mrs. Vanderdale as she watched her husband go up the steps to the top landing and then head down the hallway until he was no longer in view. Mrs. Vanderdale had the sweetest smile on her face. It was as if she was watching her first crush walk down the school corridor. "How do you guys do that?" Paige asked.

Mrs. Vanderdale turned her attention to Paige. "Do what?"

"Stay in love and adore one another so much after all these years?" Paige asked. "What's it been like for the thirty-five years that you guys have been married?"

A huge smile spread across Mrs. Vanderdale's face. "Thirty-seven," she said with such pride. "And you're right. I'm in love with that man today just as much as I was the day I married him." She looked at the steps that her husband had just scaled. She wrapped her arms around herself. "Maybe even more."

Paige sighed. She was glad to see a happily married couple so in love after all these years. At the same time, she couldn't help but be envious of them. She'd thought Blake was going to be her happily ever after. When she'd first met him, he'd been everything she had imagined in a man. He'd fit the cliché of tall, dark, and handsome to a tee. He'd been so kind, loving, and generous. He'd made Paige feel as though she was the only woman in the world.

On their wedding night, still a virgin, Paige couldn't wait to consummate her marriage. But it never happened. Well, they eventually consummated their marriage, but not on their wedding night. This hurt Paige to the core. She'd always felt that Blake was very much attracted to her, big bones, extra meat, and all. Though he had desired her, during their courtship, he'd respected her wish to remain a virgin until she was married. Still, he'd lusted after her with his eyes. She'd felt so wanted and desired. He'd looked at her like she was the only woman in the world.

Paige had been so grateful that her best friend at the time, Tamarra, had hooked them up. Well, not at first, since Paige had been none the wiser that her meeting Blake had all been a setup. He'd shown up at her job at the movie theater where she and Norman used to work together. He had supposedly been on a blind date or something. But the date had been a no-show. Paige had just thought it was by chance that the two of them had run into one another and had connected. She had truly thought it had been a divine setup by God. She came to find that Tamarra had met Blake at some catering gig she'd done. Tamarra had given him all the 411 on Paige, and Blake had taken it from there.

By the time Paige found out that her meeting with Blake wasn't as divine a setup as she'd initially thought, she was already head over heels in love with him and had exchanged wedding vows. Forgiving the two for their little scam was the easy part. The hard part was forgiving them for having slept with one another . . . twice. The first time was on the very day Tamarra and Blake met one another. The second time was just hours before Paige and Blake were married.

This explained to Paige why her man couldn't touch her on their wedding night. He'd already given himself to her best friend. Tamarra swore that those were the only times they'd been together sexually, but everything had started out with so many lies that deep down inside Paige didn't even believe that was true.

Once Paige became Blake's wife, she was still in the dark, but the guilt of having been with Paige's best friend ate Blake alive. Keeping such a secret caused him a lot of aggravation. Then, on top of that, he was overwhelmed with work. In Paige's eyes, he became a changed man, for the worse. It only made matters worse when his estranged mother sued him for most of his life savings. She claimed that when Blake's father passed, all his money should have gone to her since the two had never officially divorced, yet Blake had received it. It was a mess, as it took Blake back to a painful childhood, one in which he'd been abandoned by his mother. He grew more bitter and angrier, and he took all his frustrations out on Paige, resorting to verbal assault, physical assault, then finally sexual assault.

Blake had turned into a monster. So when Blake's so-called estranged mother shared with Paige that she wasn't even Blake's real mother, that his biological mother, her husband's mistress, had left him at the hospital, Paige kept that to herself. She knew in her spirit that would be the thing to push him into the deep end, as if he hadn't already been drowning to begin with. When Blake showed up at Paige's place of employment, calling her names and harassing her, she wanted to hurt him as much as his words were hurting her. So she let it rip that the woman he'd paid all that money to in a lawsuit wasn't even his real mother. Outraged, and wanting to one-up Paige, Blake blurted out that he'd been with her best friend.

Paige's happily ever after had turned into a happily ever never real quick. Norman had been her saving grace, making her believe in love again . . . believe in marriage again. But then he was taken from her. She knew that real love did exist and could last a lifetime. That was evident in Mr. and Mrs. Vanderdale's marriage, but what she didn't believe was that it could happen for her.

"Paige, honey," Mrs. Vanderdale said, resting her hand on Paige's shoulder. "You're gonna find true love again." Mrs. Vanderdale had read the expression on Paige's face. "You're young, you're beautiful, and you're healthy. I know you stopped working to be a stay-at-home mom for the girls."

With the money Paige had from the divorce settlement with Blake and the money she received from Social Security as a result of Norman's death, on top of Norman's life insurance policy and his inheritance, she and her girls were pretty much set for life. She had taken advantage of that by quitting her job at the theater and staying home to raise them.

"But now both girls are in school all day," Mrs. Vanderdale continued. "You don't just have to sit up at home all the time."

"I don't just stay at home," Paige said, begging to differ. "I go to church. I go to choir practice. I volunteer at the girls' school. And you know the girls are going to start taking classes at that dance school that Lorain's twins go to."

"Lorain?" Mrs. Vanderdale thought for a moment. She couldn't recall who Lorain was. "Does she attend New Day?"

"She's not a member anymore, but she does attend every now and then," Paige said. "She's the one married to the doctor."

From the expression on Mrs. Vanderdale's face, Paige knew that none of this was ringing a bell.

"I sang at her wedding, when she renewed her vows," Paige added.

"Oh, yes. I do remember her. Doesn't her mother still attend New Day regularly, though?"

"Miss Eleanor? Yes, indeed." Paige shook her head just thinking about the antics of Lorain's old-school mother.

"That woman is a hoot." Mrs. Vanderdale chuckled.

"And then some," Paige agreed.

"But back to what I was saying," Mrs. Vanderdale said. "Church, choir, a parent volunteer, and being a dance mom are all good, but what about you? What are you going to do for yourself for fun? And how do you ever expect to find someone to do it with if you're always cooped up behind four walls?"

Paige thought for a moment. Mrs. Vanderdale had a point. As long as Paige could remember, her mother had had a concern that Paige couldn't be alone with herself. Paige's mom would talk to her about getting to know herself and spending time with herself before she went jumping from man to man. Surely even her mother would have to agree that these past few years had been more than enough me time for Paige. She looked at Mrs. Vanderdale. "You know, Naomi, I think you just may have a point. Maybe it is time that I get out and experience new things. Meet new people."

Mrs. Vanderdale clapped her hands together. "See? That's what I'm trying to hear." She was delighted that Paige's frown had turned into a confident smile.

Perhaps it would be a cooking class, yoga, or painting, but Paige wasn't sure exactly what new hobby she would take up in order to go out and meet people. Her mission wasn't to go out there and find a man. She really didn't have any female friends in her life, either, as she'd been afraid to let them in after her experience with Tamarra. Besides, when it came to a man, she didn't have to go searching. One had found her a long time ago, but she just hadn't been ready at the time. Well, now she was ready. The only thing was, was he?

Chapter 6

"H2J Photography," Paige mumbled under her breath as she typed the very words she spoke into the search box on her computer. Within seconds all kinds of links, some with photos, popped up on the screen. Paige's heart began to beat fast.

After her talk with Mrs. Vanderdale yesterday, Paige decided that she was going to look up a guy she'd met years ago, when she'd arranged to have a family portrait taken of her and the girls. He'd been so flirty with her during the photo shoot, but he'd been a gentleman all the same. A gentleman who knew what he wanted, and he'd wanted Paige. He'd made that known when he eventually asked her out on a date.

Paige had considered taking him up on his offer, but it had been during a time in her life when so much was going on. Life had just kept happening to Paige. It had been one thing after the other. She had thought she was going to keel over and die when she was notified by the prison clinic that Blake had tested positive for HIV. Paige had got tested more times than she could remember, and she had had her daughters tested as well. To God be the glory, each and every test had come back negative.

Paige had ended up losing contact with the dashing photographer, but as fate would have it, she'd bumped into him again at the Vanderdales'. Samantha had mentioned wanting to do a photo shoot of the horses for a contest she was entering them in. Paige had shared the photographer's business card with Samantha, and low and behold, she'd shown up at the Vanderdales' one day, and he was there doing a photo shoot. This time Paige wasn't about to let him slip through her fingers.

The two had ended up connecting. Paige had truly been on the verge of committing herself to him, of letting another man into her life. But then life had happened again. Paige had received a letter from Blake's attorney, notifying her that he was aware of Adele's existence, that they had done the math and knew Adele had to be Blake's child. Blake wanted custody.

After having that bomb dropped on her, Paige couldn't think about a man. The only thing she'd been concerned about at the time was protecting her child from that monster of an ex-husband of hers. She recalled the day she'd broken things off with her suitor. She had been certain that he would be finished with her forever, but surprisingly, he'd said something to Paige that made her feel like, just maybe, part of her destiny would be to end up with him.

"So this is it . . . for now," he said as he looked at Paige.

"For now," Paige confirmed. "But I believe with all my heart that when we meet again, just like always, we're going to pick up right where we left off spiritually . . . and emotionally."

"And I believe that too. God says you are mine. Which is why you can take your time. Take all the time God will have you take."

"And you?"

He looked into Paige's eyes with those sexy eyes of his. "I'll wait. It's going to be unbearable, but I'll wait."

As Paige dialed the number to the photography studio where he'd worked when she met him, she took a deep breath. She hoped he was a man of his word.

When the person on the other end of the line picked up, Paige cleared her throat and asked, "May I speak to Ryan?"

"Can you hold please?" said the receptionist who had answered the phone. Before Paige could reply one way or the other, the woman clicked a button and put her on hold.

"Well, dang," Paige said, pulling the phone away from her ear and looking at it as if she were looking at the woman. Paige rolled her eyes and then placed the phone back to her ear. If music weren't playing, she would have wondered if the woman had hung up on her.

She sat in her computer room in her home, tapping her nails against the shiny black desk. Instead of the typical wooden desk, Paige had gone for something more stylish, opting for a three-tiered design made of glass and sturdy plastic. Being annoyed by the receptionist allowed Paige to deflect the nervousness she was feeling at the prospect of talking to Ryan. She wasn't sure if it was just pure anxiety or what. She and Ryan had always managed to pick up exactly where they had left off, just like old friends. But that was then and this was now.

So much could have changed in his life in the past year and a half or so. Paige wasn't seeing anyone, but that was because she'd been so busy with her two children. By the same token, Ryan had two sons. It was very likely that he had been just as busy with them. Ryan, too, had lost the love of his life, his sons' mother, and was a single parent. He could relate to what Paige had gone through in losing Norman. Therefore, he had never pressed or prodded. He had allowed Paige to do everything at her own pace. If she'd needed a time-out, he'd given it to her without argument, keeping the faith that if the two of them were meant to be together, then God would see to it that it was so.

That thought alone put a smile on Paige's face.

Almost two years was a long time, though. Raising kids was a hard job. What if he had gotten impatient with waiting on Paige and had found someone else? A feeling of horror came over Paige when it hit her spirit that there was a chance that Ryan had even married. How humiliating would that be? Her going after a married man?

"What am I doing?" Paige asked herself out loud, prepared to hang up the phone.

"I'm sorry about your wait," the receptionist said, returning to the line. "How can I help you?"

"I, uh . . ." Paige wanted to make up a lie but was immediately convicted by just the thought of telling a lie, let alone actually allowing it to come out of her mouth. "Well . . ." She was just going to hang up the phone in the woman's ear, but then she realized that some businesses had caller ID nowadays. She didn't know if the woman would call her back. How embarrassing would that be? Paige thought about perhaps telling the woman that she'd dialed the wrong number.

When the receptionist had answered the phone, she'd clearly said the words "H2J Photography." That was exactly the business that Paige had meant to call, so that still would be a lie. Ugh! There was no way out of this mess.

The receptionist helped Paige solve her dilemma when she said, "Oh, yeah. You're on hold for Ryan, right?"

Paige opened her mouth. No words came out. She still had no idea how she was going to let this thing play out.

"Hello?" the receptionist said through the phone receiver. "Are you still there?"

Paige wanted to say no. But that would be stupid, on top of being a lie. "Uh, yes, I am still here," she said, clearing her throat.

"And you asked to speak with Ryan, correct?" the woman said, reiterating. Paige could hear another phone begin to ring in the background. "I just want to make sure. It's spring. High school students are blowing us up for senior pictures. Can you hold just one more time?" the woman said. Before Paige could respond, she said, "Oh, never mind. They hung up. Anyway, about Ryan . . . He no longer works here. Well, he works for H2J Photography. He's just running his own office out in Hilliard. I can give you that number if you wanted Ryan specifically. If this Columbus location is better, we'd be happy to serve you."

"I want Ryan," Paige blurted out, and she meant that in more ways than one.

"Oh, okay," the woman said as her other line began ringing again. "I'm sorry. Please hold just one more second. I need to take this call, and then I'll give you the number to our new Hilliard location."

"Oh," was all Paige could get out in her effort to tell the receptionist that was okay, as once again, she put her on hold, whether Paige liked it or not. Within a few seconds, though, Paige heard the woman click back over. That few seconds was just the amount of time Paige needed to gather something to write on and with.

"Okay," the woman sighed. "The number is 614-555-5555."

"Thank you for all your help. You have a good day."

"You too," the woman said, ending the call.

Paige hung up and stared at the phone number she'd written down. Once again her nerves started to get the best of her. "Just call him, already," she coached herself. "What do you have to lose?" She thought for a few seconds. "Only my dignity," she declared with a sigh. She twisted her lips up. "Child, you are the same woman who got arrested in her bath towel before. Your dignity went out with the bathwater." Paige had to laugh at that comment herself.

Although it had been years ago, Paige remembered being arrested and thrown into jail as if it was yesterday. She'd gotten into it with Blake's estranged sister, who had been supporting their mother in her lawsuit against Blake. Miss Thing had talked so much trash from across that conference room table that before Paige knew it, she had that girl's weave clutched in her fist. Charges of assault were pressed against Paige, which led to a warrant for her arrest. It just so happened that when the police came to arrest Paige, she'd been enjoying a long, hot bubble bath. Wearing only her bath towel, Paige had been escorted from her home for all her neighbors to see. Yep, it was safe to say that on that day her dignity was no more. So what did she have to lose by calling Ryan in the comfort of her own home? *Nothing*.

With that final thought, Paige began to dial the number that the receptionist had given her. Before she could dial the last numeral, the doorbell rang. Paige made a puzzled face. She wasn't expecting company. The girls were in school, so it couldn't be one of their playmates coming to see if they could come outside and play. Paige erased the call and placed her phone down. She stood up from the desk and placed the piece of paper with Ryan's number in her pocket. The doorbell rang again as she made her way over to the door. She peeked through the peephole.

"Miss Nettie?" she questioned.

It wasn't strange for Miss Nettie to come to Paige's home. Ever since Adele was born, Miss Nettie had been like an official grandmother. She'd come over to help Paige with the girls, do laundry, prepare meals, whatever it took to make life easy for the Vanderdale kinfolk. Besides, Miss Nettie really cared for Paige. Paige was like the daughter she had never had and, being in her sixties, never would have.

What was unusual, though, was that Miss Nettie had stopped by without calling first. Of course, the older woman was welcome to come to Paige's home any day of the week. She'd just always given advance notice, was all.

"Miss Nettie, it's good to see you," Paige said after opening the door. "I wasn't expecting you, though."

"I know I usually put you on notice whenever I'm going stop through for a minute to help you out. But I'm not here to help you out," Miss Nettie said, then looked downward.

"Oh," Paige said, confused and at the same time concerned. Miss Nettie was not one to cast her eyes away from a person when she had something to say to them. She was a "from the hip" kind of woman. That's what Paige liked about her so much. She could always get the honest, unfiltered truth from Miss Nettie. "Well, come on in, Miss Nettie." Paige moved to the side and allowed the thick woman to enter her home, then closed the door behind them. "Can I get you something to drink? Some half and half? Half tea and half lemonade?"

Miss Nettie shook her head and put up her hand. "No, no. I'm not thirsty." She walked over to the couch and sat, staring down at the floor.

Paige found herself staring down at the dark beige carpet. With two little ones running around and still in the stage of making messes, she'd chosen the darkest carpet she could find without making her entire living room look drab. The last thing she wanted was a pretty, light carpet with red Kool-Aid stains all over it. Paige appreciated how the lighter caramel-colored sofa set seemed to pull light into the room.

Taking her eyes from the carpet to Miss Nettie, Paige said, "Okay then," and clasped her hands together, not sure what to do or say next. Paige was even more concerned as she went and sat next to Miss Nettie on the couch. "So what is it, Miss Nettie? What brings you by?"

Miss Nettie began bouncing her knee. "Like I said, I didn't come to help you today." She then looked up from the floor and into Paige's eyes. "It's your help I hope I can count on today."

"Sure. I'll try," Paige said. "What is it?"

"Before I tell you," Miss Nettie began, "you have to promise me one thing." Miss Nettie had a desperate look on her face.

"Sure, Miss Nettie." Paige was now beyond concerned. Now she was worried. She'd never seen Miss Nettie in such a state before. "I promise," Paige said before even knowing what she was promising.

"You can't tell Mrs. Vanderdale."

Chapter 7

Paige stood up from the couch, abandoning her spot next to Miss Nettie. She wrung her hands together. She didn't like the fact that Miss Nettie was asking her to keep something from Mrs. Vanderdale. She didn't want to find herself in the middle of anything or have her loyalty to either woman tested.

"I know she is your girls' grandmother and is still like a mother-in-law to you," Miss Nettie said, standing. "But I need you to promise me you'll have hush-mouth grace about this, only because it could cost me my job."

Paige noticed the fear in Miss Nettie's eyes. She looked as though she could lose everything that had ever mattered to her. As far as Paige knew, the Vanderdales were the only family Miss Nettie had. Even though Paige and Miss Nettie were close, Paige had never really pried into Miss Nettie's past. She knew Miss Nettie had a criminal history and had served time in jail.

She'd made mention of living a reckless life in her younger days but finding Jesus later in life. Not only had finding Jesus put her on the right path in life, but meeting Mr. Vanderdale, who had counseled her during her stint in jail, had played a role as well.

"I'd work for that man for free," Miss Nettie had said in the past. "Jesus saved my soul, but Mr. Vanderdale saved my life."

Mr. Vanderdale had received recognition for his past service in the community and in his field. Prior to joining the family business he had married into, which was a theater chain, Mr. Vanderdale had been referred to as the underground Dr. Phil of the Midwest. Mr. Vanderdale had been known as Dr. Vanderdale to most. He had received his doctorate in psychiatry and had practiced his profession mainly in the prison systems. He felt that if an effort was truly put forth, then the inmates could actually receive what they'd been placed in the prisons to receive: rehabilitation.

Miss Nettie had been one of Mr. Vanderdale's patients. He'd believed so much in her rehabilitation and her ability to function and thrive successfully in society without recidivism that he had hired her to work for him as the family's live-in cook and housekeeper. She'd made both herself and Mr. Vanderdale proud.

Not only did Miss Nettie not want to lose her job and the only family she had, but Paige surmised that the woman didn't want to lose the respect of Mr. Vanderdale, either.

"Miss Nettie, if it involves anything that could cause harm to someone, I don't know if I can kee—"

"Child, I'm old," Miss Nettie interrupted. "Too old to be hurting anybody." Miss Nettie's eyes filled with glee. "But not too old for love."

Paige's ears perked up. "Love?" She hurried to usher Miss Nettie back to the couch, and then the two women sat down again. "You're in love?" Paige questioned. "But that's a good thing. Why in the world would you want to keep the fact that you are in love from Mrs. Vanderdale?" Paige held up her hands, dumbfounded. Suddenly the sunshiny expression on her face was covered over with a dark cloud. "Unless it's her husband you are in love with."

Paige let out a huge breath of air as she stood to her feet, covering her mouth. "Miss Nettie." She put her hands on her hips. "You're in love with Mr. Vanderdale? Good Lord!" Paige hit herself on the forehead. "I can't believe this." She hurried back over to Miss Nettie's side. "How long has the affair been going on?" Mr. Vanderdale was a nice-looking older man, if she had to say so herself. He looked ten years younger than he actually was and had managed to keep in shape by riding horses with Samantha at least once a week, when the weather permitted. She could see how Miss Nettie might have wanted to get with him. After all, Paige had gotten with his son, who looked identical and was just a younger version.

Miss Nettie smacked Paige a good one on the leg, as if giving her a spanking.

"Ouch!" Paige began to rub her leg. "What was that for?"

"For your mind taking up residence in the gutter. Now repent and go wash your mouth out with soap for even allowing that kind of filth to come out of it." Miss Nettie pointed down the hall that led to the first-floor guest bathroom.

"But I didn't say it. You said it," Paige said. "You said not to tell Mrs. Vanderdale that you are in love, because it's her husband you are in love with."

"I said no such thing. That's maybe what your mind heard, but it's certainly not what I said." Miss Nettie huffed and then turned her body away from Paige. She folded her arms and wrinkled her forehead. She was steaming.

"Well, what was I supposed to think?" Paige asked. "Why else would you need to keep the fact that you are in love a secret from Mrs. Vanderdale? Why would she care as long as it ain't her man?"

Miss Nettie, exasperated, turned to face Paige. "There were certain conditions to the Vanderdales hiring me, to them hiring any staff member. There was no fraternizing with other members of the staff, you know, along with all the other stuff, like no stealing, no doing drugs, et cetera."

Paige nodded her understanding. Then a light-bulb went off. She snapped her fingers. "It's Stuart. You're in love with Stuart, the butler." Paige then added excitedly, "That's it, isn't it?"

Miss Nettie's facial expression was a cross between stoic and guilty.

"Ooh, I knew it." Paige jumped up. "Mrs. Vanderdale said you and Stuart had been spending time together. Then Mr. Vanderdale asked if there was anything he should know about."

Miss Nettie jumped to her feet. She was horrified and agitated by the fact that Paige seemed to be so thrilled, as well as the fact that there was a chance Mr. and Mrs. Vanderdale had an inkling that she and Stuart were in a romantic relationship. "Mr. and Mrs. Vanderdale said that?" Worry laced her tone. "Oh, Lord, have mercy." Miss Nettie put her hand on her chest.

"They know. But we've been so discreet. At least I thought we had been." She rushed over and took Paige's hands in her own. "What else did they say? Did they mention firing us for breaking the rules?" Miss Nettie waited with bated breath for Paige to respond.

Paige shook her head, feeling bad for the anxiety that was overtaking Miss Nettie. Being in love was a time to be happy, not worried. "No, Miss Nettie. As a matter of fact, they seemed pretty nonchalant about it, like they couldn't care less."

Miss Nettie stared at Paige, waiting to see what else she could add to calm her nerves.

"Miss Nettie, please." Paige shook Miss Nettie's sweaty palms. "Look at you. I've never seen you like this before. You're in love. You should be on cloud nine."

"And I would be . . . I mean, I am. It's just that there's this big ole thundercloud dangling itself on top of my cloud nine." Miss Nettie looked down, shaking her head. "Oh, dear. What am I going to do?" She pulled her hands out of Paige's and wiped them down her flower-printed dress.

"You're going to tell them. That's what you're going to do," Paige told her. "Trust me, they are going to be happy for you. I mean, yeah, maybe in your earlier years they were worried about employees hooking up, breaking up, having to work together, which could cause tension on the job and all that drama. But you two are too old for all that drama now."

Miss Nettie threw her hands on her hips, stuck a foot out and stomped it, and looked at Paige with an attitude.

"I didn't mean *old*. I meant older," Paige insisted. That was a quick cleanup on aisle six. "Here. Come sit down." Paige walked Miss Nettie back over to the couch, and the two women sat down again. "I'm sure every now and then Mrs. Vanderdale sneaks off and watches one of those crazy reality shows with you."

Miss Nettie looked at Paige and zipped her lips with her thumb and index finger. Her lips were sealed one way or the other. Paige had a feeling that she was correct in her assumption.

"Just mention it to her then. Let the chips fall where they may, but I'm telling you this, Miss Nettie. If you are in love, like you say you are, then that's the most important thing. Life is short, and as we know, tomorrow definitely ain't promised. Live your days in love, Miss Nettie. Yes?" Paige stared at Miss Nettie, her eyes watering.

Paige's little spiel had even brought tears to Miss Nettie's eyes. Miss Nettie nodded and smiled. "Okay. I'll tell her."

"Good." Paige pulled Miss Nettie in for a hug. The two women embraced until Paige pulled out of the hug. She wiped her tears away and sniffed. "Now, you said something about needing my help."

"Oh, yeah," Miss Nettie said, as if remembering the true reason she'd come to Paige's house. "You're pretty savvy with that Internet and all that Facemagazine stuff, right?"

"Facemagazine?" Paige scrunched up her nose in confusion. "Oh, you mean Facebook." Paige laughed.

"Oh, girl, you know what I mean," Miss Nettie said. "I don't know anything about that stuff. You young people putting pictures up of everything from the polish color you put on your nails to the food you eat. Well, I be getting fed off the Bible, so post a picture of that. Humph."

"I hear you," Paige said, her laughter vanishing so she could hear Miss Nettie out.

"Anyway, I need your help with all that computer and Internet business. I was told that's the best place to start searching."

"I have a laptop and a personal computer," Paige told her. "What do you need help looking for?"

"Oh, I don't just want to look for 'em. I want to find 'em."

"What?" Paige asked.

"It's not a what. It's a who," Miss Nettie said, swallowing hard. "I need help finding my child."

Chapter 8

"Miss Nettie," Paige said, dumbfounded, "I didn't even know you had children. I didn't know you had any family."

Miss Nettie looked downward in shame. "Yeah, child, there's a lot you don't know about me. Things only God knows, and of course, now Stuart." Miss Nettie stood again. "I do have some kinfolk, though. But I also have a child."

Paige remained seated on the couch. She was getting exhausted from bouncing up and down. She watched Miss Nettie walk back and forth across the living room as she spoke.

"Stuart's the one who told me I ought to go look for my offspring. I feel so bad because that's a part of my past that I just completely blocked out. To be honest with you, up until the day I found Jesus, anything before that I don't even like to count as part of my life. God knows, it wasn't living. As a matter of fact, I should be dead now. But Jesus saw fit to get up on that cross and pay the price for me." Miss Nettie raised her right hand to the heavens. "Hallelujah."

Paige watched Miss Nettie do a little two-step Holy Ghost dance. "Go on and praise Him, Miss Nettie," Paige urged the older woman. Miss Nettie was dancing so hard, it made Paige want to get up and shout with her. But this was Miss Nettie's time. She didn't need no help.

After a few more seconds, Miss Nettie was able to bring her praise down. She breathed in and out, catching her breath before she started speaking again. "I'm sorry about that," Miss Nettie said. "But if God had done for you what He did for me, you'd understand."

"Oh, no need to apologize, Miss Nettie," Paige said. "I know what He's done for me and the many times I've had to stop whatever I'm doing, even if it's picking out cereal in the grocery store aisle, to give Him praise."

The two women laughed.

Miss Nettie wiped away the sweat that had formed on her forehead and went and sat in the closest chair.

"Well, I'm proud of you, Miss Nettie. Rummaging back in the past is not an easy thing to do. But sometimes we have to do it in order to understand our present situation and to be released into the future God has for us."

"Yeah, that's just about what Stuart said." A smile jumped on Miss Nettie's lips at the mention of Stuart. "He said he wants a future with me. All of me." Miss Nettie got all giddy like a schoolgirl. "He even mentioned the *M* word." Miss Nettie blushed.

"Oh, wow," Paige said. "He's talking marriage? Just how long have you two been seeing each other?"

"Well, we've been working together for years. Always been friends. We've sorta been like each other's confidant. Can tell each other everything. As a matter a fact, he's known for years I had a baby out there somewhere. He never pressed me or judged me, which is what a real friend does."

"Yeah, I know what you mean." Paige couldn't help but notice the similarities between Miss Nettie and Stuart's relationship and hers and Norman's. Miss Nettie and Stuart had also started off as coworkers. As coworkers they had become friends. Ultimately, a bond had formed between them throughout the years, and that bond had turned into love. A part of Paige envied Miss Nettie, while a much larger part was so happy for her. Paige wished everyone could share that special type of connection with a person.

"Now Stuart and I have taken our relationship to the romantic level, where we're talking about a future together. Marriage is the rest of our lives together. He says he don't like bony women, and therefore he ain't fond of skeletons, so I need to get 'em all out of my closet."

"That's fair," Paige said, "as long as he's willing to do the same."

"Oh, that Stuart of mine is an open book." Miss Nettie chuckled. "He couldn't hide a full-blooded corpse or a skeleton bone in his closet. Man don't know what TMI is. He's so unfiltered." Miss Nettie blushed again. "But that's what I love about him. He's got a walk-in closet. He invites me in, and everything is on display. I don't have to go looking and digging around. I don't ever have to worry about him lying and carrying on." She paused. "Even though, as you put it"—Miss Nettie raised an eyebrow at Paige—"we too old for that."

Paige made a shooing motion with her hand at Miss Nettie. "You know what I meant by that. Now, don't be holding it against me."

The slight smile Miss Nettie had on her face faded. "Oh, child, don't worry. I won't. I just hope that as I begin to uncover things about myself and the past that I've buried too deep to even remember, Stuart won't hold it against me."

Paige saw the fear in Miss Nettie's eyes. She got up off the couch and walked over to the chair her friend was sitting in. Paige kneeled down and took Miss Nettie's hands in hers. "Miss Nettie, one thing I know for sure is that you are an awesome woman of God. You know what? We don't even have to get that deep and spiritual. You are an awesome woman, period!"

Miss Nettie nodded. "I'd like to think that about myself. But is a woman who abandoned her child and never looked back really awesome?"

"You are looking back now." Paige shook her hands for effect. "Miss Nettie, you know better than anybody about God's perfect timing," she said.

Miss Nettie nodded. It looked as though Paige's words were sinking in with Miss Nettie, but Paige wasn't completely sure.

"Close your eyes," Paige said.

"Huh?" Miss Nettie replied.

"Close your eyes."

Miss Nettie hesitated at first but then did as the younger woman had asked.

Once Miss Nettie's eyes were closed, Paige began to speak. "Do you remember the day you gave birth to your child?"

Miss Nettie nodded.

"Do you remember the day you took your child home from the hospital?"

Miss Nettie paused, in thought. "I think so. Maybe." She thought hard. "I really can't remember."

This was deeper than Paige had initially thought. What had happened to cause a woman not to remember the day she took her newborn home from the hospital? Or if she even took him or her home at all? Paige took another route to get to the destination she was trying to reach. "Okay, so fast-forward to a year after giving birth."

Miss Nettie looked as though she was racking her brains. "I . . . I . . ." She began to look flushed and started shifting in the chair.

"Just calm down and think."

"It's so hard. I wasn't me. I wasn't in my right mind. That woman back then, she did things. Bad things. For no rhyme or reason. Just because."

"Just because of what?" Paige asked.

Miss Nettie shook her head. "I don't know why. I think she liked . . ." Her words trailed off.

"What did she like?" Paige asked, all of a sudden feeling like a therapist instead of just someone trying to help her friend.

"Pain." A tear slid through one of Miss Nettie's closed eyelids.

Paige nodded. "Okay, so what do you think she would have done if she'd had her child in her life?"

A tear fell from Miss Nettie's other eye. "Caused it pain."

Paige ignored the tears falling from her own face and continued her conversation with Miss Nettie. "So aren't you glad you loved your child enough that you were so unselfish as to not want to bring him or her any pain?"

Miss Nettie nodded, and a smile forced its way through the tears. "Yes. That's it. I didn't want to hurt my baby. I didn't want to cause my child any pain. I would have hurt it. I liked to fight. Cause trouble. Which is how I landed in jail. I got into a fight. I cut a woman. Cut her face up. I was a bad person. I would have been a bad mother. I would have hurt my child." Tears continued to stream down Miss Nettie's face.

"So you see, Miss Nettie, you didn't abandon your baby. You saved it."

Miss Nettie opened her eyes. "I saved my child from that person I used to be." Delight at the revelation filled Miss Nettie's eyes.

"Right, Miss Nettie," Paige said, elated. "So you can wipe that guilt and shame away, the same way I'm wiping these tears away." Paige proceeded to use her hand to wipe Miss Nettie's tears away.

"Oh, Lord, child, thank you." Miss Nettie threw her arms around Paige. "Thank you for helping me see that." She pulled away and looked Paige in the eye. "That's just what I needed to uncover in order to dive into this thing headfirst without the fear of drowning."

"To God be the glory," Paige said, not about to take any credit whatsoever for what God had just done.

"Yes, to God be the glory," Miss Nettie agreed. "Now let's find my child."

Chapter 9

"There's something Miss Nettie wants to tell you both," Paige said to the Vanderdales as she stood next to Miss Nettie in the Vanderdales' parlor.

The atmosphere was calm, and the smell of food being prepared wafted through the house. Vegetable beef soup, if one had to guess. And nine times out of ten, Miss Nettie would make some homemade corn bread and rolls from scratch to go with it. Mrs. Vanderdale preferred the sweet yellow corn bread, while Mr. Vanderdale's mouth watered for the buttered-down yeast rolls. Taking in the strong scent, one could practically taste the meal in one's mouth.

Wearing an apron, Miss Nettie stood with her hands folded in front of her like a frightened teenager. Miss Nettie wasn't joking. She really did need Paige there for moral support while she confessed to the Vanderdales about her fraternizing with the other help.

Paige didn't mind at all being there for Miss Nettie. The times Miss Nettie had been there for Paige, especially after the death of Norman, were countless. Paige was going to help Miss Nettie any way she could, even in the process of finding her child. Last week, when Miss Nettie had come to Paige's home to request her help and had opened up to her about her and Stuart and the fact that she had given birth all those years ago, the girls had come home from school before they could even get started on their Internet search.

Paige had suggested that she and Miss Nettie find the time to get together and talk about some details that might help them with their search, rather than just diving in, clueless. Miss Nettie had agreed, but first she wanted to conquer the issue of telling the Vanderdales about her relationship with Stuart. So here they stood.

"Well, what is it, Nettie?" Mrs. Vanderdale asked. "I must admit I'm a little caught off guard, with Paige giving an introduction." Mrs. Vanderdale looked at Paige and then back at Miss Nettie again. "You've always been able to talk to either myself or Norm." She nodded toward her husband. "So what's going on?"

Miss Nettie looked at Paige. Paige gave her a nod of encouragement. She then faced her employees. "Well," Miss Nettie began, "let me start off by saying that I have truly loved working for the Vanderdale family and—"

"Oh, dear Jesus, she's quitting," Mrs. Vanderdale screeched, looking at her husband. "Do something, Norm. We can't let her quit." Mrs. Vanderdale stood up from her seat and walked over to Miss Nettie. "It's that Mrs. Lampkins, isn't it?" she asked Miss Nettie. "Uh-huh. I knew it." She walked over to her husband, who sat in his chair, silently waiting for his employee to say exactly what it was that was on her mind. "Every time she comes for dinner, she goes on and on about how amazing Nettie is and how, if I don't watch out, she's going to steal her from me. That witch."

"Honey," Mr. Vanderdale said to his wife in a scolding tone.

"Well, she *is* a witch." Mrs. Vanderdale walked back over to Nettie. "What's she offering you?"

Miss Nettie went to speak, but Mrs. Vanderdale raised her hand to silence her. "Never mind. It doesn't matter. I'll double it."

"Mrs. Vanderdale," Miss Nettie said, managing to squeeze in a few sentences, "Mrs. Lampkins hasn't offered me anything. I wasn't going to tell you that I quit."

Mrs. Vanderdale paused for a moment and then let out a huge sigh of relief. "Oh, my goodness, Nettie. Why didn't you just say so?" She threw her arms around Miss Nettie and laughed.

Miss Nettie hesitantly wrapped her arms around her boss and hugged her while giving Paige a "What should I do now?" look.

"Tell her," Paige mouthed, using her hands to talk as well.

"I'd never quit on you and Mr. Vanderdale," Miss Nettie said as she began to pat Mrs. Vanderdale on the back. "And I'm glad to see you react that way at just the thought of me leaving you. Which means maybe you won't fire me when I tell you what I have to say."

Mrs. Vanderdale, suddenly concerned again about what Miss Nettie had to share, went to pull away, but Miss Nettie jerked her right back into the hug. "Nettie, why on earth would we fire you?" Mrs. Vanderdale said, trying to breathe, as Miss Nettie's hug seemed to have tightened.

"I don't know how to say this," Miss Nettie began, "but I'm going to start by saying exactly what I said to Paige when I told her." Miss Nettie swallowed and then just spit it out. "I'm in love."

There was a pause as everyone waited for more.

"In love?" Mrs. Vanderdale questioned, trying to squirm out of the hug, to no avail. "Why on earth would we fire you for being in love?" she asked. "I mean, unless . . ." Mrs. Vanderdale's face turned as pale as a ghost. Suddenly she found the strength deep within to burst out of the hug. Horrified, she looked at Miss Nettie. She looked at Mr. Vanderdale and then back at Miss Nettie. "Unless the person you are in love with is . . . is . . ." She couldn't even get the words out. She snapped her neck to gaze at Paige. "And, Paige, you mean to tell me you knew about this? She told you? Nettie is secretly in love with my husband, and you didn't say a word?"

"What?" Paige's mouth dropped open to the floor. How in the world could Mrs. Vanderdale possibly think that they were there to tell her that Miss Nettie was in love with Mr. Vanderdale? But then again, that was the first thing that had come to Paige's mind when Miss Nettie had shown up on her doorstep and told her she was not too old for love.

"You heard me," Mrs. Vanderdale said to Paige. "She's been sleeping in our house, in bed at night, desiring my husband." Mrs. Vanderdale pointed an evil finger at Paige. "And you knew. You're almost as bad as her!"

"Naomi, you know darn well I would never allow such a . . . ," Paige began, but then she figured, *Why waste any more time trying to explain the situation?* She'd come to lend moral support only. It was Miss Nettie's responsibility to tell the Vanderdales about her relationship with Stuart. But things were starting to get out of hand. The last time she was in the Vanderdales' parlor, things had gotten heated between her and the lady of the house due to confusion and misunderstandings. Paige could not—would not—allow it to happen again. "Miss Nettie and Stuart have been kicking it."

Mrs. Vanderdale had a puzzled look on her face.

Paige explained, "You know, kicking it? Seeing one another. Diggin' on each other. He might even ask her to marry him. There. Dang!" Paige flung her hands up in the air, let them drop heavily, and then huffed as she made a half turn. She added a "Geesh" for good measure.

Mrs. Vanderdale stopped her ranting and looked at Miss Nettie. "Nettie, is that true? Is that what you wanted to tell us?"

Miss Nettie, whose actions resembled those of a teenager who was being scolded by her parents for missing curfew, looked at her boss and nodded. "Yes, it's true. I knew it was against the rules that you and Mr. Vanderdale set when you first hired me. And I swear, from the day I started working here, I have followed every single one to the tee." Miss Nettie, with newfound courage, lifted her head high and with an adamant tone announced, "But this is one rule I can't help but break." She stepped around Mrs. Vanderdale, walked toward Mr. Vanderdale, but stopped midway so that she was positioned between the couple. "I owe you so much, Mr. Vanderdale. You gave me a chance when nobody else would." She looked at the missus. "And you've been the best boss and confidante I could have ever imagined. But I'm in love. I'm in love with a fellow coworker. I'm in love with Stuart."

There was that smile on Miss Nettie's face again. The one that lit up the room every time she mentioned Stuart. She was a woman in love, all right. And it was written all over her face.

There was silence in the room as Miss Nettie, as well as Paige, waited for the Vanderdales' response.

Mrs. Vanderdale looked at her husband, who looked at her. She then looked at Nettie. "Is that it?" She shrugged her shoulders. "Is that what this whole meeting is about? To tell us you and Stuart are an item?"

Miss Nettie, leery and unable to read Mrs. Vanderdale's reaction, replied with a reluctant tone. "Well, yes."

Mrs. Vanderdale once again looked at her husband, who wore a frown on his face. Catching everyone in the room by surprise, she burst into laughter mixed with yelping. She clapped her hands together and stomped over to her husband. She stood right in his face, put one hand on her hip, and held the other out flat. "That's one hundred bucks, buster. You lose."

That was not exactly what Miss Nettie had thought Mrs. Vanderdale's reaction to the news would be. She got even more confused when she watched Mr. Vanderdale begin to dig into his pocket with a grunt. He pulled out his wallet, then flipped through bills as he looked up at his wife with disdain.

"What are you looking at me like that for?" Mrs. Vanderdale said, happy as a lark. "Hate the game, not the player."

Mr. Vanderdale extended a crisp one-hundred-dollar bill to his wife.

Mrs. Vanderdale snatched it up. "Yes!" she exclaimed, tucking it down into her bra for effect.

Paige got a kick out of the couple's actions. Miss Nettie was confused.

"What's going on here?" Miss Nettie asked. "You're not even the least bit mad?" She looked from husband to wife.

"Mad?" Mrs. Vanderdale said. "I'm ecstatic. I just won the hundred-dollar bet between me and

Mr. Vanderdale." She looked at her husband. "Told you." She stuck out her tongue, then patted the spot where she'd safely tucked the money.

"Told him what?" Miss Nettie said.

"I bet sore loser over there"—Mrs. Vanderdale pointed to her husband, who was still frowning—"that you and Stuart had a little something going on, and I was right."

Miss Nettie was relieved. Confused, but relieved, nonetheless. "So you knew about Stuart and me already?"

"Well, I kind of sensed something," Mrs. Vanderdale said. "We all talked about it." She turned and said to Paige, "Remember?"

Paige nodded.

"Well, later on that night Norm and I were discussing it. That's when we placed the bet," Mrs. Vanderdale said.

Miss Nettie wanted clarification. "So even though Stuart and I broke the rules about workers not fraternizing with one another, you two aren't mad?"

Both Vanderdales shook their heads.

"No." Mr. Vanderdale waved the idea off. "That rule was made back in the Stone Age, when you guys were much younger. You're older and mature now. You guys know how to handle a relationship."

Miss Nettie exhaled and clasped her hands together. "Thank you so much, Mr. Vanderdale," she said with a smile.

Now it was Paige who was frowning. "What? He calls you old, and you thank him? I say it, and I get attitude." Paige sucked her teeth. "Ain't that about nothing?"

"It's not what he said. It's how he said it," Miss Nettie replied. "Sometimes it's all about the delivery." She looked back at Mrs. Vanderdale. "I'm glad you won a hundred dollars, but I'm even gladder that you're not upset and you're not gonna fire Stuart and me."

"Fire you two?" Mrs. Vanderdale said. "This house would fall apart without the two of you."

"The house would be just fine," Mr. Vanderdale said, jumping in. "It would be this one right here who would fall apart." He pointed to his wife. "God forbid that woman had to make her bed every day."

"I'd be like Oprah Winfrey," Mrs. Vanderdale announced. "She had no problem telling the world that she makes her bed only on the weekends."

There was light laughter in the room.

"But just so we're clear," Mr. Vanderdale said, "so that there is no more jumping to conclusions, because I don't think I can bear witness to one more episode of *Three's Company* taking place right here in my living room." There was laughter again before he continued. "You and Stuart have a place here in our home for as long as you two will have us."

Miss Nettie looked at Paige with excitement. Her worries were over. "I can't wait to tell Stuart."

"By the way, where is Stuart?" Mr. Vanderdale asked. "Why isn't he here with you during your moment of confession?"

"He wanted to join me, but I thought it just coming from me, and having Paige by my side, would be better." Miss Nettie looked at Paige and winked.

Mrs. Vanderdale wasn't buying it. She whispered to Miss Nettie, "Didn't want all that testosterone in the room when talking about something as mushy as love, huh?"

"You hit the nail on the head." Miss Nettie laughed.

Once all the laughter had died down, Paige said, "Well, I'm about to go. I need to be home when the girls get off the bus."

"And Norm and I can get back to the game of Scrabble we had going on in there, on the dining room table," Mrs. Vanderdale said.

Mr. Vanderdale stood to his feet. "We'll see you later, Paige," he said, and then he and his wife headed for the dining room.

"Oh, there's just one more thing," Miss Nettie called out in a serious tone.

Mrs. Vanderdale stopped in her tracks and turned around. "What is it, Nettie?" she asked with concern.

"You know all that talk you did when you thought Mrs. Lampkins was trying to steal me away from you?"

Mrs. Vanderdale nodded.

This time it was Miss Nettie who put her hand out in the collection position. "Well, about that raise . . ."

Once again they all shared a moment of laughter. There was one thing both Miss Nettie and Paige could say. They'd all had their disagreements with one another. There had been quite a few rocky moments. In the end, though, it felt good knowing that they could all laugh together.

But just how long would it be before their laughter turned to tears?

Chapter 10

It had been such a long day for Paige. The whole situation at the Vanderdales' with Miss Nettie trying to tell her employers about her relationship with Stuart, blah, blah, blah . . . It was too much. Then, on her way home, she'd gotten stuck behind a school bus that was transporting the handicapped. She had had to wait for the bus to stop, for someone to come out of the home, and for the driver to operate the lift that allowed the wheelchair-bound rider to be lowered off the bus. Then, of course, the driver had had to roll the person off the ramp and over to the caregiver. It had seemed like she'd spent another five minutes watching the lift rise and slowly tuck itself back into the bus.

Although heated and anxious inside, Paige had thanked God that she had two healthy, beautiful daughters who were able to catch regular school buses. Besides, things could have been worse. There could have been a bad accident that held up traffic, and Paige could have found herself spitting bullets in standstill traffic that didn't even move an inch. Since Norman's death, though, Paige had become far more sensitive about car accidents. Instead of being angry that an accident was holding her up and preventing her from getting to her destination, she would pray for those involved in the accident and their families.

This time while she'd prayed to God and thanked Him for giving her healthy children, she threw in a selfish prayer—that she'd get home on time to meet Adele and Norma at the bus stop. Norma was in kindergarten, and it was the school district's policy not to allow kindergarten children off the bus without an adult being there to pick them up.

When Paige pulled up to her house, she could see the bus pulling away without having dropped her children off. She panicked at first. She had no idea where the bus took children who didn't have an adult there to pick them up. But then she realized that all she had to do was follow the bus to the next stop, which was exactly what she did. As soon as the driver turned on the stoplight and the stop signs poked out from the sides of the bus, Paige threw the car in park and then hopped out and ran to the bus door.

As kids filed out, Paige apologized to the driver for not being at the stop to get Norma off. Paige was so excited to see the faces of her daughters as they got off the bus.

"Mommy!" Little Norma was the first one to jump into her arms.

"We were worried about you," Adele said.

"Aww, how sweet," Paige said. "I was worried about you two as well. But come on. We need to get back in the car before traffic starts moving again."

Paige scurried to get the girls in the car just as the bus pulled off. "Seat belts," she reminded her daughters, and then there were three consecutive clicks in the car. Paige pulled off behind the bus, prepared to circle the block and head back home.

"They wouldn't let you off the bus, either?" Paige asked Adele. Adele was in first grade, so it wasn't against the school district's policy to allow her off the bus without an adult at the bus stop to meet her.

"Yeah, they would," Adele said. "But I wasn't about to leave my sister on that bus. Puh-lease." She snapped her neck and rolled her eyes.

Paige looked in the rearview mirror and smiled at her mini me. Full of attitude, Adele had gotten it honest.

"That's right, girlfriend," Paige said, giving Adele a high five over the seat. "You make sure you stick with your sister."

"I'm my sister's keeper," the girls said in unison, knowing that was exactly what their mother was going to say next. That was something Paige quoted frequently and explained to her daughters. She'd drilled it into them never to let anything separate them or come between them, not friends and definitely not boys.

"That's right," Paige said to them, proud that they'd been paying attention.

She got the girls back home, she did their homework with them, she cooked and fed them dinner, and then they watched some television and she got them all bathed and tucked into bed. She even read them each a bedtime story. It was at story time that Paige gave them individual attention. She visited each of their rooms, tucking them in and allowing them to pick out the book they wanted to read.

After showering and getting on her nightclothes, Paige climbed in bed, ready to dive into a book of her own. It wasn't *The Cat in the Hat,* by Dr. Seuss, or *The Secret Olivia Told Me,* by N. Joy, which were the books she'd read to the girls. It was a Brenda Jackson romance novel.

She grabbed her book off of the white Victorian nightstand, bumping the phone. That reminded her that she wanted to give her brother a call. She picked up the phone and dialed her brother. Having watched Adele and Norma today had drummed up thoughts of her and her brother when they were younger. She smiled just thinking about how close they had once been. But then, as they got older, she had felt that he was the golden boy, and she had distanced herself due to jealousy. Even though they weren't close, she loved him to death.

"Hey, little sis," her brother said into the phone receiver after the second ring. "I thought my eyes were deceiving me when I looked at the caller ID," he joked.

"Boy, quit playing. What's up? How have you been?"

Even though it had been months since Paige had talked to her brother, the two picked up where they'd left off the last time, as if it had just been yesterday. An hour later and after making plans for their families to get together for an outing, Paige ended the call.

Paige was sure some siblings talked to one another every day, every other day, or at least once a week. *Good for them,* she thought, but that wasn't the relationship she had with her brother. But one thing she knew for certain was that if she called on him, her brother would be there for her in a minute, and vice versa.

Paige sat back on her king-size bed with a Victorian headboard and footboard that matched the nightstand, dresser, and chest. She looked down at her book. It had gotten late, but she couldn't imagine closing her eyes without first escaping into a fairy-tale romance that girls only dreamed of. After about twenty pages of reading, Paige's eyelids were fluttering. She was forcing them to stay open. She did not want to stop reading her book. But she had to be up and ready to function in the morning in order to do it all over again. She closed the book and placed it back on the nightstand.

"Tomorrow it's me and you." She patted the book and blew a kiss at the hunk of a cover model. She then pulled the comforter up to her neck while nestling into her pillow. She closed her eyes with a smile on her face. Reading a Brenda Jackson book at bedtime could do that to a chick. Now, if only her real life could read like a romance novel. Only time would tell.

"Ugh!" Paige jumped out of bed. Her heart was beating faster than it ever had in her life.

She'd gotten so caught up in her reading last night that she'd forgotten to set her alarm. This wasn't the first time one of her favorite author's books had done this to her. This author had been responsible for making her late to work at least three times back when she worked at the theater. Countless meals had burned and had to be placed in the trash, and many pizzas had been ordered as a replacement, because she'd been so caught up in the great reads. If it was possible for a reader to sue an author for time missed at work, food wasted, and pizzas ordered, she absolutely would. But at the end of the day any avid reader would confess that it was all worth it!

"Come on, girls. Let's go. Let's go!" Paige shouted as she walked out into the hallway. "Rise and shine. Wakey, wakey."

She entered Adele's room first. "Hey, little one. It's time to get up and get ready for school," Paige said, walking over to her oldest daughter's full-size bed. Paige had allowed Adele to pick out the paint color of her bedroom walls. The little girl said that the soft pink walls reminded her of her favorite cotton candy.

Adele snuggled deeper under her covers. "Mommy, I don't want to get up. Can I stay home today?"

"You know you have to go to school and become the smartest girl in the world." Paige sat down on the bed next to her child, who was cocooned in her princess comforter. "Besides, this evening is your first day of dance class. If you don't go to school, then you can't go to dance class, either."

Adele snapped that comforter off her head with the quickness. "Yippee! Dance class. I'm gonna be a ballerina." Her hair was a pretty mess atop her head.

Paige patted her daughter's hair down. "Yes, you are." Paige kissed her on the forehead. "Now, go on into the bathroom and get your teeth brushed. I'm going to go get your sister started, and then I'll be back to make sure you wash your face and get all that toothpaste from around your mouth."

Adele jumped out of bed and headed into the Jack and Jill bathroom that connected her bedroom to Norma's. The entire time she sang, "I'm going to be a ballerina. I'm going to be a ballerina."

Paige shook her head and smiled. She got up off of Adele's bed and headed into Norma's room. Norma started her whining before Paige could even get a word out.

"I'm staying home with you today. I don't like my teacher. She's mean," Norma complained.

"Mean?" Paige asked. "You think Miss Walton is mean? Why? What does she do that is so mean?" Paige sat on Norma's bed, joining her on the Care Bears comforter that matched the window dressings.

"She makes us do work," Norma answered, throwing her arms across her chest in a pout.

Paige chuckled and kissed her on the forehead. "That's because she wants to make you smart."

"I'm already smart."

"She wants to make you smarter."

Norma thought for a minute. "Smarter than Adele?" That sibling rivalry showed in her eyes.

"Yep, smarter than Adele."

That perked little Norma up. She sat up in the bed, as if whatever it was she had dreamed about had finally come true. "Adele is already older than me, bigger than me, and prettier than me. But I'm going to be smarter than her." Norma stood up in her bed and began wiggling her bottom.

"Get down here before you hurt yourself." Paige laughed and grabbed Norma by her waist, then pulled her down into a hug. "Yes, Adele is bigger and older, but nobody is prettier.

Everybody is just . . ." She looked at Norma to finish the sentence.

"Pretty." Norma spread her arms wide. "Everybody in the world is pretty."

"Yep. Now get up and head into the bathroom. Adele should be finishing up."

Paige helped the girls finish getting ready for school. She packed their lunches while they ate breakfast and then put them on the bus . . . on time. After sending the girls off to school, Paige went back inside her house. Closing the door behind her, she sighed while looking around the room. "A woman's work is never done," she declared.

Her day was just getting started. She had housework to do, laundry to do, and there was some yard work she needed to do out back. The guy whom she paid to cut her grass had used a substitute lawn mower last time. The one he usually used had been in the shop. His backup didn't have a bag to catch the grass. It had started to rain before he could finish raking and bagging the grass clippings in the backyard, and Paige had told him he didn't need to finish the task. He'd offered to come back and do it, but Paige had told him that she didn't mind getting her hands dirty. He'd given her a discount on this month's service. More rain was in the forecast in a couple days, so she wanted to get the grass clippings up before then.

Four hours later, Paige had put a huge dent in her daily tasks. She had tackled getting all the grass clippings up and toting the lawn bag full of clippings to the curb. She still had laundry to do: she was going to wash all their bedding, in addition to what was in their hampers. Feeling grubby from being outside, the next thing she wanted to do was take a nice, hot shower. Paige went into the laundry room and stripped down naked. She placed all her dirty clothes in the hamper there. She wanted to avoid transporting to her bedroom any insects that might have gotten on her while she was doing the outdoor chores. Besides, Paige was the only one home. She loved those moments when she could walk through the house, naked as the day she was born. She felt so free in all her thickness. Whatever jiggled and shook, she loved it!

In the shower Paige scrubbed the outdoor residue off herself with her body sponge. Afterward, she pampered herself with Ghanaian Brown Sugar & Honey Sugar Scrub from Soul Purpose, which she'd purchased from a representative named Trina Davies, whom she'd found on Facebook. Her skin felt so soft and renewed. She put on some khakis and a button-down blouse.

She had two hours left before the girls would be home, so she put on some thick house socks to lounge around in, instead of her Anne Klein baby doll flats, which she liked to wear with her khakis.

Paige had signed up to be a parent assistant at the girls' school, which meant she did little things here and there to help the teachers out, such as going into the school to help copy papers or to assist with lunch or playground duty. Adele's teacher had asked Paige to help with some cutouts she wanted to decorate the room with. She was basically turning their classroom into a spring garden made out of construction paper. Paige had about sixty tulips and stems she needed to get cut out. She'd already cut out about fifteen. She had forty-five to go, and they needed to be done in a week. So she opted to cut out a few more before the girls got home. But first the grumbling of her belly reminded her that she hadn't eaten all day.

Paige headed to the kitchen, deciding on the way there that she'd make a turkey sandwich on wheat, with some sliced cucumbers marinated in apple cider vinegar and with salt and pepper. She had her diabetes under control—no more insulin shots—and she was going to keep it that way by eating healthy. She did splurge on those pizzas every now and then.

As Paige maneuvered from the refrigerator to the counter, making her lunch, a piece of paper sitting by one of the canisters caught her eye. "Ryan," she said softly. She didn't realize until five seconds in that she was smiling the same way Miss Nettie smiled whenever she said Stuart's name. Could it be that the book she'd read last night was still playing with her imagination, or did Paige really think she still had a shot at a happy ending with Ryan?

Paige picked up the piece of paper that she'd written Ryan's work number on. She recalled having removed it from her pocket and having set it there the day she'd written his number down. She fingered the piece of paper and stared at it for a moment. Everyone around her was in love. Miss Nettie was in love. The Vanderdales were in love. She thought about the renewal of vows ceremony she'd sung at not too long ago for her friend Lorain and her husband, Nicholas. It had been so beautiful. God just seemed to be in the blessing business when it came to love these days. And if He'd done it for all of them, then He certainly could do it for her.

Paige dropped the knife she was about to use to spread a light layer of fat-free mayo on one side of her sandwich. She then walked over to the kitchen phone. Without hesitating or second-guessing herself, she immediately picked up the phone and began dialing the number.

After two rings, a male voice finally picked up. "H2J Photography Hilliard. This is Ryan. How can I help you?"

Click!

What Paige had not expected was for Ryan to actually answer the phone. "He answered the frickin' phone!" she shouted, her hands up and her fingers spread. She was the walking epitome of shock. That caught her off guard too. Her Billy Bad act had been tested, and she'd failed miserably, as she'd hung up that phone like a big chicken.

"And I hung up in his ear!" She was horrified. She wanted so badly to pick up the phone and call him right back, but what was she supposed to say? "Hi, Ryan. It's me, Paige, the one who just hung up on you."

Of course, if she called right back, he'd know it was she who had hung up. She covered her face with her hands, as if hiding. She knew she had to call that man back. But should she do it now or later? Later she might chicken out.

The phone rang and tore Paige's mind away from her dilemma. She looked down at the caller ID. She now had a brand-new dilemma. The call was from H2J Photography.

Should she answer it or not?

Chapter 11

"Paige?"

It was Ryan's voice that Paige heard after picking up the phone on the third ring.

"Ryan," she replied. "Hello? Hello?" she added, faking phone trouble. That would be her excuse as to why she'd hung up in his ear.

"Yes, it's Ryan. Paige—"

She talked over top of him. "Ryan, can you hear me?"

"I can hear you, but you can't hear me," he said loudly, as if that was going to change things.

"Hold on." Paige took the phone away from her ear, placed it on her chest, and tried her hardest not to roar with laughter. She couldn't believe she was a grown woman playing these kinds of games. But it was the only way for her to keep from telling the truth, which was, "I got butterflies when I heard your voice, and so I hung up the phone in your ear."

"Paige, are you still there?"

Paige could hear the muffled voice of Ryan. She put the phone back to her ear.

"I'm going to call you back to see if we get a better connection." He hung up the phone.

Paige hit the END button on her phone, placed the phone down on the countertop, and burst out laughing. "Oh, my goodness. I'm a hot mess!" she exclaimed. She finished preparing her lunch and went and sat down at the table, waiting for the phone to ring again. After she was halfway through her lunch and the phone hadn't rung, she went and retrieved it from the counter. She checked to make sure that it still had battery life, that it hadn't died. Her phone indicated that the battery was at 70 percent, so that certainly wasn't why it hadn't rung.

She sat the phone down next to her sandwich. For the next five minutes she chewed, looked at the phone, swallowed, then looked at the phone again. This went on until her sandwich was gone. Why hadn't Ryan called back? Paige's ego started to deflate.

"I knew I shouldn't have called him," Paige said as she carried her dirty dishes over to her stainless-steel double sink. She looked up at the round kitchen clock that was trimmed in a heavy stainless steel. Through the silence she could hear the faint ticking. She had some time before the girls were to return home from school. She decided to go upstairs and retrieve the book she'd fallen asleep reading last night.

She returned to the living room with the book in hand, and twenty pages later Paige had not looked over at that phone one time. She was far too engaged in the book. It served as an excellent way to keep her mind off of the fact that Ryan had not called her back. After another ten pages, Paige placed the book on the coffee table and headed out the door to get the girls off the bus. By the time Paige made it to the end of the driveway, the big yellow school bus was clearing the corner, headed toward Paige. The bus's yellow warning lights began flashing as it slowed. The lights changed to red and the stop signs flipped out as the bus came to a complete stop.

"Afternoon," Paige said, greeting the bus driver once the doors opened.

"Good day to you, Ms. Vanderdale," the bus driver said with a wave.

Both Adele and Norma came tromping off the bus, chattering away. The bus driver pulled off and said a final good-bye in the form of a honk. Both Norma and Adele fought to tell their mother about their day at school.

"Hold up. Hold up," Paige said. "I can't listen to you both at once." One at a time she allowed the girls to rattle on about their day at school. They chattered all the way to the kitchen, where they knew they'd be able to pick out their desired after-school snack.

"And Johnny ate a booger," Norma said, hopping into a chair.

"Ewww," Adele said, scrunching up her face.

"You sure you want to talk about that when you're about to eat?" Paige asked, opening the refrigerator. She began to pull out Tupperware containers of sliced fruit, such as strawberries, pineapple, grapes, and melon.

"Well, I don't know if he ate it," Norma said, recanting. "I saw him pull it out of his nose with a finger on the hand he writes with. He never wiped it on anything. He picked up his pencil to write, and there was no booger. So either he ate it or it's stuck on his pencil."

"Gross!" Adele shouted.

"Well," Paige said, pulling a creamy whipped topping out of the freezer, "whatever you do, don't ever borrow a pencil from Johnny."

"I won't," Norma said. "I have lots of pencils of my own."

"Good girl," Paige said as she scooped the fruity treat into bowls and then poured each of the girls a glass of milk to go with it.

She stood in the kitchen and talked with the girls while they ate. Afterward, she allowed them a forty-five-minute play break to unwind before they dived into any homework or reading. Even though Norma was only in kindergarten, her teacher sent home a book in her bag, and Paige had to read it with her, as well as work on a phonics sheet with her. After getting the girls situated, Paige snatched up her own book and her phone off the table. She was going to go put the book up until she could find the time to get back into it, which would hopefully be tonight.

When Paige picked up her cell phone, she noticed the message letting her know that she had one missed call. It was from Ryan. She looked at the time the call had come through and realized it was when she was outside getting the girls off the bus.

"Go figure!" she sighed, thumping herself in the forehead with the palm of her hand. "Just my luck." Paige was about to set the phone back down when she saw that in addition to that one new missed call, she had one new voice message. A smile spread across her face. Looked like it was just her luck, after all.

"Hey, Paige. This is Ryan. Sorry I didn't call you right back. The phone at the office started ringing like crazy. Anyway, I was thrilled that you had called me. Then we experienced that crazy phone trouble. I'm not sure exactly why you were calling. It has been a while since that last family portrait." He chuckled. "Well, just give me a call back whenever you get this message or you have the time. If it's business you're wanting to discuss, you have my business number. If it's personal . . . 614-555-7576. I'll talk to you soon."

Paige listened to the message twice before saving it. Afterward, with a huge grin on her face and a fist pumping in the air, she shouted, "Yes!" She began doing this little jig around the living room, twitching her hips. "Uh-huh, I'm the bomb. Go, Paige. You da bomb."

Paige figured she'd continue the rest of her daily routine with the girls. She'd call Ryan back in between that and cooking dinner. But then she remembered that this was the girls' first day of dance class. "Shoot." She huffed. "I don't want to have to wait that long to call him back." Paige twisted her lips as she thought. She could always call him now, but then she might have to rush off the phone in the middle of their conversation to do homework with the girls. She wasn't about to call him and chat through the first session ever of the girls' dance class. It was final; she'd wait until tomorrow.

"Then tomorrow they'll be something else," she said, and with good reason too. That was how things had always been with her and Ryan. Right when they were about to get to the good part—to the center of the lollipop with the Tootsie Roll or the bubble gum—life would happen and Paige would always find herself having to walk away from what could be with Ryan.

"Oh, well, we'll see," Paige murmured as she headed up the steps. Midway up, she stopped in her tracks. "What am I saying here?" she said happily. "I'll call him tonight, once I get the girls settled in bed." The girls were always in bed by 8:00 p.m. That was still a pretty decent hour to call somebody, Paige figured. Then a mischievous smile spread across her face. "After all, this is not business. It's all pleasure."

Chapter 12

"It was so good seeing you, Lorain," Paige said, hugging the former New Day Temple of Faith member. Lorain left New Day and joined her husband's family church when she married him.

"You too," Lorain replied. "We're going to have to get our girls together for a playdate." She held her eleven-month-old son in her arms.

The two women stood in the lobby of the dance studio, where they had bumped into one another. Lorain was leaving the studio with her twin daughters in tow. Paige was just coming in, Adele and Norma by her side, anxiously awaiting the moment they could get their dance on. Lorain's daughters were on the competition dance team. Since Adele and Norma were just beginners, they wouldn't have any dance classes with Lorain's girls.

"Just let me know when," Paige replied. "The girls will love it."

The two women said their good-byes. Lorain and her girls exited the studio, while Paige led her girls to the locker room. After the hour-long session, Paige packed up the girls and their dance bags, helped them into the car, and drove home. By eight o'clock sharp, Adele and Norma were each tucked in bed. Paige retired to her bedroom, but not to sleep. She made a mad dash for her phone, which was charging on the nightstand. She grabbed it off the charger and sat down on the bed. She called her voice mail, as she'd saved Ryan's message. While she punched the necessary buttons to make the message play again, she retrieved a pen and paper. She was prepared to write down Ryan's cell number when he recited it in the voice message.

It was now 8:05 p.m. Her courage was on ten. She wasted not another minute before dialing Ryan's cell phone. It rang twice before he picked up and greeted her.

"Hi," Paige said, smiling. "It's Paige. I got your message."

"Clearly you did. And although I'd love to snap a picture of your beautiful face, I'm so glad you called this number and not the office." He started laughing.

Paige joined in, feeling like a giddy teenager at his compliment. He was flirting. Could that be a sign that he was single?

"So what have you been up to? How are the girls?" Ryan asked.

"The girls are great. Getting older, which pretty much tells you what I've been up to."

"They're giving you a run for your money, huh?"

"You know it," Paige said. "But I don't have to tell you. I'm sure you experience the same from your two sons."

Ryan and Paige chatted like best friends for the next fifteen minutes. There was no awkward silence, where all they could hear was one another breathing. Just like always, they picked up where they'd left off. This sat so well in Paige's spirit. All doubts about whether she should have placed a call to Ryan were no more.

"I know you are a God-fearing Christian woman and all, but I have to ask this question," Ryan said. "Are you married?"

Paige sucked her teeth. "Now, why on earth would I have called you on your cell phone if I was a married woman?"

"I don't know, but you wouldn't be the first married woman, I'm sure, to call up another guy on his cell phone."

"Well, I can assure you that I am not married," Paige declared. "And since you asked me that question, I'm going to assume you aren't, either."

"I don't know," Ryan said. "I'm sure I wouldn't be the first married man to give another woman his cell phone number for her to call him on."

Even though Ryan wasn't a hard-core church-going guy—or at least he wasn't the last time they talked—he was a good guy and had a good spirit. When he did go to church, if Paige recalled correctly, it was to a Catholic church a friend had invited him to. He had never come across to Paige as a low-down, dirty scoundrel who would cheat on his wife, although he had confessed to Paige that he wasn't the best boyfriend to past women in his life.

That was then, and this was now—for both of them. The only thing from the past that they would bring into their future was their children. His children, Paige had yet to meet. The only reason why Ryan had met her girls was that he'd taken photos of them . . . twice. But who knew? That could all change in the near future.

"Well, when you and I get married," Paige said, "I better be the only woman you give your cell phone number too."

The two of them laughed, both of them well aware that Paige had just alluded to the fact that she could end up being his wife someday. The words didn't faze either of them one way or the other. The last time they had spoken, Ryan had already practically claimed her as his wife, anyway. She was just receiving it . . . all these years later.

"You won't have to worry about that," Ryan said as his laughter died down. "I bet the girls are so big now."

"They are growing like weeds. I have to buy them new clothes and shoes every other week, which is why you will never find me spending all that crazy cash on name-brand stuff. I mean, yeah, I like to sport a designer name or two, but I ain't gon' be growing out my stuff in two weeks after shelling all that money out. Shoot."

Through the phone, Ryan could imagine Paige rolling her eyes. And that was exactly what she was doing.

"How are your boys? I bet they look like little men now," Paige said.

"Growing like weeds too, but on top of that, they are eating everything in sight. Thank God we don't live in a gingerbread house. They would literally eat us out of house and home."

For the next few minutes the couple shared more laughter than either of them had engaged in, in the past few months.

"This is what I have missed," Ryan said to Paige.

"What?"

"Laughing like this . . . with you. I've waited a long time for this. But like I told you before, I was willing to wait. No, I might not attend church regularly and know the Bible like I know the words to an old Biggie song, but I know that when the Lord makes a promise, it never returns void. I know that when He promises a person something, they may not get it right away. They may not get it tomorrow, next week, or even next year. But if you believe . . . if you really believe, then you wait on the Lord."

Listening to this man preach—correction, speak—Paige got all tingly inside. He was speaking to her heart, but he was preaching to her soul. A smile rested on her face. If she hadn't been 100 percent certain before, she was certain now that she'd done the right thing by reaching out to him.

"It's getting late," Ryan said. "But before we hang up, I want to know when I get to see you again."

"When do you want to see me again?" Paige didn't realize she'd said that more seductively than she'd intended. Just talking to this man made her so free and loose in the flesh. She said a silent prayer that Jesus, with His strength, would reel her back in.

"Now, don't start nothing you can't finish, woman, with your saved, sanctified self." He chuckled. "No, I'm just joking. But I really would like to see you again. Are you available this weekend?"

"Our church is an official partner of the Mid-Ohio Foodbank. We give out produce to the community every month, and I volunteered to help this weekend."

"What about next weekend?" Ryan asked. No sooner than he'd asked, though, he said, "No, next weekend isn't good, either."

"You have something going on?" Paige asked.

"Yes. I have a wedding to do. I think this weekend is my only free weekend this month. I mean, we could meet in between my appointments sometime during the week or something. But I really don't want to have to watch the clock when I could be watching you."

Paige blushed. If this man wasn't puffing her head up . . . "I'ma really need you to stop saying everything I want to hear. Gon' have me thinking you are too good to be true. And Lord knows, I've made that mistake before." Paige was referring to Blake. He had definitely been too good to be true.

For the first time in their entire conversation, there was awkward silence.

"Do you mind if I say something without you taking offense?" Ryan asked after a few seconds of silence.

"Go ahead," Paige said after she'd managed to get her foot out of her mouth. Everything had been running as smooth as butter before she opened up her big mouth about her ex.

"I'm not into the whole Marvel Comics series of comic books and movies and whatnot, which means I'm not into X-Men. Your ex-men."

Ryan was speaking with authority, politely reading Paige, and she liked it. A man who could speak his mind, as well as allow her to speak hers while he actually listened, was a delight.

"You and I have shared everything there is to know about one another," Ryan continued. "Sure, there are things that have taken place in our lives over these couple years we've been apart, things that we haven't told each other. But we'll have plenty of time to catch up on that. But what we're not going to do is rehash negative things from our past and compare them to our now or our future. Can we make that promise to one another?"

"Absolutely," Paige said without hesitation. She wasn't the least bit offended by the way Ryan had just come at her. He'd let her speak her mind, but if it didn't line up with the foundation of a good relationship, he was going to let her know for sure. She really appreciated that about Ryan.

"Now, back to when we can get together . . . ," Ryan said.

"I have an idea," Paige said with excitement. "We could always use volunteers at the church. How about you join me?"

"I knew it would only be a matter of time before you started trying to get me to come to church with you," Ryan said jokingly. "You Christians gon' evangelize if it's the last thing you do."

"Cut it out," Paige said. "Now, you know I don't get down like that. I have never once pressured you to come to my church."

"I know, so you've decided to use a sneak attack."

"Boy, cut it out." Paige laughed. "Can I put you down as a volunteer or not?"

"You can."

"Sounds like a plan," Paige said. "I'll text you the name of my church, the address, the time, and all that good stuff."

"All right, Miss Lady," Ryan said. "I'm sure we'll talk before then."

"I'm sure," Paige agreed.

"Good night."

"Night." Paige ended the call with the biggest smile on her face. She looked up to the heavens. "Once again you've proven that waiting on you, God, is always well worth the wait."

Chapter 13

"Goggles? What in the world would I have needed to bring some goggles for?" Miss Nettie asked as she followed behind Paige, who was heading toward the room where she kept her computer.

"I didn't say goggles, Miss Nettie." Paige laughed as they entered the room. "I said Google. We're going to get on Google. It's the name of a search engine."

"Search engine? You mean like the V-six out in my vehicle?"

Paige stopped walking, turned, and gave Miss Nettie a side eye. "If you and Naomi would stop watching all those ratchet reality shows and learn something about the real world, you would know what I'm talking about," Paige scolded.

"Don't get sassy with me," Miss Nettie shot back. "There are two things you need to remember, and one is that I'm old enough to be your mother." Miss Nettie ran her hands down the length of her body. "Although with a figure like this, I don't look it."

"Aw, shoot. Miss Nettie got a boo, and now she's feeling herself." Paige laughed. "But what's number two?"

Miss Nettie shot Paige a serious look. "That I did a bid in jail before, so you really don't wanna mess with me."

Paige shook her head. "Oh, Miss Nettie." She put her arm around the woman. "I do love you."

"And I love you too, so watch that fresh mouth of yours so I don't have to beat you down."

This time both women laughed.

Paige continued her trek over to the corner computer desk. She sat down. "You can pull up a seat next to me." Paige pointed to a rolling office chair that was just a couple feet away.

Miss Nettie followed Paige's instructions and sat beside her. By the time she did this, Paige already had the Google home page up on the computer screen.

"Okay," Paige began. "The first thing we are going to do is search your name and see what comes up, since you don't know your son's or daughter's name. We have to start somewhere, and it's always a good idea to start with what you know."

Miss Nettie nodded as she scrunched up her face while looking at the computer screen.

"So what's your full government name?" Paige asked.

"Netrice Carla Hudson."

Paige typed in Miss Nettie's government name, hit the search icon, and waited. Several links appeared, most of them for Web sites with a mug shot of Miss Nettie.

"Dang, Miss Nettie, you were gangster," Paige said, staring at the screen in awe. A younger and much harder-looking version of Miss Nettie stared back at her. The woman in the picture had wild eyes, and the hair on her head was just as wild. She turned and looked at the woman. "No one would ever be able to look at you now and know that this is the same person."

Miss Nettie's eyes never left the screen as she spoke. "That's because it's not." She looked at a confused Paige. "I ain't me no more. I've been washed and cleaned in the blood of Jesus. Honey, I got a Holy Ghost makeover." She pointed to her mug shots on the computer screen. "That woman right there is dead."

"I hear you, Miss Nettie," Paige said, turning her attention back to the computer. "But, unfortunately, if we want to find your baby, we're going to have to resurrect her."

Miss Nettie shook her head and cringed at the thought. "I guess some of that stuff from the past that I swept under the rug of my memory bank, we gon' have to pull the covers off of." Miss Nettie closed her eyes and went into immediate prayer. "Lord, we're about to pull some scabs off of some old wounds. I just pray you be the healing balm, oh, Lord. And even if I don't end up finding my baby, I ask that all I'm about to endure be not in vain. I ask that once the scabs have been picked, the wounds have been revealed again, and the healing balm is covering them, that the scar be remembrance of the glory of it all, and not the suffering." Miss Nettie paused, allowing Paige the opportunity to add to the prayer, if she was so led.

"Heavenly Father, I don't know why you chose me to be a vessel to help Miss Nettie with her endeavors, but I thank you for finding me worthy," Paige prayed. "I pray that you place resources at my fingertips. I pray for the wisdom and the know how to navigate Miss Nettie to her final destination. And when all is said and prayed, I ask that you continue to use me to be a comforter and encourager for Miss Nettie, the same way she was and is for me whenever I'm going through something. In Jesus's name, we pray. Amen!"

***

"Sister Paige, it's good to see you, as always," Deborah greeted as Paige entered the church basement, where they distributed the produce the last Saturday of the month.

"You too, Sister Deborah." Paige gave Deborah a kiss on the cheek. She looked down at the little boy tugging at Deborah's leg. "Hey there, li'l guy. You here to help Mommy?"

He nodded and then bashfully hid behind his mother's leg.

"Aw, I know you ain't trying to get shy on me with your handsome self."

Deborah looked down at her son and smiled. She rubbed her protruding belly, which showed that she was four months into her pregnancy. "Lynox is on his way to pick him up. I'd be too busy chasing after him to help load anything into anybody's car."

Paige understood, which was why her girls were at her parents' house. "Girl, you just need to be bagging," Paige said, looking down at Deborah's stomach. "You don't need to be carrying nobody's anything anywhere."

Deborah sucked her teeth. "Girl, I'm just a little bit pregnant. I'm going to do all that I can until I get big as a house. Then I'm going to let my husband cater to me like it's the end of the world."

Both women laughed.

"I know that's right," Paige said. "Milk it for all it's worth."

"Think I ain't?" Deborah said. "Speak of the devil." She looked over Paige's shoulder.

Paige turned to see Deborah's husband, Lynox, coming down the church basement stairs.

"There's the hubby now," Deborah said. "Come on, Tyson," she said to her son, taking him by his hand and going to meet up with her husband of not even one year. "I'll be back in a sec," she said over her shoulder to Paige.

"All right, girl," Paige said, heading over toward the mounds of produce in order to prepare to help box and bag it all. She grabbed a pair of plastic gloves and slid them on her hands, a step that was required of anyone who would be handling the food. She made sure her hands were well covered.

"Are you passing out cucumbers or preparing for brain surgery?" said a voice behind Paige.

A smile crept onto Paige's face as she finished putting the gloves on. She didn't even have to turn around to know that the voice belonged to none other than Ryan Coleman. But she wanted to turn around. His hypnotizing voice. His mahogany wood scent. If he still looked as good as he talked and smelled, she'd marry the man now!

"Hey there," she greeted him as she turned. When her eyes landed on him, she tried to keep the pretty girl smile on her face, but her mouth wanted to drop to the floor, because he looked so good. His medium brown skin was silky smooth. He had dark brown eyes and a smooth bald head, and his goatee still had enough gray hairs to make it attractive. He stood almost six feet tall and had a nice build. Not too slinky, not too thick.

"Ms. Paige," Ryan said. He extended both hands.

Paige placed each of her hands in his. He pulled her toward him slightly, then planted a kiss on each cheek. Paige blushed and looked around to see if anyone was watching them. She couldn't hide her embarrassment.

"Uh-oh! Did I break carnal church rule number one and engage in public affection with a woman who is not my wife?" He looked up. "And right here in the Lord's house?"

His sense of humor washed away any embarrassment Paige felt about him giving her a friendly little kiss on the cheek. Standing there, looking at him, with her hands in his, and observing the way he was looking at her, made her feel as though they were the only two people in the room.

"Unless you got a daddy who looks half as good as you, take that mess on somewhere else."

Church mother Eleanor was obviously in the room with them as well.

"Mother Eleanor," Paige said, immediately dropping her hands to her sides.

"If y'all don't stop with that mother business," the older woman complained, making a shooing motion with her hand. "I look so good, I don't even allow my own daughter to call me Mother, and she came out of my butt."

Ryan's eyes bucked at the words that had just come out of Eleanor's mouth.

Once again, Paige was embarrassed, but this time it was on behalf of the Christian standing next to them, with an unfiltered mouth. She tried to hurry up and get the situation under control before something else crazy came out of the woman's mouth. "Speaking of your daughter, I ran into her the other day at the dance studio. My girls are taking dance class now."

"Oh, yeah. I forgot you married into that rich white family. Y'all's the only kind of black folks who can afford all that dance business. If Lorain wasn't married to a doctor, them twins would be right out somewhere cheering for the Linden Eagles, talking about, 'U-g-l-y. You ain't got no alibi. You ugly,' just like all the other little black girls did when I was coming up."

Ryan tried to cover his mouth but couldn't contain his laughter.

Eleanor looked at him. "And who is this fine-looking young man?" She gave Ryan the once-over.

"This is my friend Ryan," Paige said. "Ryan, this is Mother . . . I mean miss . . . ?" She looked at Eleanor to see if the latter was a better title.

Eleanor shook her head in the negative.

Paige tried again. "Uh, Sister Eleanor?"

"That's it right there. People mistake me for Lorain's sister all the time, so call me sister."

"Ryan, this is *Sister* Eleanor," Paige said, introducing the older woman.

Ryan slowly took Eleanor's hands in his while staring into her eyes. "For a woman as fine as you, you don't even need a title. God couldn't come up with one for someone as unique as you, so why should man try?" He kissed her on the hand while still staring into her eyes. He then allowed her hands to slide out of his.

"Oh my," Eleanor said, grabbing her chest. She then looked at Paige. "Girl, if he's yours and you want to keep him, then you betta get him. Because once he gets a load of this seasoned woman, 'spite the age difference, he's going to need Viagra."

That was it. Paige couldn't take it anymore. She had to get away from Eleanor. By getting Ryan to come help out at the church, she had hoped not only that she would get to see him again, but also that he might get ministered to and consider attending her nondenominational church. That he might like it so much that he would even start attending with her on the regular. But Eleanor was giving the saints a pretty bad name right now.

"Ryan, why don't you come with me so I can show you how it's done?" Paige said, taking him by the hand.

"Oh, I can show him how it's done." Eleanor ran her hands down her body.

"That won't be necessary." Paige pulled Ryan away.

"It was nice meeting you, Sister Eleanor," Ryan called out as Paige darn near dragged him away.

Eleanor waved as they left her in the dust.

Just as soon as Paige got Ryan over in a corner, next to a mound of boxes, she asked him, "Why on earth would you egg that woman on?"

Ryan could hardly contain his laughter. "What? She's just a harmless old woman."

"There is nothing harmless about Mother Eleanor. Don't let the gray hair fool ya," Paige warned.

"Aw, you jealous of Madea over there?"

Paige snapped her neck back in shock, but then she couldn't do anything but laugh at Ryan's silliness. "Since when did you start going for Kevin Hart's crown? I don't remember you being this funny."

"Well, discovering you have a tumor on your brain can make you begin to look at things differently. Look at life differently."

"Tumor?" Thank goodness Paige didn't have any of the produce in her hands, as it would have tumbled all over the floor. She was both shocked and disappointed. She and Ryan had talked a couple times before today, playing catch-up. Not once had he mentioned anything about a tumor.

"Yeah, it wasn't that serious. It was benign. On the right side of my brain. On the surface. Three days in the hospital. Just like having a baby," Ryan said, as if it were an everyday thing.

"You say it like a woman going to give birth," Paige said. "It was brain surgery."

"I know that, but it wasn't in my brain tissue or anything. It's what they call a meningioma tumor. It's very common. Was 'bout the size of a grape." He used his hands to demonstrate the size.

"Well, a grape inside your head is nothing to shake a stick at."

"Could have been worse. Could have been the size of a golf ball. From the date the doctors found it to the date I had it removed, six months passed, and it hadn't grown at all."

"Jesus, you walked around with a grape in your head for six months after finding out about it." Paige shook her head. "I couldn't do it. That doctor would have needed to get that thing out of me quick, fast, and in a hurry."

"Well, they grow pretty slow," Brian told her. "Matter of fact, the doctor said some of his patients watch them for years and never end up having to get them removed. I figured I'd go ahead and do it while I was young and healthy. Three hours of surgery, three days in the hospital, a month recovering at home, and I was back to life as usual. On top of that, I was able to fit the surgery in around my schedule."

"Once again, you act like a pregnant woman whose doctor lets her decide which date she wants the C-section."

"Hey, with all these baby analogies, are you trying to tell me something?" He looked down at Paige's belly.

She followed his eyes. "Oh, God, no." She covered her belly with her hands. "I'm just saying, you had a brain tumor. That's serious business. Anything could have happened. I mean . . ."

Paige had to calm herself down at the thought that she might have lost Ryan during all the time she'd allowed to pass. Life was short. She'd learned that from losing Norman. She'd learned that when the threat of being HIV positive tested her faith. She'd fooled around long enough. She was not going to waste any more precious time playing games. The days of waiting around for so-called perfect timing were over. From here on out, everything would be about God's timing and His will.

Paige said a silent prayer, thanking God for keeping Ryan through his ailment. For healing him. For preserving him just for her. She was not going to allow him to slip through her fingers again. This time they were going to make it work between them, no matter what or who tried to get in the way. No playing cat and mouse. No waiting for him to tell her he loved her first before expressing how she truly felt about him. No fear of rejection. Whatever emotions welled up inside of her, by God, she was going to let them loose. Including the one that was boiling up inside of her at that very moment.

Being a woman of her word, Paige walked as close to Ryan as she could, placed each of her hands flat on his cheeks, pulled him to her face, and planted a long, passionate kiss on his lips.

"Umpf, umpf, umpf."

Both Paige and Ryan looked over to see Eleanor standing there with her hands on her hips, shaking her head.

"Look at ya," she said to Paige. "Spitting on him like a sandwich you don't want anybody to ask for a bite of. Selfish butt." She rolled her eyes and walked away.

Paige chuckled at Eleanor's comment then, looked into Ryan's eyes. "She's right, you know. I'm claiming my man. I've adored you from the moment I met you. There is no need to turn back the hands of time. We'll just move forward."

"I agree," Ryan said. "I think we've had the longest 'getting to know one another' period in history. I know everything there is to know about you." He looked her up and down until his eyes reached hers again. "And I like it all."

Paige tucked her lips in and tried to control all the sensual emotions that were brewing inside of her, her desire for the only man she'd even thought about having a relationship with since Norman's death. For the only man she'd allowed to touch her. For the only man she'd allowed into her heart completely.

"Let's, uh, do what we came here to do and help serve this produce." Paige wiped her clammy palms down her jeans.

"I think that's a good idea," Ryan said. "Where do I start?"

Paige was so mentally discombobulated that she had no idea where she and Ryan should start. But she had a pretty good idea where and how she wanted things to finish.

Chapter 14

"I got it! I got it!" Miss Nettie barged through Paige's front door with pure excitement.

This was her and Paige's third meeting in their attempt to get information on Miss Nettie's child. They'd gotten much accomplished this last go-round. She hadn't found out the name of her child, but she had found out the sex. It was a boy. Miss Nettie had a son, and she'd found proof that she was the woman who had given birth to the boy in question. Paige had helped her send off for information about the birth and what happened to the baby from that point on. They had had to reach out to the hospital for Miss Nettie's records, because their Department of Vital Statistics search hadn't fared well at all. They'd learned that there had been some complications, and that the baby had been taken from Miss Nettie by C-section. That explained a little about why Miss Nettie didn't remember a whole lot about giving birth.

"Calm down, Miss Nettie," Paige said, closing the door behind her. "You got what?"

After catching her breath, Miss Nettie spoke. "When I was leaving out the house, heading here to meet you, the mailman delivered this." Miss Nettie was waving a white envelope as if it were a flag of surrender. She handed it to Paige.

"What is it?" Paige had a smile on her face purely because the one Miss Nettie was wearing was contagious.

"Open it on up and see, child."

Paige pulled a letter out of the envelope. She unfolded it and started to read it. Miss Nettie spoke before she could even finish reading it.

"He got adopted out," Miss Nettie said.

"I see," Paige said as she finished reading the paper. "Guess we just have to find out who adopted him. If we can find that out, then—"

"A married couple took him in," Miss Nettie said.

"How do you know that?"

"I called the number on that there letter to see if they could tell me anything else. They couldn't tell me much. Said something about a closed adoption. The girl wasn't supposed to tell me nothing else. But I shared some of my story with her. I told her how heavy it's been on my heart lately, and that I just want to make things right.

I at least wanted to know what happened to him. He could have been born dead, for all I knew. But he wasn't. He was born alive and kicking."

Paige walked over and put her hand on Miss Nettie's shoulder. "Miss Nettie, you know I'm not one to pry," Paige said sympathetically. "There are a lot of things in the past I would like to forget. And I do a pretty good job of sweeping it all under the rug when it's convenient. But you best believe when I want to remember something, I can. So what I'm trying to say is—"

"How in the world can a mother forget about the birth of her own child?" Miss Nettie said, finishing the sentence for Paige. "Child, I was messed up mentally. I remember taking drugs . . . lots of drugs. Some I think that doctor might have prescribed for my head and emotions. Some I had no business with. I was doped up more often than not. Anything was better than reality. I just wanted to escape from it all. Forget my real miserable life ever existed. Suppose I succeeded."

Paige saw the look of shame on Miss Nettie's face. She hadn't meant to make Miss Nettie feel bad; she just wanted some kind of understanding.

"I do remember being pregnant, though. Those few months, I can't say I was fully clean and sober all the time, but I'm going to take a guess and say it was probably the most sober I'd been. Otherwise I wouldn't have even been able to remember being pregnant."

"Miss Nettie, I'm glad the woman was able to tell you that you gave birth to a living baby boy and that he was adopted out," Paige said on a lighter note. "But you do know that it's been almost forty years since you gave birth."

Miss Nettie got hyper. "Don't you go trying to tell me anything could have happened to him. That he could be dead," Miss Nettie snapped. "He's alive. My boy is alive. I feel it in my bones. I know I ain't felt much about him over the years, but God knows, I'm ready now. I'm ready to find my boy, come what may. Now, if you're gonna get all Negative Nancy on me all of a sudden, I reckon I won't be needing your help anymore."

"No, Miss Nettie. It's not that at all. I'm here for you. You know that. I just want to be realistic."

Miss Nettie looked at Paige pleadingly. "You're a mother. Some things you just know when it comes to your babies. Some things you just feel." Miss Nettie placed her hands on her belly. "Am I right about it?"

Paige nodded.

"Well, God didn't punish me by taking that feeling away. My boy is closer to me than I know it. Even though I wouldn't know his face in a lineup, nor would he mine, I feel some strange connection to him. I'm getting close, Paige. I'm getting close. And I have you to thank for it." Miss Nettie threw her arms around Paige.

"Oh, Miss Nettie," Paige said, rubbing Miss Nettie's back. "We're going to find your son. The same way Oprah's long-lost sister that was adopted out found her biological mother, we're going to find your son. Where there is a will, there's a way. And I think I just might know the way. Come on," Paige said, taking Miss Nettie by the hand and heading toward the front door. She snatched up her purse along the way.

"Where are we going?" Miss Nettie asked, confused. "I thought we were going to go get on that computer of yours and find my boy."

"Miss Nettie, we are going to do you one better. We are going to have your boy find you."

"Ryan, I really appreciate you doing this for us last minute," Paige said as she and Miss Nettie stood in one of the three studios located in his office.

When Paige and Miss Nettie had walked through the front door, the smell of new carpeting had greeted them. There were no markings on the eggshell-color walls, a clear sign that the recently leased office building had been updated for its new tenants.

"No problem. You sounded desperate when you called. So I called up my scheduled appointment and asked if we could push it ahead by an hour." Ryan pulled down a blue backdrop.

"And an hour is all we'll need." Paige patted Miss Nettie's salt-and-pepper hair into place. She then dug in her purse and pulled out her pink MAC lipstick.

"I don't need no lipstick. I'm taking a picture for the newspaper, not to send to the circus to see if they looking to hire a new clown." Miss Nettie swatted away Paige's hand that was holding the lipstick.

Ryan took a break from positioning the lights to ask, "You wouldn't happen to be kin to Sister Eleanor, would you?"

"Who?" Miss Nettie said, confused.

"Ryan," Paige scolded.

He shrugged his shoulders. "I was just asking." He went back to setting up.

Paige turned to Miss Nettie. "Okay, no lipstick, but at least let me—"

"Will you stop fiddling around with me?" Miss Nettie swatted at Paige. "Fixing my hair, straightening out my dress, trying to put makeup on me. You're making me more nervous than I already am. I already didn't think a picture was necessary. Why can't we just post the ad with me saying I'm looking for my boy?"

"For all you know, Miss Nettie, your son could be the spittin' image of you. He could recognize the details you're going to give, and if he sees your picture, he might think he's staring at himself. Or maybe the father will see it, or an auntie, an uncle, somebody. The more you can include in the ad, the better."

"I don't know." Miss Nettie turned away from Paige.

Paige looked at Ryan, exasperated. She threw her hands up.

"Let me," Ryan mouthed to Paige.

"You know, Miss Nettie, I've done a lot of stuff in my life that I'm ashamed of, embarrassed about, and just flat-out feel humiliated about," he said. "It's bad enough that there is a name to go along with some of it. The last thing I want to do is plaster my face next to it."

Ryan must have been talking right to Miss Nettie's ears, because she slowly turned to face him.

"You're a God-fearing woman, right?" he asked her.

Miss Nettie nodded. "Not all my life, though."

"But long enough for God to forgive you, right?"

She nodded again, taking in this young fellow's words.

"God has forgiven you, and the blood of Jesus has wiped you clean. That's all that matters. We can't hide from the things we've done in our past, but we can let them go. But you know what, Miss Nettie? This may go against what a lot of folks believe, but some of my old mess I'm going to hang on to. Not to play the 'woe is me' game or anything like that, but to show it to somebody else. In other words, to tell my stuff to help somebody else. Now, I'm not some 'every Sunday of the month' churchgoing guy, so I might not be using all the right biblical words and whatnot. But hopefully, you get what I'm trying to say."

Her eyes watering, Miss Nettie just stood there, staring at Ryan. "I know exactly what you're trying to say. And if I ever do find my boy and he wants anything to do with me, I'm going to introduce him to you. You'll be a good role model and inspiration. And whoever told you that you had to go to church to let God use you to relay His message was dead wrong. Because, young man, you just ministered to my heart more than you'll ever know."

Ryan nodded his thanks and appreciation for Miss Nettie's kind words. He then put the finishing touches on getting set up.

"Well, are you ready for this?" Paige asked Miss Nettie, a hand on each of her shoulders.

"It's been a long time coming. Yes, I'm ready."

"Then here we go." Paige helped Miss Nettie position herself on a stool.

Ryan then snapped head shots of Miss Nettie. In some of the shots Miss Nettie was smiling too much. In others she wasn't smiling enough. They managed to find a happy medium, a shot that had just the right look and feel for the article they were putting in the paper.

As soon as they finished the photo session, Paige and Miss Nettie headed back to Paige's place and went straight to the computer.

"Deborah should have e-mailed the article to me by now," Paige said as she logged on to her computer. On their way to Ryan's studio, Paige had called Deborah up and asked her to write a single paragraph about Miss Nettie and the fact that she was trying to find her son. Since Deborah was an editor and her husband was a renowned author, Paige knew they were the two people to call on. They were like the Jay Z and Beyoncé of the literary industry.

Paige went to her e-mails, and sure enough, an e-mail from Deborah was there. She downloaded it and read it silently. "It's perfect," Paige said to Miss Nettie when she had finished.

"What does it say?" Miss Nettie hadn't bothered to read it alongside Paige.

Paige cleared her throat and began to read the one-paragraph article that they would post in the daily paper, along with a photo of Miss Nettie.

"Netrice Carla Hudson is a blessed woman of God who has not been saved all her life. Prior to turning her life over to the Lord, she turned over her newborn baby, to be raised by strangers." Paige looked at Miss Nettie to make sure those words hadn't stung her in any way.

Miss Nettie nodded for Paige to continue.

"In and out of jail, and suffering from mental issues, Miss Nettie felt the baby was probably better off. But now that God has cleaned her up and given her a new life, she wants to include her son, whom she's never met and who has never met her, in her life. Miss Nettie gave birth to a bouncing baby boy on April twenty-fifth, nineteen seventy-five, at Grant Medical Center in downtown Columbus, Ohio." So far in the article

Deborah had relayed every bit of information that had been shared with her. Had they been able to get their hands on the birth certificate, they would have even given her the time of birth.

Paige continued to read. "The son she gave birth to was given up for adoption to a married couple, who remain anonymous. All records have been sealed. We need your help in finding the son of Miss Hudson, lovingly known as Miss Nettie. If this story matches up with your life or the life of someone you know, we would love to hear from you. Please e-mail us at MissNettiesson@gmail.com." Paige looked at Miss Nettie. "How does that sound?"

"Like the truth," Miss Nettie said. "Like the truth."

Chapter 15

Paige couldn't think straight as she fumbled all over her dresser, looking for the match to the earring she already had in her ear. Ryan had called her a couple days ago and had invited her to dinner. He'd mentioned that he had something very important to ask her. Paige had accepted the invite with the quickness.

Even though Paige had been back in touch with Ryan for only a little over a month, he'd had her heart for years. So it would be no surprise if that thing he had to ask her was for her hand in marriage. Paige was almost certain that that was what he wanted to do, to propose. He was the type of man who knew what he wanted and wasn't afraid to go after it. And he'd made it clear plenty of times that he wanted Paige. That God had promised her to him. He'd waited so long that Paige was convinced he couldn't wait any longer.

"And to just think that I could have lost him," Paige said to herself as she continued to search for the errant earring.

Ryan had tried his best to downplay the whole brain tumor thing, but Paige knew that anytime a doctor had to go in and open someone's head up, it was serious business. Anytime a person had to be put to sleep with anesthesia, there was a chance that he or she would not wake up.

"I could have lost my Ryan," Paige said regretfully. Her tone then changed to one of frustration. "The same way I lost that frickin' earring," she huffed. Just then her eyes landed on the missing earring. It was among all the jewelry that had just been in order, nice and neat, before she'd run through it like a tornado. She held the earring up in front of her face, admiring it. "But I found it. And I found Ryan." She began to put the earring in her ear. "And I'm not losing him again." In a playful mood, Paige looked in the mirror and did her best impersonation of Nettie from *The Color Purple*. "Nothing but death can keep me from it." She laughed at her own joke and then went to the closet to retrieve the pumps she planned on wearing with the formfitting, cream-colored Guess dress.

After Paige had gotten herself together completely, she was surprised that she still had five minutes to spare before Ryan was due at her doorstep to pick her up. She had been certain that the earring setback would put her further behind than just five minutes. It felt like she had looked for it forever. Paige decided to just sit on the couch and do nothing while she waited. She needed to get her mind right and relax herself. She was all wound up and didn't want to seem too anxious when Ryan popped the question.

She inhaled and exhaled a couple times and then found herself turning to prayer. "Lord, I just want to thank you and bless your name right now. You are so awesome and so faithful to me. You always know exactly what I need." She paused, a smile covering her face. "And who I need. And you always know the perfect time. God, you know what I can handle and what I can't. Although I would have loved to have been there to support Ryan during his brain surgery, you knew I wasn't the one. You knew I wasn't in a state where I could have even thought there was a chance I could lose that man." Paige had to take a break to catch her breath. Just the thought of losing someone she loved . . . again . . . shook her very being. "But, Lord, I thank you that you kept Ryan and that the Holy Spirit was there to be a comfort to him. I thank you for never, ever putting more on me than I can bear, and for giving me the strength to endure the things that I must. In Jesus's name, I pray . . ."

The doorbell chimed just then, drowning out Paige's "Amen."

She jumped up from the couch, straightened her dress, and then walked over to answer the door. "Well, good evening, Preacher Ryan." Paige smiled. Ever since Ryan had ministered to Miss Nettie, she'd been jokingly referring to him as a preacher.

"Will you stop it with that preacher business?" Ryan said before leaning in and kissing Paige on the cheek. "You look gorgeous, but then again, you always do. You looked gorgeous in jeans and a T-shirt, passing out potatoes and cucumbers."

Paige laughed while blushing. "And you look good too, as always."

"Okay, so now that we've determined that we are America's most beautiful couple, move over Will and Jada," Ryan said.

"Even though I could stand here all night and drown in all your compliments, a sista is hungry. So let's go."

Paige locked up her house, and she and Ryan drove to the Hickory House, a wonderful steak house that was known for its award-winning barbecue ribs. It was located in the neighboring city of Reynoldsburg, which was only a few

minutes away from Paige's home in Malvonia.
During the car ride to the restaurant, Paige tried
to get Ryan to reveal what he wanted to talk to
her about.

"I have to admit, I've been wondering what
this important thing you have to ask me is,"
Paige said, hinting, hoping Ryan would just go
ahead and tell her.

It was no use. His eyes were on the road, and
his mind was more concerned with the menu
options he'd have to decide upon. "Should I have
chicken or fish?" he pondered out loud.

When they finally arrived at the restaurant,
Paige was nervous all over again. Ryan hadn't
given her a clue as to what he wanted to talk to
her about. This had only built up Paige's anxiety
that much more. She hadn't been wrong about
calling up Ryan and rekindling their relationship. Could she be wrong about what he wanted
out of the relationship? Her nerves had even
managed to chase her appetite away. She'd just
have to order any ole thing so Ryan wouldn't
question her. After all, she'd just told him how
hungry she was.

Paige hated that after they were seated and
given menus, the waiter had to come back twice
so that he could take their order. Ryan was having the hardest time choosing his entrée. Now he

was torn between the steak and the ribs. Paige knew that he wouldn't get into any kind of deep conversation until after their order had been taken, to eliminate all interruptions. She was relieved when he ultimately ended up ordering a platter that offered both ribs and steak. Paige settled on a steak dinner.

"I can't wait for the food to arrive. Everything on that menu looked delicious," Ryan said.

"It sure did," Paige agreed. "And we'll find out if it tastes as good as it looks soon enough. But, unfortunately, we have to wait. Man, do I hate waiting." That last line was another hint that went right over Ryan's head.

Paige made a mental note that if Ryan hadn't popped the question by the time her food came, she would have to cut her steak into little bites and chew each one thirtysomething times. Putting a whole lot of food in her stomach when she had such a case of nerves could be a complete disaster. After Ryan asked for her hand in marriage, she could just imagine her going to say, "I do," and spewing hunks of steak on him.

"Yuck!" she exclaimed.

"What? What's wrong?" Ryan asked as their waiter placed some hot bread on their table.

She hadn't realized that she'd spoken out loud. "I, uh, thought I saw a bug down there on the carpet."

Ryan looked down at the carpet. So did the waiter.

"But it was just one of those squiggly little designs," Paige lied, forcing a chuckle out.

The waiter looked relieved as he walked away after assuring them their meal would be out shortly.

"Oh." Ryan grabbed a piece of bread.

Paige watched him inhale the bread like a dang caveman. She couldn't imagine how he could possibly have such a big appetite when he was about to pop the biggest question a man could ask a woman. Then again, maybe he was eating like this because he was so nervous. Whatever the reason, Paige was becoming impatient, and her hot bread was getting cold. She decided to speed things up a bit.

"When you invited me out, you said there was something you wanted to ask me," Paige said, interrupting Ryan as he was about to inhale another piece of bread.

He stopped and looked at Paige, who wasn't eating a thing. He placed the piece of bread down on his bread plate. "Oh, yeah, well . . ." He grabbed his napkin and wiped his mouth and hands. "Yes, there is something I wanted to ask you."

Paige perked up. It was about to happen. It was all about to go down. *Here it comes.* Ryan was about to ask for her hand in holy matrimony.

Ryan swallowed, making sure he had no more food in his mouth. He then looked Paige in the eye. "You know how I feel about you," he said. "I've never been one to hold back when it comes to telling you how I feel."

Paige nodded. This was true about Ryan. This was what she adored about Ryan.

"You are not some woman I just want to kick it with. You are not just some woman I want to be friends with and get benefits."

"Good. Because you know you can file that under *never*," Paige said, being playful and sassy.

Ryan smiled and continued. "You are beautiful. Your children are beautiful. You've been through so much, and it has made you a strong survivor and not a victim. You love God. I do too, but I don't know Him like you do. But maybe by being with you, that will all change. Who knows? But what I do know is that you are the most important woman in my life. Which is why I want to ask you this . . ." Ryan paused and began to pat down his pockets.

Oh my God. Oh my God, Paige was screaming inside her head as she watched Ryan pat down his pockets, desperately looking for something. This went on for a few seconds too long. *Lord, let him find it. Let him find it.*

"Oh, here it is," Ryan said.

Paige thanked the Lord in her head for answering her prayer.

"Paige Vanderdale," Ryan said, something buried in his hand.

"Yes, Ryan?" Paige squealed, no longer able to hold in the excitement.

"Will you meet my boys?"

"Yes, yes, yes, Ryan. I will ma—" Paige bounced up and down in her seat until what Ryan had just asked her completely registered in her head. "Huh? What? Come again?"

"My boys," Ryan said excitedly as he cupped a picture of himself and his two sons in his hands.

Paige tried to keep a smile on her face as she looked down to admire the boys. It wasn't like she hadn't seen them before. Ryan had shown her pictures of them on his phone. "They are so cute. They look just like you. More like you in this picture than in the ones you already showed me." She had to hurry up and say something. She couldn't just sit there, looking stupid, staring at the picture all night.

Ryan brought the picture to his face. "Yeah, that's what everybody says." He looked back at

Paige. "But you haven't answered my question yet. I mean, I get it. This is a big step. I met your girls only by default. I know you are not the type of woman who would be introducing your girls to any ole dude. Well, the same goes with my boys. I'd love for you to meet them. Then I'd love for you and the girls and the boys and me to get together. What do you think?" Ryan asked.

This was not the question Paige had thought Ryan wanted to ask her. In all reality, she hadn't even thought about the fact that she had never met his boys. Shame on her. She was all in it for the man but had forgotten that his kids were a very important factor, as were hers. As a matter of fact, she was almost embarrassed that he'd suggested the blended family meeting instead of her. It wasn't that Paige didn't want to meet his boys. They were a part of Ryan, so it was automatic that they came with the package, just like she and her girls were a package deal. She didn't care if she didn't meet them until the day of the wedding. Ryan talked about them enough and had shown her enough pictures that she felt like they were already a part of her. She would accept them with open arms and would love them just as much as she would Ryan and her own girls.

She hadn't thought about it from the boys' perspective, though. No way would it be fair to them if Ryan just bring some woman home to them and said, "Hey, this is my wife." Paige had been down that road already, as Norman had had to do that with his parents. Kids could be cruel, so given the chance, they would probably make Mrs. Vanderdale back then seem like an angel.

"You look disappointed," Ryan said to Paige. "Is everything okay? Do you not like the idea?"

"I think it's a wonderful idea, Ryan," Paige said. "I was just thinking to myself how I wish I'd suggested it first. Of course I would love to meet your boys." The waiter delivered their meals as Paige continued. "I already know I'm going to love them. Look at who their daddy is. Certainly, the apples haven't fallen too far from the tree."

"Great. Then it's settled. I'll talk to the boys, and then we'll set something up."

"Yeah, great. Fine. Just let me know." Paige couldn't even fake that she was no longer as excited as she'd been just a couple minutes ago.

"Are you sure you're okay with all this? You look . . . I don't know. Kind of disappointed maybe. Is there something going on that you need to talk to me about?"

Paige wanted to say no and allow the two of them to just enjoy their meal and call it a night. But given the way Ryan always shared everything that was on his mind with her, Paige felt she owed him the same in return. Besides, there was no way she could fake enjoying her meal when the fact that Ryan hadn't proposed was on her mind.

"Actually," Paige began, "there is something else going on. I'm actually embarrassed to say it."

"You know you don't have to ever be embarrassed around me, Paige."

"I know. It's just that . . . well, when you told me there was something important you had to ask me, I just thought that maybe you were going to . . ." Even though Ryan had assured her that she never had to feel funny around him, she couldn't help it. She'd totally jumped the gun on their relationship.

"I was going to what?" Ryan had a look on his face that reflected the fact that he was clueless about whatever it was that Paige was trying to get out.

"That you were going to ask me to . . . marry you." The last part of Paige's sentence was indecipherable, as her words ran together.

"To what?" Ryan leaned in, cupping his ear with his hand.

Paige sucked her teeth and then spit it out. "I thought you were going to ask me to marry you." She looked around to make sure no one else had heard her. Ryan hearing it was enough.

"Marry me?" Ryan said. He leaned back in his seat.

"I feel like such a fool." Paige buried her face in her hands. She didn't even want Ryan to be able to see the humiliation on her face.

"No offense, but I would never ask a woman for her hand in marriage without first asking her to meet my sons."

"I know. I know. All that just dawned on me when you said you wanted me to meet your boys. I feel like such a bad mother, because even though my girls have met you, they haven't *met you* met you. You know, as you being my man." Paige removed her hands from her face but still refused to look up at Ryan.

"That doesn't make you a bad mother. It just makes you a woman who knows what she wants, and is tired of waiting to get it," Ryan said, hoping to make Paige feel better. "I know exactly how you feel, because I'm a man who knows what he wants and who is tired of waiting to get it. Which is why I want you to meet my boys, and for all of us to get to know each other."

Paige nodded. "I know my girls took to you. I just hope your boys will like me."

"I know they will." Ryan sounded 100 percent certain. "If I wasn't one hundred percent certain my boys would love the woman I know God called to be my wife, then I wouldn't have gone out and gotten this."

Paige looked up when she heard Ryan digging around. She looked up just in time to see him pull a little black jewelry box out of his pocket. A huge mischievous smile covered Ryan's face.

"Paige Vanderdale," he stated as he stood and then walked over to Paige's side of the table.

"Ryan, oh, my God." Paige's eyes flooded with tears. She covered her mouth with her hand to hold in the yelp she wanted to let out. Tears escaped through the cracks between her fingers.

Ryan got down on bended knee and took Paige's hand in his. "Baby, stop crying, because I need you to hear this."

Paige's shoulders were heaving, and she couldn't stop the tears from coming out.

Ryan gave her a minute to let it all out before he continued. "You *are* my wife. I found you. You are a good thing. When I told you I was going to wait on what was mine, I meant it. That was a promise. You were my promise from God, which He kept, so what kind of man would I be not to keep my promise to you? You are a survivor and an overcomer, just like me. If either one of us ever fell, it feels good to know the other will have the strength to pick the fallen one up."

Paige nodded as her tears continued to flow.

"I would follow you to the ends of earth, so of course, I'll follow you to church every Sunday, if a 'going to church every Sunday' kind of man is what you want. Like ole boy from the movie *Jason's Lyric* says, 'If you're going to church, I want to be on the front pew . . . first pew. . . .' Something like that. Heck, all I know is that I want to be wherever you are."

Paige had never questioned Ryan about going to church, or rather about not going to church consistently, and she had never pressured him to go. While he did go to that Catholic church every blue moon, he wasn't a member of it. That was something she'd decided to let God work out. And so He had. Oh, He was so faithful. Paige hadn't had to say a word.

Ryan continued. "I don't just want to be everything that you want. I am everything that you want. You are one of God's best, and I know He wouldn't give you anything less than what He knows you need. The same goes for me. You are who I want. You are who I need. I want to spend every waking and sleeping moment with you. And in order for that to happen, I need you to be my wife." Ryan opened the box and showed Paige the stunning two-carat diamond ring.

It wasn't a ring that reality show divas and wives would make a fuss over. It didn't say, "My man just spent our children's college tuition on a ring." Plain and simply put, it said, "I love you."

Paige looked up at Ryan.

Ryan said, "I told you I would never ask a woman for her hand in marriage without first asking her to meet my sons. Well, I asked you to meet my sons, and now I'm asking you to be my wife."

Paige was astounded and floored. "Oh, Ryan," she said. "I will be your wife. I will be your lover. I will be your friend. I do, and I will. In Jesus's name!"

Ryan stared into Paige's eyes as he slipped the ring on her finger, all cool, calm, and collected. He then looked around the restaurant, noticed that all eyes were on them now, of course, and shouted, "She said yes!"

Some people cheered, while "Congratulations," could be heard from others.

Without a care in the world, despite the fact that practically the entire room was watching, Ryan gave Paige the biggest hug and the juiciest kiss ever. "I love you, the future Mrs. Paige Coleman. I'm in love with you."

"I love you too, Ryan Coleman," Paige said in return, oblivious to the onlookers. As far as she was concerned, it was just she and the man she loved in the room. "I'm in love with you." Paige hugged Ryan around the neck and closed her eyes as tears fell from them. She exhaled, then looked up to the heavens and mouthed, "Thank you, Lord."

Chapter 16

Paige was nervous as all get-out. She'd been sitting in her car outside Ryan's house for the past five minutes. She'd arrived ten minutes early, so she still had five minutes in which to try to gather herself.

She had never imagined she'd be so nervous to meet two nearly tween boys. Then again, yes she had. For one, boys that age were so ornery. Kids that age, period, could be so undiplomatic when expressing themselves. Paige had heard some of the craziest things come out of the mouths of some of those kids in youth church. Church was right where some of those bey-bey kids belonged, because they definitely needed Jesus . . . or for hands to be laid on them, indeed.

What if the boys didn't like her and had no problem expressing it? What if they played mean, nasty tricks on her, like those kids in that book *Operation Get Rid of Mom's New Boyfriend?* What if . . . what if . . . what if? All the what-ifs caused Paige to break out in a sweat. Paige rolled her window down to get some of that May evening breeze.

"Lord, please just touch their hearts to receive me as their future stepmother and to feel how much I love their father and will, in turn, love them all the same. Amen." That was the fifth quick prayer that Paige had prayed since dropping the girls off at the Vanderdales' and driving to Ryan's place. Prayer still worked, and "One could never pray enough," was her current motto and reason to keep praying.

As the clock ticked, Paige stayed seated in the car, rehearsing in her head how she would greet the boys. She thought about whether or not she should kiss Ryan on the cheek when she greeted him and wondered if that would make the boys jealous or upset. She had no idea. And as she sat in the car, trying to figuring out the answer to one question, a million others popped in her head.

Paige looked at the clock on her dashboard. It was 7:00 p.m. on the dot. She couldn't stall any longer. She rolled her window up and decided to say one last prayer, for good measure. She closed her eyes, and for the next minute she prayed silently to God. Just as Paige said, "Amen," and was about to open her eyes, there was a tap on the driver's side window.

Paige looked and saw two handsome young boys who looked similar to Ryan standing at her driver's side door. All the pictures hadn't done them justice. "Oh, my," Paige said, a little startled. She then rolled down her window. "Hi," she greeted, trying to suppress her nerves.

"Hi. We're Deron and Lionel," the taller one said.

"Ryan's sons," the other one said, nodding toward their house.

Paige looked at the house and saw Ryan standing in the doorway. She turned her attention back to the boys.

"I'm Deron," the taller one said and then pointed to the other. "That's my little brother, Lionel."

"Younger brother," Lionel said, correcting him. He elbowed his brother and whispered, "I'm not little anymore, dude."

Deron brushed his brother off with a rolling of eyes. Paige chuckled at the little sibling spat.

"Can we walk you up to the house?" Deron asked.

"Absolutely." Paige thought that was so sweet of them. Her nerves were totally wiped out by the young men's chivalry. "Let me get my things." Paige rolled the window up, took her keys out of the ignition, and put them in her purse. As soon as she clicked the lock to unlock her car door, the younger boy opened it for her. "Thank you," Paige said, simply flattered. She grabbed her purse and got out of the car.

Lionel closed the door behind her, while Deron extended his elbow for her to loop her arm through.

"Careful," Deron warned. "It's been raining, so it might be slick. You could hurt yourself."

"Thank you. I appreciate that," Paige said, looping her arm through his. He was about a foot shorter than her, so she bent down a little as he escorted her to the porch.

Lionel trotted ahead of them in order to open the door for Paige.

"Thank you so much, young man," Paige said to Lionel as he held the door.

"You are welcome, Miss Paige," Lionel replied.

Deron released Paige's arm and allowed her to go through the doorway first. "After you," he said. If Paige wasn't mistaken, the boy even gave her a slight bow.

Once she was inside the house, Ryan stood and greeted her with a bouquet of flowers. "Good evening," he said, kissing her on the cheek and then extending the flowers to her.

"Thank you." Paige couldn't stop smiling. She was getting the royal treatment. She looked around the three-bedroom ranch-style home. It had modern furnishings and nice art on the walls, and it was clean. That was something Paige just had not expected from a place that housed three males. "Nice place you fellas have here," she complimented.

The aroma was to die for. If Paige's senses weren't mistaken, they were having something Italian. There was no smell of old socks under the couch or stale tuna sandwiches that had been left out. It was totally not what she'd expected from a bachelor pad.

"I really like the paintings on the wall," Paige said.

"Thank you," Ryan said. "Deron"—he nodded toward the boy—"my oldest son, did those."

Paige did a double take. "Wow! I thought those were paintings bought in a store somewhere."

"That's my goal." Deron smiled. "To someday have my work in galleries across the world." He admired the paintings himself, as if dreaming of the day he spoke about. "My art teacher said I'm the most talented fifth grader he's ever met."

"I'll have to agree with your art teacher," Paige said. "And if you keep up that kind of work, that day of seeing your work in galleries will be here before you know it."

"That's what I keep telling him." Ryan patted his son on the back proudly.

Not wanting to dote all on one son, Paige addressed Lionel. "And what is your thing, Lionel?"

"Building." His eyes lit up.

"He started off when he was younger," Ryan said. "That boy could duplicate any Lego design he saw just by sight. He never even had to look at the directions."

"I went from that to building things out of scraps and supplies," Lionel said.

"Most kids want iTunes gift cards for the holidays," Deron said, jumping in. "But my geeky brother wants Home Depot gift cards." He laughed. "What fourth grader do you know who likes the Home Depot versus Toys 'R' Us?"

Lionel play punched his older brother in the arm, and the two boys laughed and tussled.

"All right. That's enough horseplay," Ryan told them. "No broken bones before dinner."

Ryan and his sons laughed.

Paige smiled at their interaction. By the way Ryan talked about his boys, she knew he was a good father who was raising two good sons. Seeing them all in action, though, was blissful validation.

"So, I hope you're hungry," Ryan said, clapping his hands together. "And I hope you have a taste for Marzetti." Ryan was referring to the dish of baked casserole with ground beef, cheddar cheese, tomato sauce, and noodles.

"If I didn't before I walked in that door, I do now," Paige said. "It smells delicious."

"Cooking is Dad's thing," Deron said teasingly, looking at Ryan.

"Yeah, he has an apron and all," Lionel said, jumping in.

"Shhh." Ryan put his index finger to his lips in an attempt to hush the boy. "You think I want her picturing me in my flowered apron? That's not sexy."

"Oh, yuck!" Both boys displayed their disgust by gagging or keeling over and grabbing their stomachs.

"Oh, please, you get worse than that watching today's television shows," Ryan said. "Anyway, go wash your hands and then help me serve," he told his boys.

The boys scurried off toward the kitchen.

"And, you," Ryan said to Paige, "allow me to escort you to the dining area." He used a sophisticated voice with a fake English accent, bowed, and then held his arm out to Paige.

"You are so crazy," Paige said, obliging.

Ryan led Paige into the dining area, which was furnished with a table that sat six, a china cabinet, and a round wooden table with a plant on it. There was one large picture of a field of flowers beneath a sunny blue sky. Paige was about to ask if it was one of Deron's, but then she saw the artist's signature on it, and it didn't match his.

"I just love your humble abode," Paige said as Ryan pulled out an upholstered chair for her. "It's not what I expected a bachelor pad, or rather the home of a single father to two boys, to look like."

Ryan leaned down. "Right. You better clean that up," he whispered in Paige's ear. "Because the bachelor thing will be history soon enough."

Paige and Ryan were interrupted by the boys as they entered the room, each with oven mitts on and carrying a dish.

"You two still at it? Geesh!" said Deron.

"Just set the food down and be quiet already," Ryan ordered Deron. He looked at Paige. "I'll be back. I'm going to go get the drinks." He looked at his sons. "Boys, come help."

Deron set down the pan of Marzetti, and Lionel set down the plate with hot, fresh garlic bread on it. They then followed their father into the kitchen.

Paige waited at the table, admiring the cheesy main dish and inhaling the smell of the garlic. A minute later, Ryan returned, carrying a pitcher of lemonade with one hand and two glasses stacked inside one another with the other hand. Deron was carrying a pot of green beans, while Lionel was carrying the other two glasses.

The gentlemen set everything down in their respective places and then sat. Ryan was at the head of the table. Paige was to his right, and his two boys sat across from her.

"All right. It's time to eat," Ryan said.

"I'll say grace," Deron announced. "Dear Lord . . ."

Paige was probably the only one who was not bowing her head, with her eyes closed, as Deron blessed the food.

Ryan and his sons had their heads bowed, their eyes closed, and their hands folded in prayer. That sight alone almost brought a tear to her eye. Paige didn't know many kids, and especially young men, who took the initiative to bless their food.

They had said their amens and had stopped praying before Paige even realized they'd done so. Ryan looked up to see her appearing dumb-founded.

"What? Just because we don't belong to a church, you think we don't pray?" Ryan asked Paige.

She shook herself out of her daze. "Huh? What?" Then she realized what Ryan had said. "Oh, no, not at all." Paige wasn't lying. She had simply been in awe of the sight before her of three males thanking God . . . no matter what it was for.

"Hey, speak for yourselves," Lionel interjected. "Those two heathens may not belong to a church, but I do." He pointed his fork at his father and his brother. "I've been a member of Grandma's church for four years now," he said proudly. Looking at his father, he asked, "Who do you think taught that one there how to pray?" He pointed at his brother again.

"I didn't learn prayer from you," Deron said.

"Then where did you learn it?" Lionel asked.

"Anyone who has ever taken math and had to learn fractions has surely learned how to pray," Deron said, as serious as could be. "How do you think I ever made it through the class?"

Everyone but Deron burst out laughing. He kept a straight face, one full of sincerity.

"I hear you, Deron," Paige said. "Some things will have you on your knees, whether you want to be there or not."

"Amen," Deron agreed.

Paige couldn't have been more impressed with these young boys with old souls.

"All right. Let's all dig in now," Ryan said, and he was the first to begin scooping up the food.

The food was passed around until everyone had a little bit of everything on their plate.

"How's it taste?" Ryan asked once everyone had taken a bite.

"Delicious," Paige said.

"As always," Lionel said. He looked at Paige. "Miss Paige, you are going to have a hard act to follow in the kitchen when you and Dad get married."

Paige just about choked on a green bean. She hurried and reached for the lemonade Ryan had poured her and used the beverage to clear her throat.

"You okay?" Ryan asked, concerned.

"Yes," Paige said. She then cut her eye at Ryan and said, "Lionel just caught me off guard a little." She raised an eyebrow at Ryan.

"About what?" he said.

Paige tightened her lips as she stared at Ryan. She gave him a look that said, "You know what."

Ryan shrugged, his body language indicating that he was pleading with Paige to tell him what she had an issue with.

Lionel, watching their little game of charades, decided to help his dad out. "She's talking about the fact that I mentioned her becoming your wife and all."

Paige quickly turned her crooked frown at Ryan into a fake smile at Lionel.

"It's okay, Miss Paige," Lionel said. "Our dad is an open book. He's talked to us about the birds and the bees. How my brother and I were made. How we need to wait until we find the woman we want to marry to . . . blah, blah, blah. You know." He took a bite of his garlic bread and then continued with his mouth full. "He told us that he made mistakes with women in the past, but that we are not mistakes. He promised to be an example to his sons by never bringing a woman around us, unless she was going to be his wife. Well, since you're the first woman we've ever met, that means you're going to be our stepmother. Welcome to the family." He then continued to eat his food, as if he'd just said another prayer.

Deron hadn't even looked up from his meal at all. He had just eaten and nodded, concurring with his brother.

Paige looked at Ryan, who was grinning from ear to ear. "Told you," he mouthed.

Paige quickly wiped a lone tear from her eye as she mouthed, "I love you."

Ryan winked and then continued to eat his food.

The rest of the meal Paige dedicated to really getting to know the boys. She asked them all about themselves, and they were eager to answer every question. After their dessert of store-bought angel food cake, Paige sat around and talked with Ryan and the boys for a little while before she had to head out.

"We can't wait to see you again, Miss Paige," Deron said. "And to meet your girls. Dad showed us pictures of them."

"And we're sorry about their father," Lionel said, chiming in.

"Oh, thank you," Paige said. She looked at Ryan and gave him a soft smile. Clearly, he'd been speaking about her to his boys.

Ryan winked.

"I've really enjoyed my evening," Paige told the boys, "and I can't wait to share another one with you boys. I'm sure the girls are going to enjoy time spent with you all as well. Your hospitality is awesome. I've met grown men who don't know how to treat a lady as special as you two do."

"Thank you, Miss Paige," the boys said in unison.

"All right," Ryan said. "You guys can go and start cleaning up."

They nodded and bid Paige farewell. She watched them walk out of the room to do as they were told.

"I'm so impressed," Paige said to Ryan. "Your sons are quite the gentlemen."

"And you were expecting what?" Ryan wanted to know.

"My brother when he was their age."

They shared a laugh.

Ryan took Paige's hands in his as their laughter died down. "So we'll do it again with the girls. This time at Magic Mountain or something. Chuck E. Cheese's. What do kids like nowadays?"

"It's the ladies' turn to host," Paige said. "We'll do it at my house. You check your calendar and let me know when you guys are available."

"I'm on it." He leaned in and kissed Paige on the lips.

"Thanks again for a wonderful evening."

"The pleasure was all mine. Now let me walk you to your car."

Ryan escorted Paige to her car, gave her another kiss good night, and then watched her taillights fade until he couldn't see them anymore. When Paige called him to let him know she'd gotten home okay, he gave her the next few dates when he would be available. They chose to meet the following Thursday. Paige couldn't wait to tell the girls about the nice little tea party they were going to have. She figured if they knew they were throwing a real live tea party, they'd be more into getting together with Ryan and his boys.

Paige had to figure out how she was going to explain to the girls that Ryan wasn't just the nice man who had taken their pictures, but that he was Mommy's fiancé. Then she'd have to explain to them that she was going to marry him. But she felt she owed someone else an explanation first.

Chapter 17

"I'm so glad you could make it to Sunday dinner," Miss Nettie said as she opened the door to let Paige and the girls in. "I've got some great news."

"Miss Nettie," Norma and Adele shouted in unison, each girl giving her a hug on each side of her. She hugged each of the girls and planted a kiss on top of their heads. They then ran off, calling for their grammy and gramps, as Miss Nettie continued talking to Paige with excitement.

"I called that attorney of yours, Mr. Fergunstein. I told him you referred me, and he acted like he would just about drop everything on his calendar to help me out. He's really taken a liking to you."

"Well, yeah, Rudy is more than an attorney. He's a friend. He's been there to help me through the roughest of times."

Paige smiled just thinking about how Rudy, when he was only fresh out of law school, had helped her get a divorce from Blake. He'd been working for legal aid at the time. Now he was a partner in his own private practice. At one point he helped Paige fight Blake once again when he tried to take Adele from her. Even though Norman had signed Adele's birth certificate, anyone with eyes could see that he wasn't her biological father. Adele was chocolate brown like her mother and didn't look like she had an ounce of white blood in her. Paige and Norman had decided that he would sign the birth certificate not so that they could hide Adele from Blake. They simply wanted Adele to be born with a father . . . her mother's husband. They wanted everyone in the family to bear the same last name.

Although Paige and Norman had never decided exactly when and how they would tell Adele about her biological father, they knew eventually they would have to. Along with that would eventually come the full story of how Adele was a product of marital rape. Paige wanted to protect her oldest daughter from that for as long as she could.

When Blake got wind of the fact that Adele existed, he and his attorney did the math and figured out that Adele had to have been conceived the last time Blake had sex with Paige, which was when he raped her. He demanded a paternity test and all kinds of mess. Paige was devastated, since the ball seemed to be in Blake's court.

Rudy saved the day when he, a usually soft-spoken cat, turned into a roaring tiger right there in the conference room, during the negotiations. He basically told Blake's attorney that Blake would get custody when hell froze over. Rudy let his claws out and played dirty when he made all kinds of threats that pushed Blake's attorney into a corner. When all was said and done, Paige came out the victor. Upon his defeat, Blake practically crawled under a rock somewhere. Disappeared off the face of the earth, with not so much as visitation rights.

After seeing the real Rudy, Paige knew that no closed adoption could stop him. He was just the person Miss Nettie needed to help her find her son. If anybody could get to the bottom of things, Rudy could.

"I'm glad Rudy could be of help," Paige said to Miss Nettie.

"I'll let you eat dinner first and talk to the family, but before you leave, come to my room and—"

"Miss Nettie, I have to talk to the family today, but you're family too, so I'd like you to be there when I say what I have to say."

Miss Nettie paused, realizing she'd been too consumed by her own news. "Oh. Good news, I hope."

Paige wanted to burst. "It's great news."

"Good, 'cause life is too good right now for all of us. The last thing we need is bad news."

"Amen to that," Paige testified.

Miss Nettie thought for a moment. "If it's such great news, though, why dinner and everyone needing to be sitting down, like you don't want them to get knocked off their feet by the news? Usually, folks can't hardly keep great news to themselves. They calling people up, texting, chirping, and that stupid Facenotes stuff."

Paige laughed. "Miss Nettie, haven't I taught you anything about social media vocabulary? It's tweeting, not chirping. It's Facebook, and those are status updates."

"Yeah, yeah, yeah." She made a shooing motion with her hand. "Anyways, let me get in here and get ready to serve. I'm having dinner with Stuart in the kitchen." She blushed. "Just make sure I don't miss when you give this great news." Miss Nettie raised her hands and made a big circle with them.

"I won't. I won't," Paige said. "Where's Naomi?"

"They're all down in the den. Sam and what's her name are here too."

Paige raised an eyebrow at Miss Nettie. "Miss Nettie, you know exactly what her name is." Clearly, Miss Nettie was still having a hard time dealing with Samantha's same-sex marriage. Paige chuckled. "Remember, Miss Nettie, we all God's children. We all God's children."

"Then we should all obey what our Father says to do and not to do." And with that, Miss Nettie went on about her business.

"I'm stuffed," Paige said, rubbing her belly as she sat in one of the dozen chairs that surrounded the long rectangle table.

"Well, let's go in the parlor and let our dinner digest, because Nettie made her famous peach cobbler, which we still need to eat for dessert," Mrs. Vanderdale said.

"I can't even think about dessert right now, I'm so full," Paige said. "I'll definitely take some to go, though." Paige looked at Adele and Norma. "Girls, why don't you go ask Miss Nettie if she would set you up in the den and then ask her if she'd join us in the parlor?" Paige instructed her daughters.

"I'm big enough to turn on the lights and the TV in the den," Adele said, offended. "I even know what channel the Disney Channel is."

"I know you do, sweetheart, but can you just do what Mommy said so that I don't have to beat you down in front of Grammy and them and get the people called on me?" Paige tried to read her daughter in as calm of a voice as she could.

"Huh?" Adele twisted her face up in confusion.

"Just go do what I told you to do," Paige muttered through clenched teeth.

"All right," Adele said, surrendering. She then looked at her little sister. "Come on, Norma." The two girls exited the dining room.

"Shall we?" Mr. Vanderdale stood.

"Yes," Samantha said, "but I don't need my food to digest. I want my cobbler now."

"Me too," Katie said.

"You have to speak for yourself, sis," Samantha said to Paige.

"Then why don't we just hang out in here?" Mrs. Vanderdale suggested.

"Sounds good to me," Paige agreed. "I don't care where we sit. I just need to let all this food settle."

"Well, I think I'm going to head on into the parlor and read the paper," Mr. Vanderdale said. He turned to walk out of the room.

"Actually, Mr. Vanderdale, I kind of wanted to talk to everyone about something," Paige said. "Do you mind staying?"

Mr. Vanderdale paused momentarily, a little caught off guard by Paige's insistent tone. He felt as if he had to stay and couldn't go read his paper. "Well, uh, no, not at all," he said and then almost reluctantly sat back down in his seat, feeling a little indifferent about what was about to come out of Paige's mouth.

Miss Nettie entered the dining room. She looked a little surprised to see everyone sitting there. "Oh. The girls told me you all wanted me in the parlor. I was heading in there."

"Change of plans, Nettie," Mrs. Vanderdale said. "Do you mind bringing dessert out? We'll serve ourselves. Not everyone is ready to eat just yet."

"Why, of course." Miss Nettie eyed Paige.

Paige nodded, signaling she was about to have the talk. Miss Nettie hurried off to get the dessert so that she wouldn't miss anything.

"So how are my nieces?" Samantha asked. "We haven't had any more incidents, you know, regarding the whole skin thing, have we?"

"Oh, no. That's water under the bridge," Paige said.

"Good. I felt so awful," Samantha said.

"No worries. Everything is good," Paige assured her.

Miss Nettie returned with a tray that held a round peach cobbler, some dessert plates, forks, and a bowl of whipped cream. She laid everything out on the table.

"Miss Nettie, do you mind having a seat for a minute?" Paige asked. "What I want to talk to everyone about, I'd like you to hear as well. That way I have to say it only once, and if anybody has any questions, I can answer them now."

"Well, what is it, Paige?" Mrs. Vanderdale had that worried look on her face.

"Please, Naomi. Let me finish. I don't want anyone jumping to any kind of conclusions, so I'll just come right out and say it." Paige cleared her throat. "I met someone. I met him years ago. We've kind of had this on-again, off-again thing. But in our hearts and souls, we've always stayed connected. Well, we've reconnected again. We have been talking every day and have gone out several times. Long story short, we're tired of letting time pass without doing what we know we each desire to do, which is to be together. So he's asked me to marry him, and I've accepted. The girls don't know. I'm going to tell them soon, but I wanted to tell you guys first, before they said anything to you, because you know how kids can be. They repeat everything they hear, and sometimes it's not translated properly."

"Didn't we learn that the hard way?" Samantha said under her breath.

Paige continued. "He's a wonderful, kind man. Because you all are the girls' family, I feel you have the right to know. A man will be entering not only my life, but also their life, so any questions you have, you are entitled to ask. I'll answer the first question everyone wants to know the answer to by telling you that his name is—"

"Robert! It's that Robert dude who took the pictures of the horses that day, isn't it?" Samantha yelled out.

Paige was surprised Samantha remembered who her love interest was, even though she'd gotten the name wrong. "It's Ryan," she said, correcting her.

"Yeah, Ryan. That's it!" Samantha exclaimed. "The way you two were acting like two fools in love . . . and you trying to ask him to ask you out to dinner. It was crazy." Samantha looked at Mrs. Vanderdale. "I told you, Ma. You owe me twenty bucks." Samantha put her hand out.

"What? Who? Wait a minute," Paige said, totally caught off guard by Samantha's comments. "You bet money that I was going to marry him? But how could you know? We reconnected only a little over a month ago."

"Oh, we made this bet a long time ago," Samantha said. "The day of the photo shoot, actually. I bet Mom twenty bucks that you two were going to end up together. It was love at first sight . . . or second sight. Or however many times it was that you two had seen each other. But you looked at him the way—" Samantha's words halted.

Everyone could pretty much guess what Samantha was about to say. That Paige looked at Ryan the same way she had looked at Norman.

Mrs. Vanderdale stood. She didn't speak. She simply exited the room.

Sadness was written all over Paige's face. She was announcing her engagement. This should be a happy time. But she had known there was a chance that not everyone would take the news well, namely, her former mother-in-law.

Paige felt a hand cover hers. It was Mr. Vanderdale's. He looked into Paige's eyes and smiled. "Congratulations, daughter. We can't wait to welcome Ryan into the family."

Paige smiled at Mr. Vanderdale's comforting words. But it was Mrs. Vanderdale she would have to go face.

***

The first place Paige went to look for Mrs. Vanderdale was the parlor. She wasn't there. She peeked in the den and saw only the girls in there. Next, Paige headed up the steps and went to the bedroom that Mr. And Mrs. Vanderdale shared. The door was open just a crack. She could see Mrs. Vanderdale sitting on the couch, which had a chair on each side and a coffee table in front.

Paige knocked softly on the door. "Naomi, can I come in?" she asked, pushing the door open a little more.

Mrs. Vanderdale didn't speak. She just nodded.

Paige opened the door and walked inside the room. There was no mistake that Paige had entered the master bedroom of the home. It was huge, almost like a five-star hotel suite. The area where the bed sat was separate from the sitting area, where Mrs. Vanderdale was currently seated. The sitting area was the size of a living room in the average home. Off to the right was a walk-in-closet that had a sitting area of its own. The closet rivaled a small, classy boutique. The attached bathroom had a shower-tub combo, as well as a Jacuzzi. Talk about his and her sinks, Mr. Vanderdale had his own sink on his own side of the bathroom, and Mrs. Vanderdale had hers.

Mrs. Vanderdale remained still on the couch. She was looking down at something in her hands. As Paige walked over to her, she realized that what Mrs. Vanderdale was holding was a picture. Standing behind the couch, Paige looked over Mrs. Vanderdale's shoulder and saw that the picture was of Norman.

"I miss my boy," Mrs. Vanderdale said. "I know it's been a few years, but I miss him all the same."

"It doesn't matter how long it's been. It's understandable that you miss him. You were his mother. You are supposed to miss your son for the rest of your life."

"I *am* his mother," Mrs. Vanderdale snapped. "It's not I *was* his mother. I still am!"

Paige jumped back. "I'm sorry," she replied, apologizing.

"Forgive me," Mrs. Vanderdale said in a calmer tone. There was silence as Mrs. Vanderdale continued staring down at the picture. "I knew this day might eventually come. I was hoping it wouldn't, though. I knew one of these days some nice fellow was going to come and sweep you off your feet and take you away from us. You'll be having dinner with his family instead of ours. You're going to start your own little family and forget all about us." Mrs. Vanderdale began to weep.

"Naomi, that will never happen," Paige was quick to say.

"I know you'd like to think that it won't happen, but what man is going to be okay with his wife hanging out with her last husband's family?"

"A man who loves me and my girls and understands that you all are a part of our lives. You all are our family, no matter what. That's never going to change. You have to believe me." Ryan knew how close Paige was to the Vanderdales. Heck, she spent more time with them than with her own parents. Paige hadn't thought to ask Ryan whether he felt awkward in any way about that. But with Ryan being who he was, if it were a problem, he certainly would not hold his tongue about it. Still, Paige made a mental note to be sure to discuss the issue with him.

"You say that now, but visits will become far and few between. That's just how life is."

"Not my life," Paige said. She walked around to face Mrs. Vanderdale. "Look at me," she ordered, and Mrs. Vanderdale lifted her face and stared at Paige with her red eyes, tears still flowing. "This family has been my rock. It goes back to what we told the girls. I don't care about color. We are family. We are connected by blood. Nothing, absolutely nothing can ever separate us. Ever. I love you. I love all of you." Paige held back tears. "I wouldn't be able to breathe without you guys. If you ain't breathing, you ain't living. I can't live without you guys. You have to believe me." She took Mrs. Vanderdale's hands in hers. "You do believe me, don't you?"

Mrs. Vanderdale took in a deep breath and then exhaled. She nodded as a smile spread on her face and her tears turned into happy tears. "Yes, I believe you. I believe you."

Paige exhaled. The last thing she wanted to do was lose a family in order to gain one. In her world, they were all going to be one big happy family. But little did she know that her world was about to come crashing down.

Chapter 18

"Thank you again for the flowers," Adele and Norma said in unison, following Paige's instructions. They'd already said thank you once, when Ryan first arrived with his two sons in tow. He'd come bearing a bouquet of roses for Paige, and each of his sons had carried a bouquet of daisies for the girls. That had been the start of what turned out to be a beautiful evening.

During a dinner of baked chicken, loaded baked potatoes, and a side salad, the six of them talked, laughed, and told knock-knock jokes. The girls had decided they didn't want to have a tea party. "They'll think we're babies," was their reasoning.

After dinner in the TV room, Ryan had this great idea that they would allow each child to share something about their parent and something about their sibling. After the kids took turns, Ryan and Paige shared things about each of their children. This drew lots of laughter and was an opportunity for them to get to know one another.

When Ryan announced that it was getting late and that he and the boys needed to get going, the girls whined their disappointment.

"When are you coming back?" Norma asked.

"Yeah, and can we take a picture again? All of us together," Adele said.

Adele and Norma bombarded Ryan and the boys with questions all the way to the door. Paige had to put a stop to their badgering and tell them to thank the young gentlemen for the flowers again.

"You girls are so very welcome," Ryan said to them.

"You're welcome," the boys told them in unison, all smiles.

"Thank you for having us, Miss Paige," Deron said.

"Thank you," Lionel repeated after him.

"You boys are always welcome in our home," Paige told them.

"Our home . . . That means it's everybody's," Adele said. "That's what Ms. Duncan said." Adele was referring to her first-grade teacher. "That means you can come whenever you want." She looked up at Paige. "Right, Mommy?"

Paige smiled and rubbed Adele's head. "Right, sweetheart." Paige looked at Ryan, who was over the moon about how well the girls had taken to him and the boys. "You heard her." Paige nodded at Adele. "It's *our* home . . . everybody's."

Ryan leaned in and kissed Paige on the cheek, then whispered in her ear, "We'll discuss the living situation at a later date."

Paige chuckled.

"Uh, do you guys mind?" Lionel said, rolling his eyes up in his head. "Come on, Deron. Let's go to the car." He elbowed his brother.

"Here's the keys," Ryan said, giving the boys the keys to unlock the car.

"Thanks again for dinner, Miss Paige," Deron said.

"It was delicious," Lionel added.

"You are welcome, boys," Paige said. "I'll see you later."

"Bye," the girls shouted and waved.

"Bye," the boys said to the girls and then made their way to the car.

"Well, ditto to what the boys said," Ryan said to Paige.

"Ditto to what Adele said." Paige winked. She looked down at the girls. "Adele, Norma, go on upstairs and start getting your clothes ready for bed."

"Okay, Mommy," Adele said.

"Good night, Mr. Ryan," the girls sang.

Ryan waved to the girls before they ran off to do what they were told.

"Man, they are getting so big," Ryan said. "And cuter by the moment."

"And they seem to adore you and the boys." Paige exhaled. "It's just more confirmation that we are supposed to be. Everything is just coming together without a hitch."

Ryan took Paige's hands in his as he continued listening to her talk.

"I told you about my telling the Vanderdales about you, and my talk with Mrs. Vanderdale that followed."

Ryan nodded.

"You didn't say much about how you feel about the Vanderdales, though."

He shrugged. "What's there to say? They are the girls' family. The girls are going to be my family, which means we're all family."

"Yeah, but they are my family too," Paige said. "I just want to make sure you understand that even if I wasn't the mother of their grandchildren, they'd still be a huge part of my life."

Ryan released Paige's hands and rubbed her chin with his hand. "You don't have to sell the Vanderdales to me, honey. I get exactly who they are in your life. Am I intimidated by the fact you were married to their son? Absolutely not. Do I feel as though I will have to compete with your deceased husband's family? No more than I feel I'm competing with your ex-husband, Blake. I'm the one who is here with you and for you now. I know what it feels like not to have you in my life. I wouldn't wish that upon my worst enemy, let alone people who love you as much as I do. So I wouldn't dare ask you to remove yourself from their lives. You are mine, and everything that comes with you. Former in-laws, credit card debt . . ."

The two laughed.

"That's why I love you, Ryan," Paige said.

"I love you too, soon to be Paige Coleman." He planted a kiss on her lips.

"Mommy's going to marry Mr. Ryan! Mommy's going to marry Mr. Ryan!"

As they stood there in each other's arms, both Ryan and Paige looked toward the top of the steps, where they saw Adele and Norma dancing around in their T-shirts and underwear.

"Girls, didn't I tell you to go wait for me?" Paige scolded. "Get y'all's naked butts in that bathroom and wait for me."

"We were just coming to tell you we were ready," Adele said.

"Okay. Now get on." Paige made a shooing motion at them.

They ran off, giggling and singing, "Kissy, kissy, poo-poo."

Paige turned around and faced Ryan. "You ready for them?"

"I was ready yesterday," Ryan said, then sealed their evening with one last kiss.

"Are you sure you're okay with this?" Paige asked as she rode in the passenger seat as Ryan drove to the Vanderdales' home.

"Yes," Ryan said, doing a double take at Paige. "And would you please stop biting your nails? You weren't this nervous when I met your parents last week."

"This is different, and you know it."

"How so?"

"A guy meeting his girl's parents is normal." She looked into the backseat to make sure the girls weren't listening. They were occupied playing patty-cake. "A guy meeting his girl's late husband's parents, not so normal."

"Well, it's our normal. Now, stop biting your nails. And why didn't I know about that nasty habit of yours?"

"I guess I've never really been nervous around you," Paige said. "But when I am, depending how nervous I am, the urge comes and goes. I guess that is what it's like with cigarette smoking."

"You don't have a secret smoking habit, do you?"

"Of course not," Paige said. She spit out a piece of nail she'd just bitten off.

"Disgusting," Ryan said. "I still don't understand why your nerves are eating at you, making you eat your nails. It's not like it's their first time meeting me. I was at their house before, for the photo shoot, remember?"

"Well, it's your first time meeting them as my fiancé."

He turned his head to the side. "I guess you have a point there. But stop worrying, love." He placed his hand on Paige's knee. "Everything has been working out just fine. What makes you think something will go wrong now?"

Paige looked out the window as they turned onto the Vanderdales' private drive. She didn't know what would make her think something would go wrong now. But for some reason, she just did.

Chapter 19

"Ryan, it's good seeing you again, buddy." Mr. Vanderdale stood from his chair and greeted Ryan as Mrs. Vanderdale escorted him and Paige into the parlor.

Even though Paige had told the Vanderdales that Ryan had two boys, Ryan and Paige had decided they'd introduce the boys at a later date. The Vanderdales had met Ryan before, but only in the role of photographer, not fiancé. They didn't want to overwhelm Mrs. Vanderdale in any way by having Paige show up on their doorstep with a whole new family.

The girls had already run off with Samantha after she greeted Ryan. She had assured him she wasn't being rude by not hanging out with them in the parlor before dinner and had revealed that her nieces didn't share when it came to her attention. Ryan had given her a pass and had informed her that the wonderful company of Mr. and Mrs. Vanderdale would make up for her absence.

"It's good to see you again as well," Ryan said, shaking Mr. Vanderdale's hand.

"It's been a couple years."

"Yeah. By the way, how did that horse contest thing go?"

"Oh, yeah. Sunrise got most photogenic. First place."

"Good. Congratulations," said Ryan.

"Couldn't have done it without your wonderful photography skills."

"Well, thank you for that."

The two men looked over at the women, who were just standing there with huge grins on their faces, watching them interact. Paige and Mrs. Vanderdale were all hugged up like two high school cheerleaders on the sidelines who were watching their boyfriends play in the homecoming game.

"What are you two up to over there?" Mr. Vanderdale asked, giving the women a mischievous look.

"Oh, nothing," Paige said. "By the way, where's Miss Nettie?"

"That woman has been running around here like she's about to explode, hasn't she, Norm?" Mrs. Vanderdale looked at her husband.

"I'd say she hasn't been her usual self these past couple days," Mr. Vanderdale agreed.

"She said she has a surprise for us at dinner," Mrs. Vanderdale said.

"She will be joining us at the dinner table, won't she, and not just serving?" Paige asked. "You know I consider Miss Nettie like blood. I want her to get the chance to meet and connect with Ryan also."

"Oh, yes. She'll be joining us," Mrs. Vanderdale assured her.

"Good." Paige looked at Ryan and smiled.

"So come on. Let's all sit until Stuart calls us for dinner," Mrs. Vanderdale suggested.

They all sat in the parlor and talked for a few minutes. Samantha, Katie, and the girls eventually joined them, and then shortly after that, Stuart ushered them into the dining room, announcing that dinner was served.

"You are going to love Miss Nettie's cooking," Paige said to Ryan as they all headed to the dining room.

The men were sure to pull the women's seats out for them.

"Everything looks delicious," Mr. Vanderdale said, admiring the food that had already been set on the table.

"That Nettie really outdid herself today," Mrs. Vanderdale said as she admired the spread. "She was running around here at a hundred miles per hour, like she had ants in her pants." She laughed. "By the way, where is she?"

On cue, Miss Nettie entered the dining room, slowing down from a light jog. "Here I am," she said.

"Will you slow your row and sit down?" Mrs. Vanderdale said to her housekeeper. "Enjoy some of this delicious food you've been wearing yourself ragged to prepare."

Paige gave the table the once-over. "Yes, Miss Nettie. It looks like you have made every item in your cookbook."

The table was covered with everything from soul food to traditional American fare. It wasn't a cohesive banquet at all, but instead about three full meals spread out.

"I wasn't sure what his favorite foods were," Miss Nettie said. "And I wanted to make sure I had something he liked."

"Well, all you had to do was call me and ask me, Miss Nettie," Paige said. "I would have told you this man can eat everything." She play tapped Ryan on the shoulder, and he smiled. "But since you actually made everything, anyhow, we're good."

"No, not him," Miss Nettie said. Then she looked at Ryan. "Although I'm glad you approve of today's menu."

Ryan nodded and smiled.

"I wasn't sure what my son's favorite foods were," Miss Nettie offered.

"Your son?" Mrs. Vanderdale said with a surprised tone. While she sounded surprised, the expression on her face indicated that she was a bit hurt.

"I'm sorry, Mrs. Vanderdale," Miss Nettie said, not looking at her boss and thus not noticing her hurt look. "I know I was supposed to give you a heads-up that I was inviting kin, but as you can see, there's enough food to invite the homeless from under the bridge." Miss Nettie frowned. "And sadly enough, that's where I found my boy." Her frown turned upside down. "But I found him nonetheless."

"Oh, Miss Nettie," Paige said, clutching her heart with happiness and relief. She knew how much finding her son meant to Miss Nettie. She was glad the mother now had some closure to the matter. Of course, Paige had no reason to feel hurt upon hearing about Miss Nettie's son, since she had been instrumental in helping the woman find her boy.

Mrs. Vanderdale inhaled and tried not to be selfish by making this moment about herself. Apparently, this was the news that had had Miss Nettie on edge. The last thing Mrs. Vanderdale wanted to do was ruin the moment by expressing her feelings about Miss Nettie not sharing the fact before now that she had a son. Instead, she opted to show her support and celebrate with her friend. She stood and walked over to Miss Nettie.

"Nettie, hush your mouth about not asking permission to invite your son to dinner. I'm just shocked to hear that you even have a son." She looked at her husband. "Norman, did you know about this?"

Mr. Vanderdale shook his head. He had talked to Miss Nettie for countless hours during their counseling sessions. She had never held back. She had shared with him everything about her life that she could remember, everything that hadn't disappeared into some dark corner of her mind. According to Mr. Vanderdale's diagnosis, Miss Nettie wasn't running from her past. Her past was hiding itself from her. Mr. Vanderdale didn't take Miss Nettie not sharing with them the fact that she had a son as personally as Mrs. Vanderdale was taking it. But then again, by knowing Miss Nettie's mental health history, he was privy to information that others weren't. There were some things in people's lives that they struggled with and had a hard time coping with, and the last thing they wanted to do was tell others about it.

"It wasn't that I was trying to keep things from you, Mrs. Vanderdale," Miss Nettie explained. "It's just that—"

"You don't have to explain a thing to us, Nettie," Mr. Vanderdale interrupted. "Clearly, this is a part of your life that you wanted to go back and atone for."

"Oh, God, it is," Miss Nettie said, her eyes watering. "And I never really knew just how much I needed to do this. I just thank God for my Stuart, for encouraging me to do it." She looked at Paige. "And for Paige, for helping me do it."

Mrs. Vanderdale looked at Paige in an accusatory manner. "You knew all this time that Miss Nettie had a boy?" The hurt expression on her face was now fully visible and undeniable.

"I found out not too long ago," Paige answered, trying not to sound defensive. "Miss Nettie came to me for help in trying to find him. We spent hours on the Internet. It got us some information, but ultimately, I had to put her in the hands of my attorney."

Paige's words didn't make Mrs. Vanderdale feel any better. Why was it that Miss Nettie felt that she wouldn't be helpful in the process? "Nettie, you know we could have hired the best private investigators in town." She looked at her husband, silently entreating him to back her up.

Mr. Vanderdale jumped in. "Of all people, we would have empathized with you and understood your wanting to get your boy back. We know exactly what it feels like to be without a son." He looked at his wife, and the two shared a moment.

"I know you would have," Miss Nettie said. "It's just that I didn't know if my son was dead or alive. I didn't want to put you all through anything that would remind you of your own son."

Mrs. Vanderdale chuckled. "Nettie, I'm reminded of my own son every morning, when I wake up. Helping you fill a void in your life or find some type of closure with your son would have been an honor. But that's neither here nor there. I'm just glad you found him." Mrs. Vanderdale gave Miss Nettie a big, warm hug. She couldn't promise that after things died down, she wouldn't have a conversation with Miss Nettie about her feelings about the matter, but for now, that wasn't as important as rejoicing with Miss Nettie.

"Congratulations, Miss Nettie," Samantha said, chiming in.

"Thank you. Thank you all," Miss Nettie said as tears of joy fell from her eyes.

Mrs. Vanderdale signaled for someone to hand her a napkin to give to Miss Nettie so that she could wipe her tears away. "Well, that explains the extra setting," she said, pointing to the table. "I thought that you'd just miscalculated or that Stuart was going to join us. But it looks like your son is the mystery guest. How special."

"Is he little, like us?" Adele said after staying out of the grown folks' business for as long as she could. "Or bigger like Mr. Ryan's sons?"

"Yeah, Adele said they're going to be our brothers," Norma added.

All the adults looked at one another and then started laughing.

"From the mouths of babes," Mrs. Vanderdale said.

"Can't get nothing past kids," Paige said.

"You're right about that," Miss Nettie said. "Now, I just hope my kid can get over the past."

The laughter died down.

"Well, what did he say when you talked to him?" Paige asked. "And when did you talk to him? How long have you had to keep this big secret inside?"

"I just talked to him for the first time a couple days ago," Miss Nettie offered. "He was shocked." Her eyes gazed off. She looked as though she was lost in thought, reflecting on the conversation she'd had with her son. "He didn't believe me at first. He actually had a birth certificate with another woman's name on it. We learned that it was an amended birth certificate, though. I had the hospital records as proof he was born to me. He was mine before he was hers. According to my boy, even though the woman he thought was his mother for years was a good-for-nothing something, it's his father who he felt should have never lied to him."

"So how were you able to convince him without a doubt that you were his birth mother?" Paige asked.

"I didn't. Mr. Rudy did. Well, not Mr. Rudy personally. He ended up having to focus on some big case that he and his own paralegal had to work on. So he had one of his partners' paralegals help me. She did the research and ended up contacting my boy's attorney, one who had worked for him in the past. We sent him all the documentation proving that I was, in fact, his birth mother. Took a blood test too."

"Attorney? You found your son living under a bridge, and yet he can afford an attorney?" Mr. Vanderdale asked.

Miss Nettie was becoming either agitated or nervous. It wasn't clear which. Nonetheless, she continued answering the questions that were being posed to her. "He's not his attorney now. He has no money to pay him now, but supposedly, once upon a time, my boy did pretty well for himself. Had the fellow on retainer for years and had spent good money on the man. Guess my son had spent enough money on him over the years that his former attorney decided to help out this one last time—pro bono—in figuring things out. We all got our answers, proof positive."

"God most definitely had His hand in this," Paige said, shaking her head in awe. "You said he lives under a bridge?"

Miss Nettie nodded.

"How did you end up tracking him down with no address? How long did it take? Who actually found him?" Paige was shooting questions left and right.

"It was actually his attorney who knew of his last whereabouts," Miss Nettie said.

Paige asked, "Who is—"

"Enough talk. We can go over the fine details of it all at another date. When is that boy of yours coming?" Mrs. Vanderdale asked.

"He's already here. He's back in my quarters," Miss Nettie answered.

Everyone looked shocked.

"When? How?" Mrs. Vanderdale asked.

"Stuart brought him in through the back a bit ago. He helped him get changed up and looking decent. "I'm sorry I didn't give you all a better heads-up." She looked at Paige. "And I'm sorry to be intruding on you and your fellow's time." Miss Nettie swallowed hard, waiting on a response.

"How many times do I have to tell you that we are family?" Mrs. Vanderdale said. "You're family." She pointed at Miss Nettie. "The way we are welcoming Ryan into our family as a son . . . is the same way we are welcoming your boy into the family," Mrs. Vanderdale continued. "Now go get him, already."

Paige looked at Ryan, took his hand in hers, squeezed it, and smiled. Everyone showed their agreement with nods or smiles.

"All right then," Miss Nettie said, clapping her hands excitedly and then taking a huge deep breath. "I'll go fetch Stuart and my boy." Miss Nettie lifted her shoulders, held her head up high, and wobbled it with confidence. "Family," Miss Nettie said as she walked off proudly. Moments later she mumbled under her breath, "Let's pray so."

Mrs. Vanderdale took her seat again. "Wow! I didn't expect all this to go down at dinner."

"God is definitely still in the miracle business, indeed," Paige said.

"Can we eat now?" Adele asked.

"Yeah. I been hungry a long time ago," Norma said.

There were some chuckles.

"Hold on just one second, girls," Paige said. "We're going to wait for Miss Nettie and them to join us, and then we'll bless the food and dig in."

"Yay," the girls cheered.

A couple seconds later, Miss Nettie opened the dining room door. "Everyone, I'd like for you to meet my son." Miss Nettie stepped to the side and raised her hand like she was one of Bob's beauties on *The Price Is Right*.

Miss Nettie's son stepped into the room behind her, and Stuart was behind him. Miss Nettie's son walked in with his head kind of down. He had a small Afro, and his face was covered in facial hair. He was kind of thin and frail and looked as though he might be wearing some of Stuart's clothes. Stuart was a slightly bigger man, so the clothes were loose. Miss Nettie's son must have lived a hard life, because he was around forty but appeared to be darn near Miss Nettie's age. Considering he was homeless and was living under a bridge, it was pretty safe to say that his life had, in fact, been rough.

Miss Nettie, smiling from ear to ear, put her arm around her son and kissed him on the cheek. He looked over at her. She gave him a smile of encouragement. She wanted him to hold his head up high. Still looking at his mother, he gave a half smile, then lifted his head higher. She nodded for him to turn, with his head held high, and face everyone to greet them.

It was almost as if he'd reverted to the little boy Miss Nettie had abandoned in the hospital all those years ago. That was how he came across—as more of a lost little boy than a grown man. By the way he was staring into his mother's eyes, it was clear that he had found himself in Miss Nettie. Looked as though this was a chapter in his life he had needed all along, whether he knew it or not.

Under his mother's encouragement, he turned toward the family seated at the table and smiled. His teeth were still in pretty good shape, especially given that he was homeless. They were bright white, and it didn't look like any were missing. A front one looked as though it might have been chipped, but other than that, any dentist would have been proud.

"Everyone," Miss Nettie said, "this is my boy, Mr.—"

"Oh, my God! Oh, my God!" Paige stood. A chill took over her, and her body began to shake. Her clammy palms were planted flat on the table, as if she was trying to keep her balance. Her eyes flooded with tears, as if a dam had broken. She stared at Miss Nettie's son. She'd gotten past the clothing; the frail, thin body; the Afro; the facial hair; and the pretty teeth. It was when she got to Miss Nettie's son's eyes that the blood could have drained from her body. Although she didn't recognize any other parts of him, she would forever recognize those eyes. The eyes that, she'd thanked God, Adele had not inherited.

Chapter 20

"Paige, wait! What's wrong?" Ryan called out as Paige knocked over the chair she'd been sitting in and began scooping up Adele and Norma like they were running from a . . .

"Monster! He's a monster!" Paige said as she snatched up her girls by their arms. "We have got to get out of here. Get my babies out of here!" Paige was frantic. Too frantic to notice the look of fear in her little girls' eyes.

"Paige, baby." Ryan stood and tried to calm her by grabbing hold of her arm.

"Don't touch me!" Paige screamed. "Don't anybody touch me." Her voice boomed across the dining room.

"My ears! Mommy, my ears!" Norma threw her hands over her ears.

Paige had Norma by her elbow and was yanking her from the table. "Let's go. We've got to go."

Mrs. Vanderdale looked at Ryan. "What's going on?"

He shook his head. He had no idea what was causing Paige to behave so erratically. He just continued trying to calm her. "Paige, you're scaring the girls," Ryan told her.

By now Paige had both her daughters in her grip and was leaving the dining room, headed for the front door. "No, we've got to get out of here. We've got to go," she said over her shoulder.

Ryan managed to block her path. "No, not until you tell us what is going on."

"I swear to God, if you don't get out of my way . . ." Paige said with such venom as she glared Ryan down.

His eyes bucked. Paige had said the word *monster*. Well, that was exactly what he felt he was standing in front of. He looked down at her girls, who were afraid and were crying. He didn't want to stir up any more drama by trying to stop Paige. He was the one who had driven her there, so he had no idea where she intended to go. Still, he stepped aside.

Mrs. Vanderdale was horrified. She looked at her husband. "Norm, go do something. I can't have her dragging my grandbabies out there in the state of mind she's in."

Mr. Vanderdale stood. "I'll go talk to her." He looked at his daughter. "Sam, come get the girls."

Samantha stood to follow her father. Ryan went to follow as well, until Mr. Vanderdale put his hand up to stop him.

"Please, Ryan. I know you're concerned. But please let me talk to her first." Mr. Vanderdale waited for a response from Ryan.

Ryan hesitated. That was his woman. He wanted to be there for her. He had to admit, though, given the way Paige had just behaved, she might very well need some professional support in addition to emotional support. Mr. Vanderdale was definitely the man for that job. So knowing Paige would be in good hands, Ryan relented.

"Thank you," Mr. Vanderdale said, knowing how hard it was for Ryan to fall back when the woman he loved was so distraught. He exited the dining room. "Paige, wait!" he called out when he saw her by the front door, hurrying to put Adele's and Norma's jackets on.

Paige was oblivious to her name being called. "Come on, girls. We have to go," she said, still struggling to get jackets on the unco-operative girls.

"Mommy, what's wrong?" Adele cried. "I want Grandma. Why are we leaving?"

"And I'm still hungry," Norma whined.

"Just put the jacket on!" Paige yelled, which only caused Adele to cry that much harder.

"Paige Vanderdale!" This time Mr. Vanderdale's voice shook the entire house.

Paige immediately looked up and noticed him.

Samantha walked around her father and over to Adele and Norma. "Come on, girls," she said softly to them. "Come with Auntie." She began to scoot them away.

"Where are you taking them?" Paige demanded to know, walking over and yanking Samantha by her arm.

Samantha was too outdone by Paige being aggressive with her. "You know I would never hurt my nieces," she said as she stood nose to nose with Paige. "Don't even come at me like that."

Mr. Vanderdale walked over and separated the two before things could get out of hand between them. "Paige, I asked Sam to sit with the girls while I talk to you."

Keeping her eyes on her daughters, with a look of desperation and fear the entire time, Paige asked, "Where is she taking them?" She then looked at Mr. Vanderdale. "She better not be taking them back in there with that . . . with that . . ." She pointed at the dining room. "Monster."

Mr. Vanderdale gently lowered Paige's hand and took it in his. "It's going to be all right. Do you trust me, Paige?"

Paige looked into Mr. Vanderdale's eyes. In all honesty, she didn't trust anyone right about now. She said nothing.

"Paige, do you trust me? Do you trust Naomi? Sam?" He nodded toward Samantha. "Have we ever done anything to hurt you?"

Paige shook her head.

"Have we ever done anything to hurt the girls?"

Again, Paige shook her head.

"Then you know in your heart we never will do anything to hurt you and the girls," he reasoned. "Now, Samantha is going to take the girls to the den, and you and I are going to talk. Okay?"

Still slightly petrified, Paige was beginning to regain her good sense. "Okay," she agreed. She then looked at Samantha sternly. "Keep your eyes on them. Don't let them go with anybody."

Samantha nodded and then exited the room with the girls.

Once Mr. Vanderdale and Paige were alone, he walked her over to the couch in the parlor and sat her down. "Would you like me to call your parents or anything?"

Paige shook her head like a frightened little schoolgirl who was in trouble and didn't want the principal to call her parents on her.

Mr. Vanderdale could tell by looking at Paige that she was truly traumatized, to the point where she was mentally reverting to earlier stages of her life. He had to handle her with care. He was a psychiatrist by trade and by heart, so this wasn't a challenge for him.

"Just now, back in the dining room, you got really upset. Tell me what happened." Mr. Vanderdale sat down on the couch.

Paige swallowed hard before she began. "Miss Nettie brought him here. Her son. He's a monster."

Once again Mr. Vanderdale could see Paige going back in time. This time he could tell by her gloomy expression that she had regressed to a dark time. He watched her rock slightly and begin to bite her nails. He placed his hand on her shoulder and slowly stopped her from rocking. "Why do you think Miss Nettie's son is a monster?" he asked.

"Because he is!" Paige shot up in anger. "He did all those bad things to me and treated me like trash."

"Okay, okay. Just calm down." He patted the vacated seat on the couch. "Come on. Sit back down next to me, Paige."

Paige stared at Mr. Vanderdale for a moment. She didn't want to sit down. She wanted to snatch her children up and get the heck out of that house quick, fast, and in a hurry. Even if it was on foot.

"Please, Paige. Talk to me," he pleaded, extending his hand.

After looking into Mr. Vanderdale's eyes, Paige loosened up. For her, in that moment, in her current state, looking at Norman Sr. was like looking at Norman Jr. Paige felt safe and secure again because she knew beyond a doubt that her Norman would never hurt her. He'd sacrificed his life to protect her. Finally, Paige slowly placed her hand in Mr. Vanderdale's and sat down.

Keeping her hand in his, Mr. Vanderdale urged Paige to tell him what was going on. "Your words are safe with me," he reminded her. "Tell me what's going on. Why has seeing Miss Nettie's son upset you? Who or what does he remind you of?"

Paige trembled before saying, "Blake."

"He reminds you of Blake?"

Paige tucked her lips in and tried not to cry while she began to talk. "He *is* Blake. Miss Nettie's son is Blake."

Mr. Vanderdale tried to remain as calm as possible and to keep his eyes from bucking out of his head upon hearing Paige's words. He needed to remain as neutral as possible. "Blake, as in your ex-husband, Blake?" He swallowed, hoping it wasn't so, before asking the next question. "Blake, as in Adele's biological father?"

Tears dripped from Paige's eyes as she nodded.

"Dear God," Mr. Vanderdale said under his breath. He could absolutely understand why Paige had had such a reaction upon being introduced to their housekeeper's long-lost son.

Paige could see complete empathy in Mr. Vanderdale's eyes. "See? Now do you see why I have to get my girls out of here? He's going to hurt us. He's going to take Adele from me." Paige began shaking.

"No, he's not," Mr. Vanderdale assured her. "I won't allow him." He thought for a moment.

"What are you going to do?" Paige interrupted his pondering.

Mr. Vanderdale knew that he had to go in there and ask Miss Nettie's son a couple questions. It was possible that he was not Blake but simply reminded Paige of Blake. If it turned out that he was, in fact, Adele's biological father, then Mr. Vanderdale would have to ask him to leave their home. It was a given. They loved Miss Nettie like family. They also loved Paige, and they loved their grandchildren. Those four people were their first priority. They didn't know Miss Nettie's son from a bum on the street—no pun intended—so that was not where their dilemma lay. It was with Miss Nettie, the woman who had worked for them for almost twenty-five years. She was family, just as much as Paige was. But the girls, the grandkids, they were blood. Blood was thicker than water. So Mr. Vanderdale would have to figure out how to tell Miss Nettie that her son could never step foot in their home again. He knew that might mean losing Miss Nettie. Losing their grandchildren wasn't an option, though.

Mr. Vanderdale told Paige exactly what he'd been thinking. "I'm going to go talk to Miss Nettie, and if need be, I'll have to ask that her son leaves, and I'll express that he is never welcome in our home again."

Her eyes softened. Her fear began to subside. "Really? But Miss Nettie is family. She's been your family far longer than we have. She has been here for Naomi and is so loyal to you all."

"Paige, time has nothing to do with this. Loyalty has nothing to do with this. You are the mother of our grandchildren." He squeezed her hand. "You all mean more to us than anything in this world. If we have to close off the entire rest of the world to protect this family, by God, that is what we'll do. We love you, Paige. You've been hurt enough in life, and you won't be hurt ever again, not under my watch."

Mr. Vanderdale's words filled Paige's heart. She couldn't even come up with any words to express how the ones he'd just spoken made her feel. "You really mean that?" she asked him.

"Yes, Paige. I'm here for you as long as I have breath. Not only are your words safe with me, but you are safe with me."

Paige was looking down at her hand as Mr. Vanderdale caressed it. She closed her eyes and took in the feeling of love, support, and security he had just displayed. It was just what she needed to override the feeling she was overcome with just moments ago.

"Thank you so much," Paige said. "I love you too."

Mr. Vanderdale pulled Paige in for a hug and was surprised when he felt Paige's lips press against his.

Chapter 21

"Paige!"

Mr. Vanderdale and Paige pulled away from each other when they heard Paige's name being yelled out. They turned to look at the dining room doorway, where Ryan stood. His face displayed different emotions. Shock. Hurt. Confusion. Anger.

"What the h...? What is going on here?" Ryan said, walking toward them.

"Ryan, I'm sorry. . . . I . . ." Paige stood and held her hand up. When Ryan kept charging toward them, she began walking toward him to stop him in his tracks. He was like a raging bull.

"Move out of my way, Paige!" Ryan said, raising his hands, glaring at Mr. Vanderdale with rage.

"No, Ryan." Paige threw her arms around him and hugged him. "It's not what it looks like. Please let me explain."

Ryan kept his hands up, not touching Paige. "Paige, move. Get out of my way," he said in the calmest tone he could muster.

Paige stood still, pressing her weight against Ryan so that he couldn't take another step toward Mr. Vanderdale.

Mr. Vanderdale wanted to explain. "Ryan—"

"Old man, don't you say ish to me!" Ryan spat. "You're supposed to be helping her in here. You got your wife in there, telling me you're a doctor, you're a professional, you know what you are doing, and you'll be able to calm Paige down. All the while you're in here, taking advantage of her. Man, white folks. Y'all some freaks."

In Mr. Vanderdale's past line of work in the prison system, he had been called worse and had heard more racist comments than he could remember, so Ryan's comment raised an eyebrow slightly but didn't get him all up in arms. Ryan was speaking from an emotional point right now. Mr. Vanderdale understood that.

Ryan looked at Paige. "He's the one you need to get your daughters away from." Ryan pointed at Mr. Vanderdale.

"No, Ryan. He didn't do anything. It was all me," Paige admitted. "Mr. Vanderdale . . . white people in general . . . is not a freak. He's not the one who abused me, who raped me, who cheated on me, who contracted HIV, and who then tried to take my daughter from me. That black man in there did all that." She pointed to the dining room door.

"What . . . what do you mean?" Ryan was utterly confused now.

"Where's Miss Nettie's son?" Mr. Vanderdale asked.

"Man, don't you talk to me," Ryan snapped. Mr. Vanderdale was the enemy until he got to the bottom of what all was going on here.

"Ryan, baby, calm down," Paige said. The roles had somehow been reversed. Now it was Paige who was trying to calm down an erratic Ryan. Paige asked Ryan the same question. "Where is Miss Nettie's son?"

"I don't know. He left right after you did. Miss Nettie and Stuart went chasing after him. I've been in the kitchen with Mrs. Vanderdale, giving her water, trying to keep her from having a heart attack." It was no surprise that Mrs. Vanderdale was having one of her episodes. "I finally got her calmed down and decided I'd come out here and check to see what was going on with you," Ryan said to Paige. "And boy, oh, boy, did I see what was going on." He shook his head and began biting his lower lip, like it was killing him to keep from going over there and putting Mr. Vanderdale in his place.

"Ryan, there is so much you don't understand right now," Paige told him.

"Then somebody help a brotha understand before I go all ham up in here," he said. "Because from what I could tell, when I walked into this room, your tongue was down Mr. Vanderdale's throat."

"Oh, Jesus Christ, mother of God!"

Everyone looked at the dining room doorway and saw Mrs. Vanderdale putting her hand across her forehead and falling against the wall.

Mr. Vanderdale rushed over to catch his wife before she hit the floor. He put his arms around his wife and held her steady. He managed to balance her so that she did not hit the floor. But after what she'd just heard, mess was about to hit the fan.

"Stuart, can you fetch Naomi some water please?" Mr. Vanderdale yelled out as he helped his wife over to the couch in the parlor.

"He's off with Miss Nettie," Ryan said. "I'll go grab some." For a minute, Ryan's concern about Mrs. Vanderdale's condition overrode the anger he was feeling toward her husband.

"Oh, Jesus," Paige said as she stood there, biting her nails. She paced the floor a few times before Ryan returned with a bottle of water.

"I grabbed this out of the fridge," Ryan said, reentering the parlor. He carried the water bottle over to Mr. Vanderdale.

"Thank you," Mr. Vanderdale replied. He fed his wife several sips of the water, until she seemed to regain her composure.

Mrs. Vanderdale sat up on the couch. "Whew," she said, shaking off her feeling of being dazed and confused. "I had the craziest dream. I dreamt that I was in the kitchen and I heard all this arguing. I came out here to see what was going on, and Ryan here was fussing at you. . . ." She looked at her husband. "Something about kissing Paige. I tell ya, it was more like a nightmare. I have to stop eating so late in the evening." Mrs. Vanderdale looked up at everyone's faces. The only one making eye contact with her was Ryan. Paige was looking downward, was pacing, and was still biting her nails. Mr. Vanderdale had simply buried his face in his hands. "Dear God, it wasn't a dream, was it!" Mrs. Vanderdale exclaimed. "It was a real live nightmare."

Ryan crossed his arms, with a scowl on his face. "Trust me, Mrs. Vanderdale, you and me both are owed some answers here."

Mrs. Vanderdale stood. She stumbled slightly before she was able to balance herself. Mr. Vanderdale went to help her, but she swatted his hand away and rolled her eyes at him. She then went stomping over to Paige. "You, you . . . jezebel!" she spat.

Mr. Vanderdale was able to catch up with his wife and hold her back.

"I'm sorry, Naomi," Paige said. "Truly I am. You know I would never disrespect you or do anything to hurt you." She looked at Mr. Vanderdale. "I'm sorry, so sorry I kissed you. I don't know what I was thinking."

"Wait. You kissed him?" Ryan said, jumping in.

"Yes," Paige answered.

At the same time Mr. Vanderdale answered, "No."

Both Ryan and Mrs. Vanderdale looked back and forth from Paige to Mr. Vanderdale, confused.

"Somebody better tell me what the h-e double hockey sticks is going on before I go reality show up in here," Mrs. Vanderdale warned.

Mr. Vanderdale made an attempt to explain. "Yes, it was Paige who kissed me, but she wasn't herself. I could use all kind of fancy terminology to help explain what happened, but I'll just try to make it plain and simple." When Mr. Vanderdale saw that everyone was open to hearing him out, he continued. "Seeing Miss Nettie's son triggered a traumatic reaction in Paige. She reverted to a helpless state. In my trying to show her compassion and understanding, the . . . let's just say, the little girl in her . . . didn't see me as Mr. Vanderdale, the therapist or her former father-in-law."

"And clearly she didn't see you as another woman's husband, either," Mrs. Vanderdale added.

"Honey, please." Mr. Vanderdale held his hand up to his wife. "Let me finish."

Mrs. Vanderdale crossed her arms and looked away.

"Anyway, she wasn't in her right mind," Mr. Vanderdale concluded. "It's the truth, and it's not unusual at all. Our Paige, in her right mind, would have never behaved that way."

All eyes went to Paige.

She nodded in agreement. "I am so sorry." She looked from Ryan to Mrs. Vanderdale. "I truly have no idea what I was thinking." She put her hand on her forehead. "Seeing Blake again just—"

"Blake?" Mrs. Vanderdale interrupted. "As in your ex-husband, Blake?"

"Yes," Mr. Vanderdale answered on Paige's behalf.

"Dear God!" Mrs. Vanderdale turned pale.

Ryan stood there, speechless.

Mrs. Vanderdale began, "That man was . . ."

"Our granddaughters' father," Mr. Vanderdale said.

Mrs. Vanderdale, feeling way more sympathetic, said, "Paige, sweetheart. I'm so sorry. We didn't know." Mrs. Vanderdale hugged Paige.

"I know. I know," Paige said, hugging Mrs. Vanderdale back. Paige pulled from the hug and turned her back to everyone. "And to just think, I'm the one who helped her find his sorry a—" Paige cut off her own words. She wasn't about to disrespect the Vanderdales' home by resorting to expletives.

Just then Paige noticed that Ryan was being pretty quiet. She looked over at him. He was staring down at the floor. "Ryan, you okay?" Paige asked him.

He lifted his head to look at her. Words escaped him. He had never imagined in a million years that he'd find himself caught up in this type of soap opera drama. Was this what he was signing up for when he asked Paige to be his wife? Was this what came with it?

"I don't know what I am right now," Ryan managed to answer. "This entire scenario feels surreal." He rubbed his head. "Talk about six degrees of separation. I can't believe the connection here."

"I know, right?" Paige agreed. She slowly walked over to Ryan and put her hand on his shoulder. He eventually looked into her eyes. "I don't know what's about to happen now. This changes the game, I'm sure."

Ryan took Paige's hands in his. "I'm not playing a game," he told Paige. "This is real life. I said I wanted to spend the rest of my life with you, and that's what I meant." He paused. "No matter what all comes along with it, I guess. I know I'm not about to leave you to fend for yourself. We haven't exchanged vows yet, but we are one. This might not be a game, but it might turn into a fight, the fight of your life. A fight for Adele's life. And I'm going to be right here by your side, with ammunition on my back." He kissed Paige on the lips. "And for the record, those lips better not touch another man's ever again. That's your one pass."

"Pass?" Paige said. "Does that mean I have to give you a pass? Do I have to worry about you eventually paying me back?"

Ryan thought for a moment, twisting his lips. He then walked away from Paige and over toward Mrs. Vanderdale. He stopped in front of Mrs. Vanderdale and looked at Paige with a mischievous expression on his face. He then surprised everyone by walking over to Mr.

Vanderdale and kissing him . . . on the cheek. "There," Ryan said. "We've both kissed Mr. Vanderdale. Now we're even."

Chuckles filled the room.

The way Ryan had just turned this whole kissing situation around was such a relief. Paige couldn't have asked for a better fiancé.

"Well, that takes care of the whole kissing game," Ryan said. He then looked at Paige. "Now what are we going to do about Blake?"

Chapter 22

About an hour after Miss Nettie brought her long-lost son into the Vanderdales' dining room to introduce him to the people she called her family, she returned to the house, entering through the front door. Stuart followed behind her.

Paige, Ryan, and the girls had already left the house, and so had Samantha and Katie. Mr. and Mrs. Vanderdale were seated in the parlor, watching television.

Mrs. Vanderdale stood when the couple walked in. "Nettie," she said, looking past Miss Nettie and Stuart.

"My son is not with us, if that's what you're looking for," Miss Nettie said.

"Speaking of your son," Mr. Vanderdale began. "Paige seems to believe that he is—"

"Blake," Miss Nettie said, finishing his sentence. "My son's name is Blake. He is exactly who Paige thinks he is."

There was a brief moment of silence. No one really knew what to say.

"How are you, Nettie?" Mr. Vanderdale asked. He decided it was best to show concern for Miss Nettie, versus jumping right in and banning her son from their home.

She shrugged her shoulders. "A little shook up, I guess, about everything that happened today."

"I imagine," Mr. Vanderdale replied. He then looked behind Miss Nettie. "How about you, Stuart?"

Stuart stepped forth. "This is my fiancée. I feel what she feels." He put his arm around Miss Nettie. "And I'm going to be there to see her through it, no matter what."

Stuart and Miss Nettie stood there, looking like an older version of Ryan and Paige. Those men were going to stand by their women and surmount everything that came along in the bags they were carrying.

"That's good, Stuart," Mr. Vanderdale said. "Because I'm sure Nettie is going to need all the support she can get."

Miss Nettie raised an eyebrow. "And hopefully that includes the support of both of you as well."

Mr. and Mrs. Vanderdale exchanged looks.

"Nettie, you know beyond a shadow of a doubt that this family loves you," Mrs. Vanderdale said, stepping up to her. "And though we understand that your son is a part of you, I'm sure you understand why he can never step foot in our house again."

Miss Nettie remained silent for a moment while she processed what her employer was saying to her. She then looked at Mr. Vanderdale. "My son has a past. I have a past. I've paid for my crimes. He's paid for his crimes. I've been rehabilitated. He's been rehabilitated. And you do believe in rehabilitation, don't you, Mr. Vanderdale?"

Mrs. Vanderdale jumped to her husband's defense. "Nettie, that's not fair, and you know it."

"And you?" Miss Nettie turned to Mrs. Vanderdale. "You believe in forgiveness, right?"

"I know where you are going with this, Nettie, and it's not fair," Mr. Vanderdale said. "You know that we have special and unusual circumstances here." Mr. Vanderdale took a step toward Miss Nettie. "Nettie, I'm going to ask you something, and I hope you aren't offended by it." When Nettie didn't object, he continued. "When you brought your son into this house, did you have any idea who he was?"

Miss Nettie put her head down.

"Nettie, how could you?" Mrs. Vanderdale's voice was laced with disappointment.

"Hold on now." Stuart raised his hand for Mrs. Vanderdale to back off. "Blake told us a little bit of his story, but not all of it."

"But I did know it wasn't a coincidence . . . his story matching closely to Paige's story," Miss Nettie confessed. "I honestly thought this was the best way to go about things. I felt that if we all just got together in the same room, we could work it out. Had I mentioned it to you all beforehand, you would have never allowed him to step foot in this house." She looked at the Vanderdales accusingly. "Just like you're doing now."

"He tried to take our grandchild from Paige," Mrs. Vanderdale said.

"That was years ago," Miss Nettie proclaimed.

"Yes, but who is to say he won't try to take her again, and right from underneath our noses?" Mrs. Vanderdale reasoned.

"And just where is he going to take her? Back under the bridge where he's now living?" Miss Nettie asked. "My son lost everything, including his will to live. Everything he had, every dime he had, he gave it to Paige and Adele, not to mention all the legal fees he had. He has no interest in Paige or anything she has. My boy doesn't even have an interest in living. His days were numbered before I found him. If I hadn't stepped in, Lord only knows if he'd even be alive today. He needs me. The same way I needed you all after I thought my world was coming to an end, he needs me. Mentally, he's drained, and I know how that feels."

Miss Nettie looked at Mr. Vanderdale. "But you helped me, Mr. Vanderdale. You were a godsend. I was days away from taking a sheet and hanging myself in my prison cell. I felt I was a lost cause and life just wasn't worth living anymore. But you saved me. And I was hoping . . . It was my prayer that maybe . . . just maybe . . . you would save my boy too."

The discomfort of being put on the spot like that showed in Mr. Vanderdale's expression. "Miss Nettie, I honestly don't know if that's possible."

Miss Nettie was taken aback. "I guess I don't understand your response. Helping folks in that manner is your calling in life."

"Nettie, you know I retired from that field a long time ago," Mr. Vanderdale reminded her.

"You retired from it as far as getting a paycheck for it. But I know you still got the gift, Mr. Vanderdale," Miss Nettie reasoned as she walked over to Mr. Vanderdale. "You saved me when I thought there was no saving me. You know what I went through, Mr. Vanderdale." Tears of pain filled Miss Nettie's eyes. "You know what they put me through before you came into the prison to help me. . . . I mean the so-called treatment. The ECT."

Mr. Vanderdale stared into Miss Nettie's knowing eyes. He could only imagine the pain she'd been subjected to prior to him working with her. The doctor who had been treating Miss Nettie before him had diagnosed her as a psychotic depressive. He'd ordered her to have ECT, which was electric shock therapy. This was a treatment Mr. Vanderdale was strongly against. It included a huge amount of electric current passing through the brain. The treatment had been known to fry a patient's memory, stealing hunks of their life from their memory bank . . . forever. This could very well have played a part in Miss Nettie's inability to recall details about the birth of her son. At the mere thought of this, Mr. Vanderdale felt a huge amount of empathy for Miss Nettie.

Mr. Vanderdale put his hands up. "Okay, Nettie, okay."

Miss Nettie immediately got excited and bounced up and down.

"Whoa. Hold up. Okay, I'll think about it. I can't promise you I'm going to do it, but I will at least think about it," Mr. Vanderdale promised.

"And I'll pray," Mrs. Vanderdale added. "But, Nettie, regardless of Norm's decision, I must reiterate that your son is not welcome in our home."

"You say that now, Mrs. Vanderdale," Miss Nettie said. "But I'm believing God that when all is said and prayed, He'll soften your and your husband's hearts regarding the matter. With the help of God and His vessel"—she looked at Mr. Vanderdale—"my boy is going to be a changed man. The same way I'm a changed woman." She looked at Stuart. "The same way Stuart here is a changed man." Miss Nettie had tear-filled eyes. "Isn't it just amazing? You will be responsible for the healing of my entire family." She looked up to the heavens. "Thank you, dear God. I praise you in advance. Thank you."

Stuart hugged Miss Nettie, who was about to start shouting praise. He kissed her on the forehead and led her out of the room.

Mr. and Mrs. Vanderdale were left there, alone in their thoughts about the entire matter.

"Well, honey, what are we going to do?" Mrs. Vanderdale asked her husband.

"Just like you said to do." Mr. Vanderdale looked at his wife. "Pray."

Paige looked down at her ringing cell phone. Once again, she allowed the call to go straight to voice mail and didn't answer it. That's pretty much what she'd done for the past two days whenever Ryan called. Whenever anyone called, for that matter. The only person she wanted to talk to about the whole Blake situation was God. And that was just what she'd been doing.

Ever since Ryan had driven Paige home after leaving the Vanderdales', she'd been on her knees. The ride home had been silent. The girls were in the car and not too much could be said in front of them. After dropping them off at home, Ryan told Paige he would call her. And he had. She just hadn't picked up the phone to talk to him.

Paige didn't want anyone in her ear right now. She didn't even want to hear her own voice. She'd been through so much in her life. She'd made decisions without thinking—without praying. She'd allowed others to make decisions for her. When she felt God wasn't doing what He should be doing or what she wanted Him to do, she would even kick Him to the left, like a boyfriend who wasn't spoiling her rotten and giving her everything she wanted. But all the while, God had been giving her everything she needed.

She'd come a long way for sure in her relationship with God. She didn't have time for wishy-washiness. She'd learned her lesson about that. Not following God's lead only made the journey longer. Now she was bound and determined to do whatever the Lord sayeth, even if it meant drowning out everyone else's voice.

Paige looked at the clock. The girls still had two and a half hours of school left. She decided she would go up to the school and volunteer to make copies for the teachers. Time alone in the copy room was another opportunity to hear from God.

In the year and a half that Blake had been out of jail, Paige had not run into him once. She had not heard from him or his attorney. She'd felt safe in the comfort of God's bosom, knowing He'd protect her from any evil Blake wanted to spew her way. So even though she didn't understand why God had allowed Blake to resurface in her life—and not just in her life, but in the lives of darn near everybody she was connected to—she was not angry. She didn't even question God. For the first time in a long time, she simply trusted Him.

Paige gathered her purse and keys, then slipped on her booties that were in the laundry room. She was just about to set the alarm and walk out the laundry room door that was connected to the garage when she heard her doorbell ring. She paused in her tracks, wondering who it could be.

"It could be anybody," she told herself. After all, she'd been dodging everybody. Any one of them could have come to see about her. At first thought, Paige was just going to let them knock until they went away. But what if they stayed out there and saw her pulling out of her garage? She didn't want to seem like a prisoner in her own home. So with that thought, she decided to go answer the door.

When she looked out the peephole and saw that it was Miss Nettie, her heart rate sped up. She no longer saw her as just Miss Nettie, her friend and confidante. She was now the mother of her psycho ex-husband. She looked out the peephole again at the older woman standing on her porch. Paige loved Miss Nettie. Loved her to life and death. She could not—she would not—make her pay the price for her son's sins. After all, the fact that was the mother of her psycho ex-husband meant that she was Adele's grandmother.

Paige unlocked the front door and opened it. She pushed the screen open enough for Miss Nettie to enter her home. Miss Nettie looked up at Paige with what looked like regret in her eyes. She then entered the house. Paige closed the door and locked up. When she turned around, Miss Nettie was just standing there, looking at her. Both women seemed to fill up with emotions. Before either one of them knew it, they had charged toward one another to embrace in a heartfelt hug. The tears were unstoppable as each woman cried.

Miss Nettie spoke first. "I'm so sorry."

"Miss Nettie, you don't have to apologize," Paige said.

"I do. I owe you several apologies."

The women hugged for a few more seconds, then finally separated. Paige went and got them both some tissue to wipe their faces.

"Thank you," Miss Nettie said, taking the tissue from Paige and then blowing her nose with it.

"You're welcome." Paige wiped her tears away. She then looked at Miss Nettie. "You said you owed me several apologies. I don't understand."

Miss Nettie took a deep breath and then gave her one of those "Here it goes" looks. "First off, let me just say that I honestly had no idea who my boy was. I didn't even know if my child was a boy or a girl. I would have never asked you to help me search for him, had I known."

"I know that, Miss Nettie," Paige said.

"Wait. Please let me finish." Miss Nettie found the courage to continue speaking. "I did know who he was, though, by the time I brought him to the Vanderdale house to meet everyone."

"Miss Nettie," Paige said with such disappointment.

"I didn't do it that way to hurt anyone. I just felt it was better that way. I knew if I had told you all in advance, he would have never been allowed to step foot in the house. No one would have ever given him a chance." She put her head down. "Not that anyone gave him a chance this way, either."

Paige just stood there. She really had no idea what to say about Miss Nettie's confession.

"I wasn't betraying you or trying to trick you," Miss Nettie offered. "I love you like a daughter. Like you was my own child." Miss Nettie's eyes filled with tears. "You truly are the daughter I never had. And to think that once upon a time you really were my daughter, my daughter-in-law . . . but because of me, my son treated you like a dog on the street." Miss Nettie keeled over in tears.

"Miss Nettie, I won't let you blame yourself for what your son did to me," Paige said, putting her hand on Miss Nettie's back. "You weren't the one who raised him to treat women like that."

"Exactly. I wasn't there for him in the beginning . . . from the start of his precious life. That's when I really needed to be there, and I wasn't. I might not have been the one who raised him to treat women like that, but I wasn't there to raise him on how, in fact, he is supposed to treat women. When a mother fails her son, she fails all the other women in his life too. And I'm sorry. I'm so sorry, Paige. Will you forgive me?"

Miss Nettie was crying hard. "I was such a broken woman when I gave birth to Blake. His father was another woman's husband at the time. He was born into a broken situation. He was raised broken by a woman who I'm sure was broken as a result of the role I played in breaking up her marriage. My boy was then abandoned by yet another woman, who at the time he thought was his birth mother. Even though he was a man when he married you, that broken boy was still inside of him. Still controlling his life. He was angry inside. He might have been good at hiding it, but only for so long."

Paige could almost feel the pain that Miss Nettie was in as she cried out, apologizing. Just watching the woman caused tears to fall from Paige's eyes. Paige still didn't feel as though Miss Nettie owed her an apology for what Blake had done to her.

"I've apologized to Blake. He's forgiven me. Now I have to apologize to you," Miss Nettie said to Paige. She took Paige's face in her hands. "Baby, I'm sorry for what my son did to you. I'm sorry I was the first female in his life to show him that he couldn't trust women. I left him in the hands of another woman, who ended up leaving him. And I can only imagine what he felt like when he found out that the two mothers he had had both abandoned him. We taught him that a woman would hurt him, leave him. I'm sorry that I didn't nurture him with the love a mother ought to nurture her child with. I'm sorry I didn't teach him how to love a woman, how a woman loves, and how to receive that love. I'm sorry for my role in breaking him. I'm sorry that he broke you. Dear Jesus, I'm sorry," Miss Nettie cried out.

Paige threw her arms around Miss Nettie. "I forgive you. I forgive you, Miss Nettie." Following the instructions of the Holy Spirit, Paige forgave Miss Nettie, even though at first she didn't feel as though an apology was owed to her. But hearing Miss Nettie speak, and hearing the proverbial chains break and fall with her every word, Paige knew beyond a shadow of a doubt that Miss Nettie's apology wasn't for anyone but herself. It was for her own deliverance. Her own freedom. And if Paige could help set that woman free by simply accepting her apology, so be it.

The women once again found themselves in a tight embrace as they cried, their shoulders heaving up and down.

"I forgive you, and I love you, Miss Nettie," Paige repeated once the two women had finally separated.

Miss Nettie brushed her hands down her coat. "Dear Lord, I must look like a crazy woman."

"Oh, no," Paige said, begging to differ. "You look like a free woman."

Miss Nettie nodded. "Yes, Lord. Thank you, Jesus." She exhaled. She took Paige's hands in hers. "Thank you so much for forgiving me. It means a lot."

"You are welcome, Miss Nettie. God has forgiven me so many times without hesitation. Who am I to deny forgiveness?"

"I'm so glad to hear you say that," Miss Nettie said. "Because there is someone else who needs your forgiveness too."

Paige stopped breathing for a moment when she heard the next word that came out of Miss Nettie's mouth.

"Blake."

Chapter 23

"Mommy, I can't. I can't stand in that man's face and give him the pleasure of hearing me say that I forgive him," Paige said to her mother as she paced the kitchen floor of her mother and father's home. "I don't want to be in his presence. I've forgiven him in my heart as much as I can. I've confessed my forgiveness to God. Why do I have to say it to him? God knows my heart." Paige paused for a moment, then continued her rant. "I'm questioning whether I've ever truly forgiven him in my heart at all. Even if I've forgiven him, the man, perhaps I haven't forgiven the things he's done. Is that possible? Does that make sense?" Paige grabbed her head. "I don't know. It's just all so confusing."

"Shhh. Calm down, baby, before the girls hear you," Mrs. Robinson said.

Adele and Norma were out in the living room, watching television with their grandfather. That was their favorite pastime when spending time at the Robinsons'.

"How much do the girls know about all this, anyway?" Mrs. Robinson asked. "And come over here and sit down with me at the table. You making me dizzy with all that walking back and forth."

Paige stopped pacing and walked over to the kitchen table and sat down. "Adele doesn't know anything. All she knows is that Mommy got upset at Miss Nettie's son, who is a monster."

Mrs. Robinson shook her head. "This is all just a mess. Have you talked to your pastor?"

"I've talked only to God. I'm asking Him to soften my heart." Paige made a fist in anger. "All the trouble Blake has caused in my life has resurfaced and has taken over my mind. Now, all of a sudden, there is a part of me that wants him to pay for all he's done, not be forgiven for it."

"Paige, honey." Her mother raised an eyebrow at her.

"I know that's an awful thing to say." Paige stared off into space for a moment. "Besides, I think he's already paying for it." Paige looked at her mother. "Mom, you should have seen him. He looks bad. Well, not *bad* bad, but he's not the Blake you would remember. I almost didn't recognize him at first. As a matter of fact, I didn't recognize him immediately. I had to look into his eyes. He's bone thin. He's covered in so much facial hair, like he doesn't own a razor. His *GQ* wardrobe is no more."

"Miss Nettie said he's homeless now, right?"

"Yeah, but I just don't understand how."

"Didn't he pay you quite a bit in the alimony settlement? Then there's the money for Adele, not to mention that woman who raised him suing his pants off. He was in jail for what? Four years? He surely wasn't making any money while locked up. Sounds like he lost everything."

Paige thought for a moment. "Or gave it all up."

"What do you mean?"

"I know when I found out I might have HIV, it felt like a death sentence. I had one foot in the grave. For a split second it felt like I didn't have anything to live for. But I did. If nothing else, I had Adele. Well, Blake didn't even have that as a motivation. I took that hope from him. And maybe that's why he just wants to give up. Why he gave up." Paige began to feel an ounce of sympathy. Once she realized that was the emotion taking over her, she quickly snapped out of it. "No, no, no. I will not feel sorry for that man." Paige tried to shake it off.

Mrs. Robinson took her daughter's hands in her own. "Baby, so much compassion has been shown to you by so many others. If you couldn't find it in your heart to have compassion for someone else, wouldn't that make you the monster?"

Paige looked down. What could she possibly say to that? "I know this is something I might have to do. Just seems like every time I look up, I'm continuously having to forgive him, though. I haven't had anger for him in my heart. I can honestly say that. I haven't felt anything about him. I've completely blocked him out. When you aren't forced to deal with something, you don't think about it one way or the other. I figured I could either be that person who clung to all the wrong someone has done to them in order to justify hating them, or I could let it go and live life. Well, I chose the latter, and I've been living life. I never stopped to think about Blake being Adele's father and how I would handle it."

"That's probably because you felt that if you didn't think about it, it would just stay under the rug and never come to pass."

"Out of mind, out of sight in my case, huh?" Paige chuckled. Her chuckle then died down and became a sigh.

"It's going to be all right, baby girl." Mrs. Robinson patted Paige's hand. "What's Ryan saying about all this? After all, he is your *fiancé*."

"Why did you say it like that?" Paige asked, not missing the emphasis her mother had put on the word *fiancé*.

"Maybe because this man has been in and out of your life for some years now, yet whenever the rough gets going, so do you," Mrs. Robinson pointed out.

"Mom, right now, in all honesty, I'm a little bit consumed by my ex-husband, rather than by trying to get a new one."

Mrs. Robinson became silent for a moment. "Well, does Ryan know that?"

Paige shook her head. "Like I said, I haven't had a chance to talk to him. I've just been trying to hear from God and not focus on what other people think. But when Miss Nettie showed up on my doorstep, wanting me to meet with and forgive Blake, I had to come talk to you."

"So, you haven't talked to Ryan since the day at the Vanderdales' last week?"

Paige shook her head.

"You know what? You just playing with that boy. Yeah, you just keep taking him on over to the Vanderdales and playing house over there. You bring him to our doorstep after you say, 'I do.' Then I'll know you're serious about this boy." Mrs. Robinson stood up from the table and walked over to the coffeepot, still mumbling. "All this on-again, off-again business." She turned around and shot Paige a look. "Real love don't have no on-and-off switch. So that ought to tell you something right there." She grabbed a cup from the cabinet and began pouring herself a cup of coffee.

"I do love Ryan," Paige said. "It's just that there is always some storm cloud in my life that decides to bust open every time Ryan and I are in a good place. I know marriage is hard work and has enough ups and downs of its own. Why add to that burden by going into a marriage messy?"

"Have you ever thought for one single moment that God has been trying to put Ryan in your life just so that when that cloud does burst open, there is someone there for you to dance in the rain with?"

Paige took in her mother's words, and her heart seemed to open up wide, like a rain cloud actually, pouring out good energy. That revelation lit the room up. Paige stood. "Mommy, I think you're right."

"Child," Mrs. Robinson began and then took a sip of her hot coffee. "I know I'm right. I'm always right, or have you forgotten?"

Paige ran over and hugged her mother, making her spill some of the coffee in her cup. "Yes, you are always right, which is why God sent me over here today." Paige kissed her mother on the cheek. "Thanks, Mommy. I gotta go."

"What's your hurry?"

"Life," Paige shouted over her shoulder as she exited the kitchen.

"Thank you for meeting with me," Paige said to Ryan as the two of them sat in a coffee shop. The heavy scent of the blended beans was like an aphrodisiac to those who needed a caffeine fix. The smell seemed to entice even the non–coffee drinkers and lure them into purchasing one of the caffeinated beverages, hot or cold, on the menu.

Ryan nodded. Paige could tell by his body language that he wasn't too happy with the fact that she'd given him the cold shoulder the past few days. After the first couple days of calling and texting Paige, with no acknowledgment, he'd let it go. He'd been down that road before with her.

"I know you're upset with me, Ryan, as you should be—" Paige began, but Ryan decided not to let her finish.

"Listen, let's not even play this game. You did what you always do when you and I are in a good place. You run."

"I don't mean for—"

"No, no, you listen to me. You leave me hanging and then call me up when you're good and ready to pick up where we left off, and I'm tired of it. I've told you I want to be in your life. I want you to be in mine. I asked you to marry me. You met my kids, I've met yours, and they've met each other. This isn't a game to me. This is real life, so when real life happens, I'm supposed to be there for you. And vice versa."

"I know, Ryan. I get that now. Honestly, I do. I'm sorry. I'm sorry for being so selfishly independent and trying to do everything on my own. All the while God has truly placed a helpmate before me," Paige said. "The whole situation with my marriage to Norman, Blake being Adele's biological father, Norman signing the birth certificate, and all that other stuff was just so messy. I didn't want you to have to stand by and bear witness to come what may."

"Don't you get it? I want to be in it knee-deep with you. That's what a man is supposed to do for his woman. So let me be your man for real this time. Please, because the next time life happens, I need to know that you are not going to turn your back on me and leave me hanging. I love you, but I can't. I won't, especially now that our kids are involved. So I need you to really think about this, think about us, and let me know what you really want to do."

Ryan had put Paige in her place, and she liked it. He'd taken from her the option of running away. Either she was in this thing or she wasn't.

"I'm in," Paige said, smiling. "I'm in this thing until death do us part. No more running . . . unless I'm holding on to your hand and you're running right beside me."

Ryan stared at Paige for a moment, reading her eyes. He had to be sure that she meant what she was saying.

"No more running from the rain. We stand there and get wet together," Paige added.

That put a smile on Ryan's face. He leaned in and kissed Paige on the lips. "Then it's settled. Looks like we've got a wedding to plan."

"Indeed we do," Paige said. "But before we start planning our new life together, and before we combine our families, there's something I have to do that might change the dynamics of it all."

"And what's that?" Ryan said, almost afraid to ask.

"I have to tell Adele who her father is."

Chapter 24

"He doesn't look like a monster, Mommy."

Paige had just helped Adele out of the tub and was drying her off.

"Huh?" Paige said.

"Miss Nettie's son. You said he was a monster, but he doesn't look like one. Monsters are supposed to have fangs and horns." Adele began to twist up her face and use her hands to make a scratching gesture. "And claws like this."

Paige just sat there, watching Adele, and then it hit her. She'd done something she hadn't done in all six years of Adele's life. She'd talked badly about her father in front of her. No, Adele didn't know that Miss Nettie's son was her father, but he was, and there was no denying that fact. Ironically, tonight was the night Paige had planned to tell Adele all about Blake. Reminded that Adele was under the impression that he was a monster, Paige decided that perhaps this wasn't such a good time to break the news, after all. But then again, maybe it was God opening up the door for Paige to broach the subject.

"No, he doesn't look like a monster, does he?" Paige asked as she continued to dry off Adele.

"Nope." Adele shook her head. "So why did you call him one?"

Paige thought of what to say. "I guess I made a mistake. Sometimes grown-ups make mistakes. Besides, it wasn't nice of me to call that man a name."

"Name-calling and bullying are not nice," Adele scolded.

"I know, and Mommy is sorry."

"Did you tell the man that? And Miss Nettie? Because she looked sad that you called her son a bad name."

As if Paige hadn't been convicted enough. *Leave it to the mouths of babes to add salt to the wound,* she thought.

"I haven't apologized yet."

"But you are going to, right? You said when a person does something bad and hurts another person, they should apologize. Like that time Norma took my doll, and I hit her. You made me apologize."

Her daughter was right. An apology was owed when a person hurt someone. So why was it that Paige was the one doing the apologizing? Hadn't

Blake hurt her far more than she'd hurt him? Had he hurt her more when he put his hands on her and physically abused her? When he belittled her in an effort to abuse her mentally? When he slept with her best friend? When he raped her? When he risked giving her HIV? When he tried to take her daughter? Why wasn't God convicting him to the point where he should apologize?

Paige's insides began to boil as she lotioned Adele up. All Paige could remember thinking was that Miss Nettie had some nerve asking her to meet with Blake and express her forgiveness. The more Paige thought about it, the more she wanted to receive an apology prior to her giving one. When he was sending her letters from his attorney, one of those letters should have been an apology from him.

Miss Nettie knew only secondhand what that man had done to Paige. She hadn't had to live through it. What Blake had done to Paige was pure evil in her book. But he hadn't looked evil that day in the dining room. Helpless, maybe, but not evil. Clearly, Blake was a changed man, at least physically. Perhaps he'd changed mentally as well. Did all that even matter? Even if he hadn't changed mentally, Paige setting him free by forgiving him, even without receiving an apology of her own, could be that very thing to change him.

All of a sudden Paige felt uplifted and encouraged. Just the thought that God might be choosing her to help save a soul, that God was considering her for something great and awesome, was enough to raise her spirits. Blake's eternal life could depend on her obedience. *What an honor,* she thought.

Many a time Paige had sat in church, telling God that she would go where He wanted her to go. That she would do what He wanted her to do. God was not one to lie, so why should she? Wouldn't it be great if people were as faithful as God? Paige couldn't speak or act for people in general, but she could be accountable for herself.

"Mommy is going to apologize to the man," Paige told Adele as she slipped the little girl's nightgown over her head.

"Good. Because he had a sad face when you got mad. I want him to be happy." She raised her hands and made a huge circle with them. "I want the whole world to be happy. If everybody is happy, nobody will be mad and do bad stuff, and we can all live happily ever after."

Paige smiled. "You are so right, baby."

"Yes, just like Grandma Robinson always says."

"Which is?" Paige asked.

"I'm always right," Adele replied, mocking her maternal grandmother.

Paige smiled and kissed Adele on the forehead. "Yes, indeed she is." Which was exactly why first thing in the morning, right after Paige got the girls off to school, she was going to pay Miss Nettie a visit. She needed her to arrange a meeting between her and her son . . . before the devil talked Paige out of doing what she needed to do.

The next morning, as planned, Paige got the girls on the bus and then headed over to the Vanderdales' home. As she drove down their private drive, she didn't bite her nails, not a once. She wasn't nervous at all about the prospect of coming face-to-face with Blake. She was more excited than anything. It wasn't just about her freeing Blake with forgiveness. It was about freeing herself as well. This entire Blake issue would be out in the open. There would be closure. She would not have to take the unknown into her marriage with Ryan, nor would she have to look over her shoulder, fearing the day Blake might decide to pop up in Adele's life and tell her the truth. God was making it so that everything was on Paige's terms. Wasn't God good?

Paige parked her car and then went and rang the doorbell of the Vanderdales' home. After a few seconds the door opened a crack.

"Paige, dear, what are you doing here?" It was Mrs. Vanderdale who answered the door instead of Miss Nettie or another member of the staff.

"Hi. I stopped by so that I could speak with Miss Nettie."

"Oh, well, uh, Nettie is busy right now," Mrs. Vanderdale said.

Paige thought it peculiar that the door was still open only a crack and Mrs. Vanderdale was not inviting her in. "Well, is she home at least? I can wait for her to get unbusy."

Mrs. Vanderdale paused, thought for a moment, and then opened the door. "Well, yes, I suppose that would be okay." She slowly stepped to the side to allow Paige in the door.

"Is everything okay, Naomi?" Paige asked, entering the home. She took off her jacket and hung it on the coatrack. "You're acting a little . . . weird."

"Yes, everything is just fine," Mrs. Vanderdale was quick to say. She then hurriedly grabbed Paige's arm. "Did I tell you I redecorated the guest room? Come upstairs. Let me show you." She dragged Paige toward the staircase.

Just then Paige noticed Miss Nettie coming around the corner from the direction of the den. Paige paused. That was when she saw that Miss Nettie wasn't alone. There was a figure behind her—two, to be exact. She recognized Mr. Vanderdale as the person taking up the rear. Between him and Miss Nettie was Blake. Paige's heart dropped, and she had to catch her breath. Although she was there to ask Miss Nettie to set up a meeting with Blake for her, she wasn't prepared for that meeting to take place today.

"Paige, dear, I'm . . ." Mrs. Vanderdale began, but then she was at a loss for words. How could she explain having Paige's sworn enemy in their home?

"Blake." That was all that Paige could say.

Mr. Vanderdale came up from the rear and stood in front of both Miss Nettie and her son. "Paige, we can explain."

"Not that you really owe me an explanation," Paige stated. "This is your home. You can have in your home whomever you choose." Even though Paige said those words, a part of her still felt a little betrayed. The Vanderdales had no idea Paige was there in the name of forgiveness. Seemed like they would have at least asked her how she felt about them allowing Blake into their home, knowing Paige could show up and run into him at any given time. Right now was a prime example of that.

Paige considered the fact, though, that Miss Nettie had been their housekeeper since forever and a day. She was family, which meant they had a sense of obligation to her as well. They were truly between a rock and a not so soft place. Paige wasn't about to make them feel any worse than their faces reflected they already felt.

"As a matter of fact," Paige said, "I'm glad he's here."

"What?" The Vanderdales and Miss Nettie all spoke that word in unison.

"I actually came to see Miss Nettie today," Paige continued. "About arranging a meeting between Blake and me." Paige gave a chuckle. "But I see you're all a step ahead of me."

"About that . . . ," Mr. Vanderdale said, jumping in again. "Nettie asked me if I would counsel Blake. At first I didn't want to, but then I decided to think about it."

"And I prayed about it," Mrs. Vanderdale said. "I had to listen to my spirit, and of course, God, and advise my husband. God said—"

"I know what God said," Paige declared, cutting her off. "If there's one thing Pastor Margie has taught me, it's that God is not going to tell people something different regarding the same situation. So clearly, God has spoken to all our hearts and told us the same thing regarding . . . Blake." How many more times would she have to say his name? Something about saying his name was starting to get to her. It made it seem as though they were friends. It was kind of like how people called the serial killer Theodore Bundy simply Ted, as if they were on a friendly basis with him.

Paige didn't want anyone to get the wrong idea. She planned on forgiving Blake, but that didn't mean she had to be friends with him, be in his presence, or entertain him. She'd proven that when she forgave Tamarra. Of course, God hadn't challenged Paige to be in Tamarra's presence, like He was now doing with Blake.

Miss Nettie stepped up and said, "You're being here . . . does it mean you thought about what I asked you the other day?"

Paige took in a breath and exhaled. "Yes I have thought about it. And my answer, apparently, is yes."

"Oh, dear Jesus," Miss Nettie said. Her eyes immediately filled with tears. "Prayer still works. Yes, it does."

Mr. Vanderdale waited for Miss Nettie to come down off her spiritual high before he spoke. "Perhaps we should all go back to my office."

He pointed back toward the den area. His home office was located right off the den. He looked at Blake, who had been standing there the entire time with everyone talking about him like he wasn't there. "Is that okay with you, Blake? You want to go back to my office to talk with Paige?"

Blake looked at Paige while he responded to Mr. Vanderdale. He looked into her eyes for a few seconds, until Paige cast hers downward. He finally spoke. "I shamed and humiliated her in the open. I need to apologize in the open."

When Blake took a step toward Paige, she immediately stepped back. He put his hands up to let her know that it was okay, that he wasn't going to move any closer to her, because he could see she was uncomfortable. He hated knowing that he had instilled such fear in her.

"Paige," Blake began, "I want to apologize, but 'I'm sorry' won't suffice. If I'm going to seek your forgiveness, then you need to know exactly what you are forgiving me for. As a man, I need to acknowledge each of my wrongdoings and not try to lump them together."

He looked at Mr. Vanderdale for approval about his wording. Just moments ago, when he'd been speaking with Mr. Vanderdale about seeking forgiveness from Paige, Mr. Vanderdale had informed him of the importance of acknowledging each of the harmful actions he'd committed against the person he had wronged. It was as important for Blake to admit these things to himself as it was for him to confess them to his victim.

"Our entire relationship was built on a lie," Blake continued. "I wanted to create this fairy tale for you. I wanted you to believe our chance meeting was some divine setup. I knew that you were a churchgoing woman and that this would encourage you to start seeing me." He bowed his head. "And then there was the part Tamarra had in it."

It was obvious Blake was uncomfortable bringing her name up by the way he began to shift from one foot to the other. It had been Tamarra's bright idea to set Blake up with Paige in the first place, under fictitious circumstances. Tamarra had viewed Blake as an egotistical, self-centered alpha male after the way he'd treated her following their one-night stand. She knew that someone like Paige, who was outspoken, would chew up someone like Blake and spit him out. Paige was Tamarra's secret weapon to get back at Blake and put him in his place. Tamarra's little scheme went awry when Paige actually fell for the smooth talker and their whirlwind romance led to marriage. Blake knew this was a sore subject for Paige, but it was one he had to address. In this forgiveness thing, he could leave no stone unturned.

Mr. Vanderdale cleared his throat. Blake looked up at him, and Mr. Vanderdale encouraged his pro bono patient to continue.

"I kept secrets from you," Blake said. "I betrayed you with your best friend. I neglected you as my wife in my desire to be a successful businessman and earn boatloads of money. I needed to hide behind work and success, otherwise you would know I was a broken soul." He shook his head. "I'd been in this dark place for most of my life. But I can honestly say that when I met you, the light you shine, it brought me out of the darkness. So I used you. I used you for your smile. I used you for your happiness and peace. I tried to steal your light, instead of finding my own way to shine. Your light was yours. It wasn't enough for both of us. So I sucked all the light out of you, and I'm sorry." Blake's bottom lip began to tremble.

"That's where you're wrong," Paige said. "You didn't suck all the light out of me. I had plenty. As long as I had Jesus, I had plenty of light. But I chose to stay in the dark. I chose to hold on to all the bad things you'd done to me as an excuse to just walk through life mad at the world. Blaming everybody else, including God Himself."

"And I'm sorry for all those things I did to assist in putting you in that mind-set. The abuse . . ." He swallowed hard, then gathered the courage to go on. "The rape . . . accusing you of being unfaithful, when I knew that was not who you were. That was just me taking out the anger I had toward my mother on you." He looked at Miss Nettie. "Or at least the woman who I thought was my mother at the time." He turned his attention back to his ex-wife. "I thought you were going to pack up and leave, like she'd done."

"I was team Blake," Paige said. "I honestly was. I truly loved you. Even after the abuse started, I couldn't just turn off my feelings for you. I wanted to fix whatever was wrong. I wanted to fix you."

"And that was never going to happen," Blake said. "I needed to want to be fixed. But once I found myself back in that dark place, I rested in it. It was my comfort zone, so I made a choice to stay there. My excuse was that it was justified. All my actions were justified, so I could see no wrong in them. Even while I was rotting away in jail, I was still angry. Then, when I found out I was HIV positive, I got even angrier."

"Did you think I'd given it to you?" Paige asked.

Blake shook his head. "No, no. Like I said, I knew you would never have been unfaithful to me. Again, me accusing you of having an affair was just me trying to hurt you because I was hurting. And you know the saying. Hurt people hurt people. I was the epitome of that. Unfortunately for you, you were the only one around for me to take it all out on, so I hurt you. And I kept hurting you when I tried to take Adele from you. I knew I was wrong, which was why I didn't even show up at the meeting between our attorneys. I couldn't show my pitiful face, and I couldn't look at your face, for fear I'd cower and drop everything."

Blake chuckled and shook his head. "But you and that attorney of yours put up a heck of a fight. When my attorney came back to me with the results of the meeting, I just threw in the towel. It was over. The battle, the war. My life. After all, I had been diagnosed HIV positive. It was a death sentence to me. What was I going to do? Take that little girl from you so she could watch me die? I had nothing to live for. How I saw it, my life was this miserable existence. I was going to die. What did I need money for, or anything else, for that matter? I'd never have another relationship again, because what woman is going to get with a guy who is HIV positive? So after turning over everything I owned to Adele's trust fund, I crawled up under a bridge to die, literally."

Blake swallowed and then continued. "There's this outreach ministry that comes and feeds and ministers to the homeless. They are always talking about how much Jesus loves us, about forgiveness and all that stuff. Some of the things you used to talk about." Blake cracked a smile at Paige. "Reminded me of you. More importantly, it reminded me of all I'd done to you. So before I die, I need you to forgive me, Paige. Please. Will you forgive me? I need to hear you say the words." Blake's eyes became moist. "I can hardly live with myself, knowing what I've done to you, how I jeopardized your life, and how I never even got the chance to apologize. And I don't want to die without your forgiveness. I need to go in peace."

Paige took in all Blake's words before she spoke. "It's not my forgiveness you need to take to your grave, Blake. It's Jesus's." She stared into Blake's eyes. "I know when we were married, you never got saved or baptized or anything. Did you while you were locked up?"

Blake shook his head. "My soul is dirty. I'm jacked up. I was a felon in jail for beating and raping my wife. God don't want that nasty soul."

"Blake, was I that bad of an example of a Christian that you didn't know that's exactly how God wants you to come to Him?"

"But you were so perfect," Blake said. "You never hurt me, or anyone else, for that matter."

"No, sir," Paige was quick to say. "Only Jesus was perfect, and that was the Jesus in me that you saw. But the fleshly Paige, the one made from dirt, she got cleaned up by the blood of Jesus. And I'm sorry that I never made that plain. But will you allow me to make it up to you now?"

Blake looked somewhat confused.

"Will you allow me to go to the throne with you and seek true forgiveness?"

"I . . . I don't know. . . ." Blake began. He was very apprehensive. In all his years in jail, so many folks had tried to convert him to so many different religions and theologies. He'd become BFFs with the majority of his own demons. He couldn't dare betray them and forsake them. The one sure thing about his demons was that he knew they would always be there for him when he needed them. He couldn't say the same for God, because he'd never taken a chance on giving himself completely to God. He'd heard Christians warn that once you turned your life completely over to God, that was when the real hell began. *So,* he figured, *why bother?* As long as the devil already had him, demons wouldn't bother him.

"Paige, my life is pretty much over," Blake told her. "I live on the streets. I'm a homeless, HIV positive man with practically no health care besides whatever I receive at the free clinic when I decide to go. It's too late for all that religious and spiritual stuff now."

"But it's never too late for Jesus," Paige told him. She took a step toward Blake. "You saw what life with the devil on earth was like. Can you imagine what it will be like once he gets you on his own turf? Here, in this life, you're in control. You have a choice. But, Blake, when you close your eyes for the last time and take that final breath, it's judgment day. I know I don't have a heaven or hell to put you in. I have no idea what kind of covenant your soul can and will make with God, regardless of whether you're saved or not. But do you really want to take that chance? Do you really want to take the chance of death, which is eternal, being a hundred times worse?"

Blake thought for a moment and then shook his head.

"Then however many days you have here on earth, why not just give them to God? The one who will never leave you and will never forsake you? The one who will never cheat you or cheat on you, because He's, oh, so faithful?"

"Yes, Lord." Miss Nettie raised her holy hands.

Paige continued stepping toward Blake. "Why not just say yes and watch what He can do?" Paige raised her hands and spread them wide. "Look what He's already done. Do you think anybody but God could have orchestrated this?" She looked at Miss Nettie. "Brought you to your biological mother, the place where true healing begins. Because that's what you want, right?" Paige asked Blake. "You want to be healed, right?" Paige's voice got louder and more commanding, the closer she got to Blake. "You want that pain to go away, don't you? You want to send those demons that have been tormenting you back to the pit of hell, where they belong, don't you?"

Blake began to nod his head as a tear fell from his eye.

"God can do that for you," Paige told Blake. "The blood of Jesus has already done that for you," she shouted.

"Yes, glory!" an emotional Miss Nettie shouted.

Mrs. Vanderdale was becoming emotional. Noticing this, Mr. Vanderdale went and wrapped his arms around his wife.

"You've heard your mother's testimony, right?" Paige asked, pointing at Miss Nettie but looking at Blake.

Again, Blake nodded. Again, a tear fell.

"So she told you what God did for her. So if He did it for her, why would He not do it for you?"

"He'll do it for you, baby," Miss Nettie cried. "He'll do it. He's a healer," she declared.

"Now I ask you, do you want it?" Paige said to Blake, now back to her normal tone. She was more comforting and consoling now.

"Yes, I want it. Dear God, I want to be healed." Blake broke down in tears.

Paige took his hands in hers and led him into the prayer of salvation. Afterward, the room was full of rejoicing. Miss Nettie threw her hands around her son and was praying for him in tongues, as well as thanking God for healing, redemption, and deliverance.

"And to answer your question, Blake," Paige said as she watched mother and son embrace, "Yes, I will. I forgive you."

Blake broke down even more. Miss Nettie clapped her hands and did a two-step.

The moment felt surreal to Paige. She had truly never imagined the day where she would not only stand face-to-face in the same room with her ex, but would also pray for the man and lead him to salvation. God really did have jokes. Paige herself had to laugh at that one.

After a small chuckle escaped her mouth, and as Miss Nettie and Blake finally parted, Paige addressed Blake. "Welcome to the kingdom," she said. "Now, I just have one more question for you. Would you like to meet your daughter?"

Chapter 25

"Bye, Mr. Blake," Adele said as she wrapped her arms around Blake's neck. "Thanks for the dolly."

"And thanks for my dolly too," Norma added.

"You both are so welcome," Blake said, smiling, as he stood in the doorway of the Vanderdales' home. He'd been in the Vanderdales' home the past couple of hours, getting to know both Adele and Norma. He was now about to leave.

A week had passed since Blake had received Paige's forgiveness. When Paige had asked him if he wanted to meet Adele, he had absolutely agreed to. He had one stipulation, though: that Paige not tell the little girl that he was her father. He had his reasons, which he'd shared with Paige.

One was that he just wanted to get to know the child, with no burden to carry. By that he explained that he could not present himself to that little girl as her father in his current situation of being homeless. That was not the kind of father he had ever imagined being; therefore, it wasn't the kind of father he wanted to be to her. Secondly, he was still finding himself. He was saved but still broken. His brokenness could not be fixed overnight. Maybe not even over the course of a year. He had a lot of work to do. But he now had hope. He had faith. He had a reason to live, if for nothing else, for his daughter.

Mr. Vanderdale was helping Blake do the work on himself with therapy. Blake had attended church with his mother as well, and her pastor had agreed to minister to Blake. Blake was both grateful and confident that when he presented himself to his child as her biological father, it would be as a whole man.

Lastly, he was aware that Norman had signed Adele's birth certificate and that the little girl believed he was her father and the Vanderdales were her grandparents. Ryan did not want to confuse things even more by having to explain that it was Miss Nettie, who, in fact, was her biological grandmother. It all just seemed like too much for a small child to bear. Paige agreed, recalling one point in her life when it had been even too much for her, as a grown woman, to bear. They decided that everything would be done in due time. But for now, they'd just start with a simple introduction, and Paige apologizing for calling Blake a monster.

The Vanderdales' home seemed to be a safe haven for everything to go down. So they'd all met up there. Paige had come over after the girls had gotten out of school.

"Are you sure you can't stay for dinner?" Mrs. Vanderdale asked Blake. "You know your mother's cooking is out of this world."

"I know. But unfortunately, I can't stay," Blake replied. "I have to be at the shelter by six to keep my bed."

"A shelter?" Adele asked. "You live in a shelter? The park Mommy takes me and Norma to sometimes has a shelter. We barbecued under it once. I bet it's real fun camping out there at your shelter." Adele looked at Paige. "Mommy, can we please, pretty please, stay at the shelter too?" she begged, her hands clasped together. "We can roast marshmallows and stuff."

Norma followed suit. "Sleeping bag!" she cheered.

All the adults in the room—namely, Paige, Blake, Mrs. Vanderdale, and Stuart—laughed. Miss Nettie had gone off to the kitchen to prepare dinner.

"It's not that kind of shelter," Paige told her girls. "It's a building. It has four walls. They call it a shelter because it's just that. It's not a permanent place to live, but just a temporary place that provides a covering . . . provides shelter."

Adele frowned and then looked at Blake. "So where are you going to live forever?"

In order to take some of the pressure off of Blake, Stuart chimed in. "He's actually going to live with me." Stuart put his arm around Blake. His car keys were in his hand, as he was the one who was going to drive Blake to the shelter. "I'm moving into a new place next month, and Blake here is going to move in with me. Blake and my new wife." Miss Nettie and Stuart had already applied for their license to marry.

Adele wore a huge smile. "Mommy, you were right!" she said to Paige. "Miss Nettie is going to be Mr. Stuart's wife." She turned back to Stuart. "You're going to be the daddy." She pointed at Stuart. "Miss Nettie is going to be the mommy." She then pointed at Blake as she said, "And you are the little boy who is going to live with them."

All the adults laughed again.

"Well, I'm not quite the little boy anymore," Blake said, "but something like that."

"Mr. Ryan has two little boys. Soon he's going to be the daddy in our house."

Norma nodded to confirm what her older sister had said.

There was a bit of awkward silence in the room.

Paige wasn't sure how Blake was processing all this. Norman had already claimed Daddy duty when he signed Adele's birth certificate. That had been tough enough for Blake to deal with while he'd been incarcerated. Now he had to stand there and listen to how, once again, another man was going to be taking over Daddy duty.

Blake bent down to Adele's level. "This Ryan, is he a nice man?"

"Yes," both Adele and Norma said in unison.

"Then I bet he'll make a great daddy." He pinched both girls' cheeks.

Paige let out a silent sigh of relief. Everything appeared to be going smoothly. She didn't want anything to trigger something negative. Taking this thing step-by-step and one day at a time was a great idea. She truly felt in her spirit that it was the right thing to do. Even more so, she was glad that she and Blake were on the same page. At least for now. But Paige was no dummy. The man might have now been saved, but that didn't mean she wasn't going to use her wisdom and sleep with one eye open.

***

"So how did everything go?" Ryan asked Paige through the phone receiver.

Paige had gotten the girls to bed. She was sitting on her own bed, taking off her shoes and socks. Her plans were to shower and go to bed. But she had wanted to give Ryan a call before it got too late.

"It actually went very well. The girls were nice and pleasant."

"Of course they were. That's how you raised them to be."

"Well, I must admit I was a little nervous. I was just waiting for Adele to mention me calling him a monster."

Ryan chuckled. "Oh, yeah, that."

"I had a talk with her about how I shouldn't have called him a bad name. So clearly, it must have worked."

"Good."

There was silence.

"What?" Paige said.

"Nothing, I was just thinking," Ryan answered.

"About what?"

"About how frickin' amazing you are. That and about how your story is turning out."

Paige smiled and thought about how, despite all she'd been through with Blake, she had been able to forgive him, to be peaceful, and to afford him the right to meet his daughter. She was darn proud of her own self, if she didn't say so herself. "Yeah, I am pretty frickin' amazing, aren't I?" She laughed. "Not more amazing than God, though. After all, He is the author of my life. And it is all turning out well."

Paige thought back to the past few years and shook her head. "The glory truly does outweigh the suffering. I may have had two marriages that ended tragically, but I know for sure that this third time will be the charm. I have no fears. Baby, I'm more confident than ever. And I just thank you for being obedient and for having the patience to allow me to get myself together. Because, like Blake, I was truly broken, and I felt worthless and wanted to give up. I needed to be saved. I couldn't put that on you. You shouldn't have to save a person in order to love them. No, I needed to come to you ready to love and loving myself. So that I can love you that much more."

"Well, woman, I'm ready to be loved by you like never before. So what are we waiting for? Let's do it."

Paige got a little choked up and couldn't speak.

"What's wrong? Your throat dry from all that talking you were doing just a minute ago?"

"No. It's just that I'm not quite sure what you mean."

"I meant what I said. Paige, let's do this. Let's hop on a plane, train, boat, or automobile and just go. Do you have a passport?"

"Well, yeah, but—"

"No buts. As a matter of fact, I got a Groupon e-mail earlier today. It's to the Dominican Republic. An all-inclusive resort that even includes airfare. It was dirt cheap. I think up to six people can go."

"So you want to bring the kids?"

"Heck, no! I was thinking more like bringing your parents and my parents. Maybe your girls can stay with the Vanderdales. My boys can stay with my neighbor. The couple next door and their daughter, who just started college, have helped me out a lot with the boys over the years. I trust them to keep them while I'm off making you my wife," Ryan said. He then envisioned it all. "It would be like a dream come true. That way our parents can get to know each other in paradise. What more could we ask for?"

The excitement in Ryan's voice was contagious. Just listening to him go on and on about how amazing and fairy tale like it would be pumped up Paige to the point where she was in total agreement.

"Our parents are going to flip," Paige said.

"Our parents are going to love the fact that they get a free vacation."

"So we're going to flip the tab for this?" Paige questioned.

"It would be the same cost as throwing a wedding, getting a dress, having a reception, going on a honeymoon. Heck, we'll probably come out cheaper this way. Besides, I'm flipping this tab. I'm going to show my new wife the time of her life. What would I look like, making you put five on it?" He laughed.

Paige had never really talked with Ryan about how financially set she was. She still lived a regular and simple lifestyle. Even though she knew she wouldn't live forever, by God, she wanted to. And just in case God did decide to answer that prayer, because He was a God who could do anything, she would have the finances to do so. The cherry on top of it all was that however many more days she did have on this earth, she planned on spending them with Ryan. She didn't think she'd ever disclose her financial situation to Ryan. He'd never asked, and he planned on being the man and taking care of his woman. But she wouldn't have him sign a prenuptial agreement, either. What was his was hers and what was hers was his. That included both money and the children.

Just the thought of it all made Paige shout out, "Let's do it! What the heck. You get on the phone with your parents, and I'll get on the phone with mine. Let's shoot for boarding that plane not this weekend, but the next. Do you think that's too soon?"

"It's not soon enough, in my opinion. Both our parents are retired. I run my own office. You don't have to report regularly anywhere." Ryan knew better than to flat out say that Paige didn't have a job. Although she didn't clock in on a time clock, he knew her day was full of work.

Paige wiped the tears of excitement and joy from her eyes. "Babe, this is a dream come true."

"After the nightmare you have had to endure in your days, you deserve for all your dreams to come true. And I'm going to be the man to make sure that happens."

"Ryan, I love you. I'm ready to love you. I'm so ready for this." Paige was 100 percent sure.

"Paige?"

"Yeah?"

"Woman, I've *been* ready for you."

Chapter 26

"Oh, I just love that man," Mrs. Robinson said. "He's just perfect for you."

"Yep, just as perfect as this dress is going to be on me when I say, 'I do.'" Paige spun around in the long sand-colored dress with lace trim, which she'd just walked out of the dressing room in.

"It's lovely," Mrs. Robinson said, walking over and fingering the sleeves. "It's going to be hot there, though. I'm going to have to cut off these long sleeves and make some spaghetti straps or something."

"I know. That's what I was thinking." Paige twisted and turned in the mirror a couple more times. She ran her hands down the dress, her fingers indulging in the silky material. She tingled inside, just imagining Ryan running his hands down the dress on their wedding night, not to mention slipping it down her body so that she could step out of it and into his arms.

"I can't believe this. It's a dream come true," Mrs. Robinson declared, snapping Paige out of her daydream. "Ryan really knows how to give his woman a fantasy. And you deserve it. Like I said, he's just perfect." Mrs. Robinson clasped her hands together and stared off, as if she were envisioning rainbows. A smile rested on her lips.

"Mom, you've been around him only a couple times," Paige stated. It was true that Mrs. Robinson had met Ryan when Paige first introduced him and his boys to both her parents. And the second time she saw him was when they all had dinner with Ryan's parents and the girls. "Yet you've said how perfect he is about a hundred times." Paige raised an eyebrow. "Are you living vicariously through me, Ma? Is he perfect because not only is he up and taking me out of the country, but he's letting you and Dad tow along too?"

"Well, that's not the only reason." Mrs. Robinson let out a mischievous giggle.

"Uh-huh. I knew it."

"Well, honey, can you blame me? Your dad and I got married at the courthouse. Exchanging vows on a faraway island somewhere had always been what I imagined when I was a little girl. So what if it's not my wedding? A sista is going to the Dominican Republic, baby!" Mrs. Robinson clapped her hands and stomped her foot.

Paige laughed. "Well, I'll have you know you needn't have guilt or shame. Ryan's mama is acting just as bad as you. I think she's texted me about twenty different outfits she plans on packing, to get my opinion."

"Twenty outfits?" Mrs. Robinson scrunched up her nose. "I thought we were going to be there only a week."

"Exactly."

Mrs. Robinson thought for a moment. "Well, I ain't mad at her. A free vacation . . . I'd live it up too. Besides, she looks like she has really nice taste . . . the way she was dressed at dinner in that Donna Karan outfit. Nice. Both Ryan's parents are really nice people. Makes me feel that you're even safer with him."

Paige paused for a moment. "What do you mean by that?"

"Well . . . ," Mrs. Robinson began. "I think our family has been blessed in the sense that for generations back, we have all been raised by both parents. The women didn't leave. The men stayed and helped raise the babies. We weren't the Huxtables, but there was the biological mother and the biological father raising the children in our family in the same home. It goes way back to my great-great-grandmother and grandfather. We didn't have to deal with the void and the brokenness so many people have to deal with today. That feeling of abandonment. That feeling of seeking validation. Just carrying that hurt and pain into their own relationships, then causing pain and hurting the person you are in a relationship with."

Mrs. Robinson went and sat down on a stool in the dressing room area. She continued her words to her daughter. "I've never told you this before, Paige, but I understand why you did what you did with the whole having Norman sign Adele's birth certificate and whatnot. No, I don't believe in telling lies and keeping secrets, even by omission. But at least you knew that eventually you were going to have consequences to face and deal with."

Paige sighed. "And, boy, did I have to face them, all right."

"But you faced them. You didn't run, and you didn't try to hide. You were even the one who suggested to Blake that he meet Adele."

Paige nodded.

"So, like I was saying, I understand why you did it. To protect your child. To protect your baby girl from just being so broken at an age when she wouldn't know how to deal with or process not having a daddy or having a daddy that was in jail. It's too much for a child. And what good parent in their right mind would want to purposely do that to a child? I know people like to say that black women have an attitude problem. They say that's why black men turn to white women to get with."

She went on, "What I say to the black man is, 'If you don't want a black woman to break her foot off in your butt, then don't break your promise to her. Don't lie to her. Don't cheat on her. Don't betray her. Don't leave her and her children for dead. Oh, you will see the ugly side, indeed. Black women, women in general, are the most caring and nurturing creatures on this earth. But do something to make us lose respect for your sorry self and see what happens.'" Mrs. Robinson rolled her eyes.

"Ma, you crazy. But I did hear Iyanla Vanzant say something like that to one of the guests on her show."

Mrs. Robinson nodded her head. "I agree one hundred percent. But Ryan gets it." Mrs. Robinson stared off into space and smiled. "Yeah, that boy gets it. And I'm not saying that men and women who don't come from two-parent homes are just jacked up and can't make it. I'm just saying for me"—she pointed to her chest—"as a mother, my preference is that my children marry partners with a history of a two-parent home in the family."

Paige put her hands on her hips. "Uh-huh. I remember Naomi had a preference for who she wanted her kids to marry as well." Paige was referring to how Mrs. Vanderdale had felt the best thing for her children was to marry within the white race.

"Well, she got her wish. Kinda, sorta. Her son might not have married a white woman, but her daughter did." Mrs. Robinson doubled over in laughter.

"Mama, stop. You bad." Paige made a shooing motion with her hand. "Let me go take off this dress."

"You know I'm just playing. Sam is my girl."

"Yeah, whatever, Ma," Paige said as she walked into the dressing room to remove the dress.

"But back to our serious conversation," Mrs. Robinson said. "Take Ryan's sons, for example. He's been raising them in a single-parent home, but those boys are amazing."

"Aren't they?" Paige agreed through the dressing room door. "They are going to be the perfect husbands for a couple of young women out there. And that was long before a stepmother ever stepped in to raise them and turn it into a two-parent home. Ryan did the thang with his boys."

"That's because he knew how. He had men before him who had raised him up well and had taught him. He was able to pass that on to his boys."

"And he finally got the fact that he's a promise to a woman, her godsend. He learned that the hard way with the boys' mother."

"Again, that's what separates Ryan from some other men. He realizes that everything in life is to learn from, and he learns from it, and then he teaches it. He passes it on. If we could get all men to do that, we could have the trickle-down effect and change the way a man loves a woman and a woman responds to his love."

Paige came out of the dressing room, dressed in her own clothes again. "Dang, Ma, you ought to make a YouTube video for this. You are dead serious."

"Child, I am. I must admit, I be watching them trifling reality shows as well. At first I thought it was funny to see those women acting like that. But then I realized that they weren't acting. Some of that mess ain't scripted. It's who they are. It's been in 'em, and they've been acting like that long before a camera ever came around. They just be acting crazy over those men who be dogging them out. Their emotions be all over the place having them do some crazy things."

"Homeless emotions," Paige said.

"Huh?" Mrs. Robinson asked.

"T. D. Jakes said that anytime someone proves that they are not safe to love and you have the unfinished business of loving them, anyway, the torment that you feel is the homelessness of your emotions. Those women are tormented."

"That's deep, and that's good, but I'm not sure he was talking about them crazy broads on that show." Mrs. Robinson shook her head.

Paige chuckled. "Come on, Ma. Let's go pay for this dress and then go find you one." Paige went to exit the dressing room area.

"Two dresses."

"Two?" Paige stopped in her tracks.

Mrs. Robinson stood. "Well, if Ryan's mother is going to have twenty outfits, the least I can do is one-up her by changing into a second dress for the wedding."

"Mom, that's something only the bride does. And I'm not even going to do a dress change." Paige rolled her eyes and continued her trek to the checkout counter.

"Well, I'm starting a new fad." She followed behind Paige. "The mother of the bride gets to show out to. After all, you get it from your mama." Mrs. Robinson started snapping her fingers and twisting her hips.

"Oh, Lord," Paige said, looking over her shoulder at her mother. "Let's go before this ends up being the honeymoon you and Daddy never had, instead of my wedding."

Both women laughed as they went to the cash register to pay for the dress. On the way there, Paige's cell phone rang. She fumbled in her purse to get to it. By the time she had it in her hand, it was too late. She'd missed the call. "It was Pastor Margie. I'll call her back after I do this transaction. Lord knows, I need to tell her about the pending nuptials. She wasn't too thrilled the last time, when I came to her after the fact."

"I know the feeling," Mrs. Robinson said, rolling her eyes and sucking her teeth.

Paige ignored her mother's little dig as the two of them stood at the checkout counter and the clerk rung up the dress.

"Where to?" Paige asked her mother as they exited the store.

"I'm thinking some of those consignment shops over there on Fifth Avenue," Mrs. Robinson answered. "I don't want to pick up something off the rack at the department store and risk one of Miss Thing's twenty outfits duplicating mine."

"Trust me, I've seen everything my future mother-in-law is packing in her suitcase. I'll know whether you two are going to end up being Twinkies. I say we go to Easton." Paige pulled out her keys as they walked across the parking lot. "They have a lot of new shops there now. And if we don't find anything there, we can always hit the consignment shops another day."

"We're leaving in five days. We don't have time like that," Mrs. Robison spat as they approached Paige's car. "By the way, have you and Ryan taken care of everything you needed to take care of? The wedding license or whatever?"

Paige used her key fob to unlock the car doors. "We went downtown, to the courthouse, and took care of that on day one," Paige answered as she laid her dress across the backseat. "But we didn't really need to do that here in the state of Ohio. We're working with a wedding planning company that's taking care of everything for us over in the Dominican Republic, though." The women got inside the car. "Ryan has been fooling around with me for long enough. If things don't go right and I don't show up, ready to marry that man, he's going to be done with me. He'll write me off and find someone else to put the ring on."

"Well, we don't even have to worry about all that," Mrs. Robinson said.

"You are right about that," Paige agreed as she started the car. "Nothing is going to keep me from getting on that plane and marrying the

man I'm going to spend the rest of my life with."
Paige drove out of the parking lot, none the
wiser that she was only partially right. Nothing
would keep her from getting on that plane, but
perhaps someone would.

Chapter 27

Paige compared her checklist against everything she'd packed in her carry-on and large suitcase. She wasn't missing a thing. She'd placed her passport in her laptop bag, which she would keep on her person at all times. She'd already checked everyone in online the day before and printed out their boarding passes. It was such a convenience that airlines allowed passengers to check in within twenty-four hours of the flight's departure. Not only had she printed everyone's boarding pass, but she texted them to both her and Ryan's cell phone as well.

Ryan had arranged for an airport shuttle to pick everyone up at their homes later on that day, which was a Friday. The flight was scheduled to depart at six thirty that evening. Final boarding was around six, six fifteen. It was the best flight available that had seats for all six of them on such short notice.

The shuttle would pick up Ryan first, then his parents, and lastly the Robinsons. Paige was the only one who was going to meet the group at the airport. She was going to pay seven dollars per day to park at the airport. The girls had dance class on Friday evening, and it began at 5:00 p.m. sharp. That meant the girls had to be dressed and ready to begin class at five, so Paige and the girls usually arrived at the dance studio at around 4:30 p.m. Paige would be away from her girls an entire week. She wanted to spend every last minute with them before her departure.

She had put them on the school bus that morning. She would be getting them off in a few minutes. She'd give them a snack, talk about their day, and before she knew it, she'd be dropping them off at the dance studio. Samantha had agreed to meet her at the studio, where she would take over the care of her nieces. While Paige was away, the Vanderdales would help out with caring for the girls as well.

Paige and Ryan had spent a little bit of time discussing what their living arrangements would be once they returned, and they would devise a more concrete plan while honeymooning. What mattered the most to them now was that even if they did have to live briefly in separate homes, in a couple of days they would be joined as one spiritually forever.

Their families would be joined as well, but right now Paige had to make sure she got everything loaded into her car, including the girls' luggage. Because Adele and Norma spent a decent amount of time with their aunt and paternal grandparents, they had quite a number of items at their respective homes, so Paige didn't have to pack too much for the girls. By the time Paige finished loading up the car and double-checking her list again, as if she was Santa Claus, the girls' bus was dropping them off.

"Mommy," the girls yelled as they exited the bus and ran into Paige's arms.

"I thought you was gonna be on the airplane," Adele said.

"I am," Paige answered. "But remember Mommy said she wanted to spend every minute with you and your sister that she could?"

Adele nodded.

"Well, I meant that. So I'm going to take you guys to dance class, and Aunt Sam is going to meet us there. Then she and your grandparents are going to take care of you while I'm gone."

Paige led the girls into the house. They had snacks, told Paige how their day was at school, and started their school assignments. By 4:15

p.m. they were in the car and on their way to the dance studio. They encountered a traffic jam due to a broken-down vehicle, which put Paige a few minutes behind schedule. When she arrived at the studio, Samantha was already waiting for her in the lobby.

"So sorry I'm late," Paige said, ushering the girls into the studio.

"Oh, no problem," Samantha said, giving Paige a hug. "I've been here only a couple minutes myself."

"Okay, well, why don't you come on back with me so that when you bring them yourself next Friday, you'll know where the locker room is, their studio, the viewing room, and all that jazz?"

"Sounds good to me," Samantha said. "Then, after you give them their kisses good-bye and they're off dancing, we can go transfer their stuff from your car to mine."

"That's a plan," Paige said. Paige got the girls to the locker room and all changed. "Be good girls while Mommy is gone, and I'll bring you back something really nice, okay?"

"Yay!" the girls cheered, jumping up and down.

"Remind Mr. Ryan that he's going to be our daddy after he marries you," Adele said.

"I will." Paige smiled. It was an added bonus that the girls were excited about her marrying Ryan.

"Hurry back, Mommy," Norma said. "We're going to miss you."

"Yeah, and hurry back because we want our present too," Adele said with a straight face.

Paige and Samantha couldn't help but laugh.

"I'm going to miss you girls too," Paige said. "Mommy loves you both very much."

"We love you too," the girls chorused.

After all the hugs, kisses, and farewells, Paige got the girls to their studio to practice. Afterward, she and Samantha went out to the car and put the girls' things in Samantha's car.

"Thanks, again, Sam. I truly appreciate you," Paige said.

"Oh, no problem. What are sisters for?" Samantha said, hugging Paige. "You all have a safe trip, and do everything I would do and then some." She winked.

"Girl, you already know." Paige laughed.

Samantha hurried back into the studio, while Paige got in the car and secured her seat belt. She did one last sweep of the car. That was when she looked down at the floor on the passenger side and saw that she'd forgotten to give Samantha the girls' book bags. "Dang it the snap!" she shouted. She undid her seat belt, grabbed the book bags, and then got out of the car.

She did a light jog into the studio. As soon as she walked through the door, she stopped in her tracks, only because she walked smack-dab into a dance mom who was exiting the studio.

"I'm so sorry," both women said at the same time, then looked at each other.

"Lorain, I'm so sorry," Paige said, realizing she knew the person she'd almost taken out, like she was a quarterback on a football field.

"Paige, how are you?" Lorain asked.

"Good." Paige looked down at the twins, who were lagging behind their mother. Practice must have been intense. The girls looked worn out. "Hi, girls."

"Hi," they said in unison.

Paige looked at Lorain. She looked equally as worn out as the girls. "How are you?"

"A little tired. I was up all night."

"With your little one?" Paige asked, assuming that was the case. "By the way, where is he?" She realized Lorain's son wasn't with her.

"The baby is with my mom. I was up all night, sitting with Unique. She—"

"Oh, Unique is back in town?" Paige asked, not meaning to cut Lorain off. She blamed it on the anxiety of wanting to make sure she caught her flight. "She moved to Atlanta, right?"

"Yes, she's been back a week now," Lorain said. Her tone became somber. She leaned in and, trying to be discreet, whispered, "They gave her only about another week, you know."

Paige threw her hand over her mouth. "Oh, Jesus, Lorain. I'm so sorry. I had no idea that Unique was even sick." Paige looked down at her watch. "I feel so bad that I can't stay and talk. I have a flight to catch, but I'm so sorry." Paige hugged Lorain tightly. "I'll definitely be praying for her, though."

"Oh, no. Unique is not sick," Lorain said upon being released from Paige's hug. Once again she whispered. "It's Tamarra. Unique stays at her bedside until she falls off to sleep," Lorain explained. "You know, when she first found out and got sick, she never really told anybody. I don't blame her, not with such a stigma being attached to the disease. Since she was self-employed and a small business owner, the insurance benefits weren't the best. Her bills pretty much bankrupted her. Her home is in foreclosure. She was able to sell the catering business, but she even depleted those funds.

"You know she left New Day years ago. She kept in touch only with Unique, and then, when Unique moved away, Tamarra no longer had a connection to New Day. Last week Pastor

Margie just happened to be visiting someone
else in the hospital when she walked by a room
that had Tamarra's name on the door. Pastor
Margie peeked in, and lo and behold it was
our Tamarra." Lorain's eyes filled with tears.
"Unique told me that Pastor said when Tamarra
saw her, she just burst into tears."

Lorain sniffed. "Just to think she's been fighting the disease alone all these years. Even when
she first got sick, Unique was working for her in
West Virginia. She asked her to come back to
Malvonia and run the business for her. She told
Unique she wasn't well but never told her that
she . . . you know . . . had *it*."

Anyone walking by would have mistakenly
believed that Paige was either in a Lamaze class
or was going into labor. Her breathing in and out
was becoming heavier and heavier.

Lorain put her hand on Paige's shoulder. "You
okay?"

Paige couldn't respond. She couldn't talk. She
couldn't breathe. Lorain had been talking; she'd
been talking a lot. She had been saying so much
that Paige could barely take it all in. Tamarra
was sick. The woman who had been her best
friend once upon a time was sick. She'd been
sick for a while. She wasn't just sick. She was on
her deathbed. She'd been given a week to live.

"How could this . . . what . . . I mean . . ." Paige's world was spinning. The words were whirling around in her head. It was like a tornado. She was in the eye of the storm. She didn't know how to process everything that Lorain had just said. She wobbled, slightly losing her balance.

"Paige!" Lorain grabbed Paige. "Come sit down." She escorted her over to a bench by the door.

"Is everything okay?" the receptionist asked.

"Uh, yeah, yeah . . . I think," Lorain replied, then turned and faced Paige. "Are you okay? Do you need me to call someone?"

Paige tucked her lips in to help hold back the yelp she wanted to let out. Her lips trembled like they were levies trying to hold back an explosion of water.

"Paige, breathe." Lorain sat down next to her. "Can you breathe? Nod or something, or I'm going to have Rebecca call nine-one-one." Lorain nodded toward the receptionist.

Once again Paige began to breathe in and out heavily. "Where is she?" was what Paige finally managed to force out.

"Huh?" Lorain said, not catching what Paige had asked.

"Where is she now? Tamarra?"

"She's home now. At her house. It's in fore-closure, but they haven't sent the sheriff to put her out or anything. They're trying to do a quick sale or something like that. I heard the church she now belongs to took up a collection, but it wasn't enough to pay off all her debts. They were able to put a dent in her medical bills, though. She worked hard all her life, building that business. They wanted her to die with as much dignity as she could. I even got together with my doctors' wives' club, and we donated and raised money. The bills keep piling up, though. At least she doesn't have any children, a husband, or anyone who will have to worry about her debt falling on their shoulders. It's just a shame. At the very least, a person wants to die with a good name, you know."

Paige nodded. "Yes, I know."

Lorain rubbed Paige's back. "I'm sorry I had to be the one to tell you this. I know you two had a falling-out some time ago. I just knew you two would have patched things up by now." Lorain chuckled. "You two were as thick as thieves."

Paige just sat there rocking back and forth.

"I'm surprised Pastor Margie didn't say anything to you about it."

A light bulb immediately went off in Paige's head. She'd missed church last Sunday. She'd attended Ryan's mother and father's church, taking them up on their invite. Pastor Margie had called and left her a message while she was in the shop with her mother, buying her wedding dress. She'd forgotten to return the call, though. Paige couldn't remember the last time she'd checked her messages.

"I uh, missed church last Sunday," Paige said in Pastor Margie's defense. "Pastor called me, but I had no idea. . . ." Paige's words trailed off. She shook her head, still in disbelief.

"Well, I'm just glad I ran into you and was able to let you know," Lorain said. "I don't know exactly what happened between the two of you. But one thing I have learned in my own life is that the last thing you want to do is let time pass without saying what is truly on your heart. Good or bad, release it."

Paige heard everything Lorain was saying, but hearing this devastating news about Tamarra had taken her heart and mind to places they hadn't been in a long time. She'd prayed for her enemies. She'd forgiven them. She'd told Tamarra to her face that she'd forgiven her, and she'd meant it. But on the same day she'd

forgiven Tamarra, she'd walked away from both
her and their friendship.

The Bible said that one must forgive. It didn't
say that one still had to associate with someone
or entertain him or her after forgiveness had
taken place. Tamarra represented a time in
Paige's life that was dark. She'd been intimate
with her husband, and this had formed a connection between the three of them that Paige
didn't want to deal with every time she saw
Tamarra. That was when a thought occurred to
Paige.

"Disease. You said Tamarra has a disease,"
Paige said, turning to Lorain. "What . . . what is
it?" Paige was almost afraid to ask, which was
why she stammered.

Lorain said softly, "She's having complications from AIDS."

Paige threw her head back. Thank God there
was a wall behind her, or else she would have
fallen right off that bench. Still, the wind felt like
it had been punched out of Paige. All the dots
were beginning to connect. Blake might have not
discovered that he was HIV positive until he was
in jail, but clearly, he'd contracted the deadly
disease long before ever going to jail. Blake had a
pretty colorful sexual history. Tamarra had
claimed that he was a womanizer, that he used

women for whatever he wanted and then tossed them aside like trash. His sexual past had caught up with him, and Tamarra had been caught in the cross fire.

"Are you sure I can't call someone for you?" Lorain asked. "Did you say you had a plane or something to catch?"

"Ryan," Paige said out loud. She'd truly forgotten all about the fact that she was supposed to go meet at the airport the man who she was marrying and with whom she planned on spending the rest of her life. She looked down at her watch. The plane was scheduled to leave in less than ninety minutes. That meant that everyone was surely waiting at the airport for her. Time had truly gotten away from Paige. "I've gotta go." Paige jumped up.

Lorain stood up. "Are you sure you're okay to drive? I can take you where you need to be or call you a cab or something."

"No, no. I'm fine," Paige said. She pulled Lorain in for a hug. "Thank you so much."

"Oh, no problem. You take care of yourself."

"Yes, I will. You too." Paige headed for the door.

"Wait, Paige. I think you left these."

Paige turned around to see Lorain standing there, holding the girls' book bags.

Paige sighed but then had an idea. "The girls' aunt Samantha. Blond hair. Tall. Thin. She's in the viewing room for studio two. Will you give them to her please?" Paige had one foot out the door as she backpedaled out of the building.

"Yes, sure. You go ahead," Lorain said.

"Thank you. Thank you so much. For everything." Paige darted out the door and raced to her car. She got in the car and started it. She looked in the rearview mirror before she backed out of her parking space. She locked eyes with herself in the mirror and prayed that within the next five minutes she could come up with the answer to the question her eyes were asking her.

Where are you going?

Paige could give only one of two answers: to the airport, to be with the man she wanted to spend the rest of her years with, or to the house where her former best friend didn't have years to live but only a matter of days.

Chapter 28

As Paige pulled out of the dance studio parking lot, her phone rang. She looked down at the center console, where she'd left the phone while she'd taken the girls inside. She picked the phone up. Ryan's name flashed across the caller ID, along with a picture of him with his boys smiling next to him. It was a picture she'd taken of them with her phone when they came to her house for dinner.

A loud horn blowing tore Paige's eyes away from the phone. She'd almost hit the car coming into the parking lot. She hurriedly swerved over to the right to keep from nicking the front end of it and causing a fender bender. The phone fell from her hand when she grabbed the steering wheel with both hands.

"Sorry," she said, waving an apologetic hand at the other driver. Paige put the car in park and reached down to pick up her phone. She felt around until she could grasp it with her finger-

tips. By the time she got control of the phone
and had it up to her ear, the call had already
gone to voice mail.

Paige sat and thought for a minute while she
looked at the phone, noticing that she had four
missed calls and a couple text messages and that
the voice mail symbol was displayed.

"Lord, guide me," was all Paige said as she
exited the parking lot.

Fifteen minutes later Paige was pulling up
to her destination. She parked and sat in her
car for a few seconds. The clock was ticking.
While driving for the past fifteen minutes, she
had weighed all her options. The pros and cons
of getting on the plane. The pros and cons of
not getting on the plane. This was one of the
hardest choices Paige had had to make in a long
time. But for some reason, she felt as though
the choice really wasn't hers to make. It felt
more like a no-brainer. Like a given. God wasn't
wavering on what He'd put in Paige's heart
to do. It was her flesh that was doing all the
wavering as it fought against what her head kept
urging her to do.

Paige put the car in park. She turned off the
engine and pulled the key out of the ignition. She
leaned her head back against the headrest, closed
her eyes, and asked for the Holy Spirit to continue

directing her path, ordering both her steps and her words. She did not want to stray and change the course of her entire life, although she felt with the decision she was making, that was exactly what was about to happen. With that final thought, Paige got out of the car and made her way inside the airport.

She looked down at the boarding passes she'd retrieved from her laptop bag. She double-checked the airline, then looked up to find their counter. She figured she would find her family nearby. She hadn't even made it to the desig-nated ticket counter before she heard her name being called.

"Paige, right here."

She spotted Ryan waving and walking toward her. His fast-paced walk turned into a light jog before he caught up with her.

"Honey, where were you?" Ryan pulled Paige into a hug and kissed her on the side of her head.

Paige didn't say anything.

"We all just checked our luggage," Ryan told Paige, coming out of the hug. "I had our parents go on through security and head back to the gate." He looked down at Paige, noticing she didn't have any luggage. Just her purse. "Where's your luggage? Did you do curbside check-in?"

Still, Paige remained silent. All she could do was look into the eyes of the man who expected her to board a plane, get married in two days, then honeymoon for five before returning to the States to combine their lives and the lives of their children. In his eyes she saw it all taking place. A dream come true. Well, she was about to wake him up out of that dream.

"Ryan, there is something I have to tell you." Paige cast her tear-filled eyes downward.

Ryan stared at Paige for a moment before he started shaking his head. "Don't do this to me, Paige. Don't get cold feet on me now." He pointed toward the security gate. "Our parents are already waiting on us to—"

"Ryan, please," Paige interrupted him. "I do not have cold feet. I want to marry you now more than ever," she said.

Ryan exhaled. The gust of air that came from his lungs could have knocked her over. "Thank you, God," he said, hugging Paige again.

"But I can't."

Paige's words stung Ryan. They paralyzed him. He couldn't move as he held Paige in his arms.

After more seconds of silence than Paige could stand to suffocate in, she spoke. "Not like we planned to."

Ryan slowly pulled away from Paige. "What are you saying?"

"I just got some really horrific news," Paige said.

A look of concern filled Ryan's eyes.

"It's Tamarra."

Ryan's look went from concern to confusion. What in the world could Tamarra have to do with why Paige couldn't marry him?

"You know how Blake tested HIV positive and I had the whole HIV scare?"

"Yes." Now Ryan sounded nervous. "But you tested negative . . . a million times . . . right?" Now he felt fear.

Paige could sense what Ryan was thinking. "Yes, absolutely. I'm negative. I don't have HIV," Paige confirmed.

Ryan exhaled.

"Blake didn't give me HIV, but he gave it to Tamarra."

Ryan didn't know what to say at first. "Oh, my. That's . . . that's awful." He felt bad for Tamarra, but he still didn't understand what that had to do with the two of them not getting married.

"I just found out that . . ." Paige held back tears. "She's dying. She's on her deathbed. Literally. She was in the hospital, but she wanted to die at home. So she's at home, I think with hospice care."

Ryan shook his head. "I'm sorry to hear all this, Paige, but I still don't understand how this has anything to do with us. I know it's hard hearing that someone you used to be close with is dying. But you haven't talked to Tamarra in years. You stopped being her friend, so . . . I hate to sound cold, but I don't get it."

"Ryan, the doctors don't see her making it through the week. We have plans to be gone a week. If I got on that plane without going to see Tamarra, and if I learned when I got back that she'd d—" Paige couldn't even finish the word as a tear fell from her eye.

"Baby, don't cry." Ryan wiped Paige's tear. "I'm being real selfish right now," he admitted. "I want you to go through security with me, get on that plane, and return bearing my last name. Because if you don't—I hate to say this—I don't think you ever will."

"Ryan, that's not true. I love you. I don't want anything more than to be your wife. I promise you that."

"But . . ."

"But my soul . . ." Paige's shoulders began heaving up and down. She couldn't even finish her thought.

Ryan pulled Paige to his chest. He hugged her and consoled her as much as he knew how, even though he felt like he was the one who needed consoling right about now. He hadn't been able to sleep the past two weeks. All he'd been thinking about was their trip to the Dominican Republic, where God's promise would finally be manifested. He had imagined the two of them connecting on a much higher level than ever. But now, with this news that Paige had learned about Tamarra, Ryan knew that even if Paige's body was with him in the Dominican Republic, her mind would be back in Malvonia. He wanted all of her, or he wanted nothing. And what he didn't want to do was force her to be somewhere her heart didn't want to be. He'd question her "I do" forever. So even though he wanted so badly to shake some sense into her, or even go caveman and drag her through security, he thought better of it. He'd rather be left at the altar than know he'd dragged her to the altar.

"Say no more, Paige," Ryan said. "I understand what you have to do." That was what his lips said. His heart was hurting, and his head was pissed. But he had his reasons for allowing words to come out of his mouth that he really didn't mean.

"Do you really?" Paige pulled away, glad that Ryan understood.

Ryan was unable to look Paige in the eye.

Paige sensed that even though Ryan might have understood, he didn't support her in this. "Ryan, I'm so torn. I've been torn since finding this all out. I ran into Lorain when I was dropping the girls off at dance class, and she told me. I prayed on it all the way here. Do I get on this plane, or do I go make peace with Tamarra?"

"I thought you already made peace with her. I thought you forgave her," Ryan said.

"I did. I forgave her, and then I walked away. Even after I dismissed her from my life, she tried to be there for me, and what did I do? I sent her away when she showed up to support me in court during my trial with Blake. I beat her down at Mother Doreen's wedding." Paige shook her head in disgust at her own actions. "Now who is the one who needs forgiving?" Paige let out a muted wail. It wasn't loud and piercing, but it held just as much pain as if it were.

Passersby started looking at the two of them. Ryan looked around at the inquiring eyes. Some passengers were practically running into others, they were so deep into his and Paige's business.

"What's he doing to her?" he heard an older woman ask the woman she was walking with. They looked at Ryan as if he were a woman beater.

Ryan was slightly embarrassed about the scene he and Paige were making. He pulled her to him once again. "Don't. You don't have to stand here and explain to me anymore. Just do what you need to do, and I'll . . ." He thought for a minute. "I'll go on vacation with my parents and yours."

Paige quickly lifted her head. She'd forgotten about how many other people would be affected by her not getting on that plane. "Oh, yes, that's right." Paige looked horrified. "What are we going to tell our parents?" Paige thought some more. "And the kids?" She turned her back to Ryan. "Dear God. What's happening here? Why can't my life be like peach cobbler with extra ice cream for just five minutes?"

"Because you have diabetes," Ryan joked.

"Yeah, well, my diabetes is under control." That was true. Paige hadn't had to take insulin shots for years since first being diagnosed with the disease. "But when will I get my life under control?"

Ryan turned her around. "Your life *is* under control. And you have a life."

Conviction hit Paige like a ton of bricks. Was she really complaining about her near perfect life, knowing that Tamarra's was about to end? "You're right. You are so right." Paige immediately wished she could take the words back.

"Passengers Ryan Coleman and Paige Van-derdale, your flight is about to reach the final boarding stage. Paging Ryan Coleman and Paige Vanderdale to US Airways gate forty-two."

When Paige and Ryan heard those words over the intercom, they both looked at each other.

"Well, sounds like I have a plane to board," Ryan said. He extended his hands to Paige. Paige placed her hands in Ryan's. "Are you sure this is what you want to do? Because I'm going to be honest. I want you to get on that plane with me and start a new life with me and not run back to your old life." Again, those were calm, diplomatic words that Ryan spoke. Inside, he was screaming for Paige to get her behind on that plane.

"Ryan, that's not fair. I'm not running back to—"

"Like I said, I was just being honest. You are talking to a man who has been both patient and obedient for so long. What I've longed for was right at my fingertips, and now it's not going to happen. Why? Why has my dream seemed so close, and yet I can never mange to reach it?" Ryan looked deeply into Paige's eyes. "My arm is tired of stretching. Perhaps it's time to just let it go."

Paige's mouth fell open. "Ryan, what are you trying to say?"

"Final boarding call for Ryan Coleman and Paige Vanderdale." The flight attendant made her last announcement instructing Ryan and Paige to come to gate forty-two. The plane would be departing in fifteen minutes. Once the door to the aircraft was closed, no more passengers would be permitted on the plane.

"You heard her," Ryan said to Paige in reference to the announcement. "Final call."

Paige shook her head. "Ryan, don't do this to me. Because it sounds to me like you're giving me this underlying ultimatum."

Ryan shrugged. "Look, I better go." He nodded toward the security checkpoint. "I'm sure our parents are fit to be tied. At least one of us needs to board this plane." He kissed Paige on the forehead. "You take care. I'll say a prayer for your friend." Ryan turned and headed toward the security checkpoint, his heart wanting to jump out of his chest because it was so full of disappointment and heartache. But like he'd concluded before, if he had to fight and drag her to come and marry him, he wouldn't.

"I love you, Ryan," she called. Paige said it like she was trying to convince not only Ryan but also the entire world. What would her parents say, her mother especially? She'd already questioned Paige's true feelings for Ryan. Would her mother think that once again she was right? She watched the back of Ryan's head as he walked away.

Go with him.

Paige didn't know if it was her head, her heart, or a whisper from God directing her.

"And I'm going to marry you," Paige called out, making another attempt to reassure Ryan. To reassure the world. "I promise. It's just that—"

Without turning around, Ryan raised his hand in a wave. He was either waving good-bye to Paige or cutting her off.

Paige's stomach ached. It ached with regret for letting him walk away. It ached over the hurt she knew she must be causing him. It ached with the pain she felt for Tamarra's predicament. It ached from the fact that she could possibly be making the biggest mistake of her life by allowing Ryan to walk away. It ached from the fact that she could possibly be making the biggest mistake of her life by going to see about Tamarra.

Even though just moments ago Paige had entered that airport confident that she was following the direction of her spirit woman, doubt began to seep in. Her flesh and her spirit were at war, which was always a terrible thing. One never knew which one would prevail.

Paige just stood there as Ryan managed to get airport assistance in passing through the security checkpoint ahead of everyone else in the line so that he could catch his plane. Fortunately, Columbus's airport was fairly small. It didn't have trains and whatnot that passengers had to take in order to get to their gates. Paige knew Ryan would get to his destination in time.

She took a deep breath in and then exhaled. Now would she get to hers in time?

"It could be me," Paige mumbled as she drove to Tamarra's home. She decided she wouldn't waste any time going back to her house. "Dear God, that could be me. Blake was my husband. I was the one sleeping with him every night. And yet Tamarra caught the virus."

Paige just kept shaking her head in disbelief as she drove to Tamarra's house. She was in disbelief that Tamarra had caught the virus. She was in disbelief that she hadn't. She felt guilty after thanking God that she didn't have it, knowing that Tamarra did. She prayed during the entire drive. Paige was consumed with thoughts of how Tamarra would receive her and wondered if she would even agree to.

"Lord, what if she won't even let me in the door, the same way I wouldn't let her in the courtroom to support me?" Paige asked in her conversation with God. "This could be a waste of time. I could be sacrificing my relationship with Ryan for nothing."

Paige was absolutely horrified at the thought. While she was at the airport, she hadn't once stopped to think about the fact that Tamarra might not even want to see her.

"God, you wouldn't send me to her home, knowing she wouldn't receive me, would you?" Paige didn't even have to wait on an answer from God to that question. She smiled. "Then again, you sent your Son here, knowing that not everyone would receive Him, huh?"

Relief and peace settled over Paige's heart. She had managed to convince herself again that she was doing what God had instructed her to do, and that was all that mattered. Paige repeated aloud words Pastor Margie had once said. "If God sends you somewhere, it doesn't matter whether anyone else shows up or not. As long as you are where you are supposed to be is all God's concerned about."

As Paige pulled up in front of Tamarra's house, she saw about three cars in the driveway, and so she parked in front of the house. Paige was now where she was supposed to be. She put the car in park, turned it off, and then looked up to the heavens. "So now that I'm where I'm supposed to be, Lord, tell me what I'm now supposed to do."

Chapter 29

Not sure how long she would be inside Tamarra's house, if she was even allowed to step foot in there, Paige decided to send Ryan a text, asking him to apologize to both her parents as well as his. Paige's parents didn't do cell phones, or else she would have sent them a text directly. She was certain, though, that her mother would call her just as soon as she could to get from the horse's mouth the reason why Paige hadn't gotten her butt on that plane.

After sending the text, Paige got out of the car and walked up the walkway to Tamarra's house, passing the FOR SALE BY BANK sign that was planted in her front yard. Paige crept up to Tamarra's doorstep. The more steps she took, the longer the walkway seemed to get. She wanted to turn around a million times, afraid of what was going to happen when she knocked on that door. Well, the time had come to find out. Paige stepped up on the porch and rang the doorbell. Her stomach was doing somersaults until finally the front door opened.

"Hi. May I help you?" an older woman asked.

Although Paige had never met Tamarra's mother in the flesh, she'd seen enough pictures of her to know her when she saw her.

"Mrs. Evans?" Paige said.

"Yes." The woman stared at Paige. Clearly, Paige knew who she was, but Mrs. Evans couldn't place Paige.

"I'm Paige. We've never met before, but I've heard so much about you," Paige said. "It's good to finally meet you."

"Oh, Paige, Paige." Mrs. Evans's eyes lit up. "Dear God, I can't believe I finally get to meet you in person." She opened the door wide and gave Paige a big, warm, welcoming hug. Come on in here." She moved to the side to allow Paige in the house.

Paige hesitated, shocked that she'd at least been granted access to the home. Of course, Tamarra had the right to put her out, though. She would just have to take that chance. Paige stepped inside.

"Tamarra talked about you so much. I had just never made it down from Maryland to meet you." She escorted Paige into the front room, where an older man was sitting and watching television. "Honey, this here is Paige," Mrs. Evans said.

The room still had the same furniture, as far as Paige could remember. It looked as though Tamarra had rearranged things some, but that wasn't what made the room look different. It was the lighting. The curtains on the large triple-pane front window were drawn. It was evening, and the sun was going down. But for some reason, Paige felt as though even if the sun had just risen, there still would be darkness in the room. Perhaps it wasn't the lighting that was making the room so dark. After all, the lamp on the end table was on, and there was light coming from the television. Paige surmised that it was the feeling that was dark . . . the mood.

"Hi, Mr. Evans," Paige said and waved. She used an upbeat, bubbly tone, trying to bring just a hint of light to the situation.

"Hey, suga. Good to meet you," Mr. Evans said from his chair. He immediately turned his attention back to the show he was watching on television.

Paige didn't press by asking him any questions, like the standard "How are you holding up?" It was clear he didn't want to engage. Paige could only imagine how hard it must be for him to think about the fact that he was about to lose his daughter, let alone talk about it.

Mrs. Evans decided to trample on the silence. "Every time I ask Tamarra about you, she always says you're doing fine. I know she said you got married, had some babies or something. She told me you two don't talk as much, what with you busy with family and her so busy with running and building her own company all these years. Her daddy and I have visited a couple times and never got to see you. I was hoping we would now that . . ." Mrs. Evans's words faded.

Paige honestly didn't know what to say. It sounded as if Tamarra had never told her parents that the two of them had had a falling-out, which was the real reason they were estranged.

"Anyway," Mrs. Evans continued, "I'm glad to finally meet you. I just wish it wasn't under these circumstances." She was becoming teary eyed. She wiped a falling tear away. "Anyway, I'm sure you don't want me standing here, talking your ear off. You're here to see Tamarra. She's in her room." Mrs. Evans turned and headed up a flight of steps, passing the dining area, which hosted bouquets of flowers Tamarra had received.

Mrs. Evans was halfway up the steps when she realized Paige wasn't behind her. She stopped, turned around, and looked at Paige, who was standing at the bottom of the steps. "You all right? You coming?" she asked Paige.

Paige just stood there. It had been so long since she'd been in this house. Since she'd gone up those steps to the bedroom where she and Tamarra had had many grown-up slumber parties. They'd put away countless pizzas, tubs of ice cream, popcorn, soda, brownies, and potato chips. And they had done a lot of trash talking about the male species and gossiping about church folks. Paige chuckled, just thinking about all the times they'd shared up in Tamarra's room. It truly did feel bittersweet for Paige to be back in that house again. Was what she was about to see going to forever taint her good memories? Would Tamarra look frail and weak, like Blake? It was those questions that gave Paige pause, literally, at the bottom of the steps.

"Paige, honey. It's okay," Mrs. Evans said, nodding her head toward the top landing and proceeding up the steps.

Paige took a deep breath and fought to lift the weight of her legs, which felt like tons, as she climbed the steps. Her mind was still struggling with her decision to go through with this. Her legs were paying the price, wanting to stay planted, as if her feet were buried in cement.

Mrs. Evans stopped outside of Tamarra's door. She turned to Paige. "A couple folks are in there with her right now. Her nurse, a couple friends from church, and a gal she used to work with."

Paige nodded. She could hear some light chattering going on, on the other side of the door. Given all the cars parked outside, Paige had figured Tamarra had guests. She just hoped that she wasn't an unwelcome guest.

Mrs. Evans gave a light tap on the door and then pushed it open. "Hey, baby girl," she said, entering the room. "I'm back, and I brought someone with me." She entered the room and, with a huge grin on her face, stepped off to the side. "It's Paige."

When Paige walked through the doorway, the room fell completely silent. The world just seconds ago had been spinning so fast, Paige thought she'd lose her balance. Now it had abruptly stopped, and Paige nearly toppled over, because she was still spinning. Her mind was, anyway. What was Tamarra going to say to her, if anything? What was Tamarra going to do? Could Tamarra even see and speak? Would she know who Paige was? These were the questions that had just hit Paige's mind. It had been so crowded with so many other thoughts, she guessed that these had been waiting in the wings until there was sufficient room for them to join in.

Tamarra was lying there in her California king–size bed. She was surrounded by four king-size pillows with burgundy and gold linen pillowcases and was covered up by a nice thick matching comforter. She looked like a woman on her own private island. Paige used to tease Tamarra about being single yet having that big ole bed. She'd tried to tell her that if she got a smaller bed, it would make her bedroom look bigger and roomier. Tamarra had always replied that just in case she never found that man who treated her like a queen, she'd make sure the place where she laid her head was fit for a queen, and that it was.

Tamarra had hired a decorator to come in and decorate her room. From the drapes to the sitting area set up by her bay window, it was definitely like a throne. And right now Paige was feeling a little bit like Esther in the Book of Esther. She hadn't gotten prior permission to enter. Would it be off with her head?

"P-Paige," a weak Tamarra managed to get out.

Her voice was so low and flat, Paige couldn't read it one way or the other. Because Tamarra's body was covered, Paige couldn't see it, but if her sunken-in face was any sign, Tamarra was probably paper thin.

"Hi, Tamarra," Paige greeted.

Tamarra just lay there, staring at Paige. She was in pure disbelief. "Paige, is that really you?" she finally asked.

Paige nodded, still not sure in which direction things were going to go. "Yes, Tamarra, it's really me," she confirmed.

Tamarra stared at Paige for a few more seconds before she parted her lips to say, "Get out."

Paige stood frozen stiff at Tamarra's words. The way her blood seemed to chill, she probably really was frozen. Her breath got caught, and she couldn't breathe out. Good thing, because all of a sudden it was so icy in the room that if she had been able to breathe, a puff of frost would have formed before her face.

"Tamarra, what did you say?" Mrs. Evans asked as she walked toward her daughter.

With her eyes still glued on Paige, Tamarra repeated, "Get . . . out. . . ." She swallowed and steadied her breath. "Please." She looked around at everyone in the room. "Do you all mind? Just for a moment?" She looked at her mom. "I'd like to talk to Paige alone." Tamarra began to cough.

"You okay?" asked Unique, Lorain's daughter, as she sat next to Tamarra. "Here. Drink some water." Unique grabbed a water bottle filled with ice and water that was sitting on the nightstand next to the bed. She lifted it to Tamarra's mouth and squeezed it.

Tamarra looked relieved to take in the cold liquid. After a few seconds, Unique moved the water bottle away from Tamarra's mouth. "Ahhh," Tamarra said.

"You need some more?" Unique asked with much concern.

Tamarra shook her head.

"Okay, well, we'll give you guys some time alone," Unique said. She stood up.

There was a woman in scrubs, who Paige assumed was the nurse, in a chair over in the sitting area. She had been reading a book but had been torn away from its pages by Tamarra's coughing fit. She stood as well. There were two other women in the room, and they were standing on the opposite side of the bed from where Unique had been sitting.

"I'll fix everybody some tea and coffee," Mrs. Evans offered. She was the first to exit the room, patting Paige on the shoulder as she walked by.

Unique followed Mrs. Evans, and when she got to Paige, she stopped and gave her a hug. "Hey, Sister Paige," Unique said, squeezing her tightly. She knew Paige and Tamarra's history. It blessed her soul to see that Paige had come to see about Tamarra in her final days. "I'll be praying out there," Unique said as she broke from the hug and headed out the door.

The other two women, Paige did not recognize. They could have been women from the church Tamarra now attended or maybe her new best friends. A twinge of jealousy bounced throughout Paige' spirit. She smiled at the women, and they each gave her a friendly smile as they exited the room. The nurse followed behind them.

"Can you close?" Tamarra asked Paige, nodding to the door.

Paige looked behind her at the open door. "Oh, sure." She immediately turned and closed it. She then just stood in front of the now closed door.

"Hot in here," Tamarra complained with a frown.

Paige walked over and pulled Tamarra's covers down some. She stared at Tamarra's frail body and her skin, which looked so aged due to dryness and wrinkling. Her hair was long, and it flowed in front of her shoulders and down to her breasts. Her eyes looked lifeless, almost as if she'd given up even before her body had. Seeing Tamarra like this melted any remnants of coldness Paige might have ever exhibited with this woman. She felt no bitterness and no hate, only sympathy and compassion.

"Sorry, I didn't call," Paige began.

Tamarra raised her bony, flimsy arm. She struggled to hold her hand up to halt Paige's words. She shook her head. "Thank you so much for coming," she said, and she then coughed.

The cough, to Paige's ears, sounded so painful. Apparently, Tamarra had had something in her throat, because after she finished hacking, she seemed to be able to speak in clearer sentences.

"I don't know if you came to cuss me out, to come spit on my grave, to tell me this is what I deserve, or to—"

"Please, Tamarra, don't. None of those are reasons why I'm here," Paige said. "I would never come here to say those things to you."

"Bet you're thinking it." Tamarra coughed.

Paige walked over and retrieved the water bottle she'd seen Unique give Tamarra a drink from. She lifted the bottle to Tamarra's lips and squeezed. Back when Paige used to listen to rap music all the time, she recalled how a very popular rapper died from complications from AIDS. He had AIDS-related pneumocystis pneumonia. His death had been so sudden that it rocked the hip-hop world. She wondered if that's what Tamarra was experiencing, but didn't dare ask. None of that had anything to do with her just being there for her friend right now. Tamarra took a drink and then held up her hand to signal that she'd had enough. Water dripped from her mouth. Paige looked around and saw a box of tissue on the nightstand on the opposite side of the bed. She walked over, grabbed one, then dabbed the water that was dripping from Tamarra's mouth.

"Thank you," Tamarra said.

"You're welcome." Paige sat the water bottle down next to the tissue box.

There was silence. During the silence Paige allowed her eyes to wander, as if she was admiring the room. She could hardly bear seeing Tamarra like this.

Tamarra started to speak. "I'm sorry, Paige. Don't want to beat around the bush. My days are numbered. Years have already passed. Don't want another minute to pass without saying I'm so sorry." She took a deep breath, as if saying the words had used up a lot of her breath.

"Tamarra I've already forgiven you," Paige said. "Truly I have."

"I know you said you forgave me, but you kept away from me like I had the plague." She looked down at her body. "Guess now I really do have the plague." She gave a laugh, which turned into a cough. Paige reached for the water, but Tamarra held her hand up to let her know she was okay.

"Tamarra, you do not need to apologize to me again."

"Please, Paige, let me do this. I've carried it with me for years. Please don't let me have to take it to my grave." She swallowed and paced herself. "I want to own up to everything. I want to apologize for everything."

Paige put her head down and shook it. "Tamarra, I didn't come here to rehash the past. When I heard my best friend was sick, I came running. I practically left my fiancé standing at the altar in order to come see about you. Girl, my being here should show you that I forgive you, that I love you. That at the end of the day, nothing you ever did or ever said matters. What matters most is you, and me being here to make sure that you know that no matter what, I love you. I've always loved you. I will always love you."

"If you break out in Whitney Houston's most famous song, I'm going to die . . . not that I'm not going to die, anyhow." Tamarra laughed. She coughed.

"I see you still have your sense of humor," Paige said, laughing lightly.

"Yeah, at this point all I can do is laugh. I gotta laugh to keep from crying." Tamarra turned serious. "Because every time I thought about leaving this earth without talking to the best friend I've ever had in my life, all I could do was cry."

Paige nodded her understanding. There had been times when she'd thought about Tamarra and her past relationship, and it had brought tears to her eyes that they were no longer even cordial with one another. But then the tears would turn into tears of hurt. All the pain would try to come to the forefront. So in order to push it away, she had had to push all thoughts of Tamarra away.

"We were like Laverne and Shirley, huh?" Paige said.

"Lucy and Ethel."

"Frick and Frack."

Both women laughed.

Once their laughter died down, Tamarra spoke. "I'm sorry I ruined all that with the whole Blake incident. Secretly setting you up with him. Having slept with him."

"Please, Tamarra." It was like nails down a chalkboard for Paige to hear it all. She'd just had to hear it all over again from Blake. Enough was enough, already.

"Paige, this guilt and shame I've been carrying were killing me long before I ever knew this disease was. I did you wrong. You might not believe me when I say that I truly never meant to hurt you, but I didn't. I hooked you up with a man I had already been with, and then I slept with him again . . . after you two got together. When people who weren't there to witness our downfall ask me about how come I don't hang out with you anymore, I can't even bring myself to tell them the truth. Not even my own parents know what a low-down, conniving, and back-stabbing friend I was to you." Tamarra coughed a few times while she spoke, but managed to get out everything she wanted to say.

"Come on, Tamarra." Paige hadn't even put Tamarra down as much as she was now putting herself down. She honestly had not come there to get a deathbed confession from Tamarra.

"It's the truth. Call a thing a thing. I've watched *Iyanla: Fix My Life* enough times to know that I'm a thing. But I'm sorry. I'm so sorry about it all. Every lie, every moment of deceit, and about connecting you with a man who I knew meant the female species no good. I placed you in death's path, and now look at me." She raised her arms as best she could and then allowed them to fall.

"For the record, yes, I was upset," Paige admitted. "And hurt and disappointed. But some of the things you are saying, I never—"

"You never said them to me," Tamarra interrupted. "You never said them to anyone else, at least not that I heard. But at your angriest times, you had to have thought it, felt it. Because I know I sure did," Tamarra said. "When we were friends, when I used to hurt, you would hurt. When you would hurt, I would hurt, so when I hurt you . . . I was hurting as well. If that makes any sense."

"It does," Paige said. "And even though I did not come here seeking any type of apology from you whatsoever, I hear you. I hear your apology and the things you are apologizing for specifically, and I accept your apology. It is truly water under the bridge. I don't want to speak about it, and I don't want to think about it ever again. Okay?"

Tamarra nodded. "Okay."

"But since we are apologizing, I'm sorry for just completely cutting you off."

"I did hand you the scissors," Tamarra acknowledged.

"I'm sorry for getting physical with you," Paige continued. "I'm sorry for turning you away when you were trying to be there for me when I was going through that mess with Blake. I may not have wanted to be a friend to you, but in the midst of it all, you were still willing to try to be a friend to me. And Lord knows, I could have used one." Paige looked down.

"I get it," Tamarra said. "And I accept your apology. Like you said, it's water under the bridge. So we can start anew in fresh waters. How about that?"

Paige smiled. She began to fight back tears. "I just wish I hadn't waited so long," she said as her tears fell faster and flowed down her face. "There is just so much wasted time. So many things we could have done together. Moments we could have shared." Paige sniffed. "You were supposed to be my children's godmother."

Tamarra became teary eyed as well. "I thought we agreed to move forward, not backward."

Paige grabbed a tissue and wiped her tears away. "Yeah, you're right."

"So, this fresh start . . . Is it as friends, associates, or can we pick up where we left off and just be best friends?"

Paige looked at Tamarra. "Looks like what you need right now is a best friend."

"I think you're right," Tamarra said. "So in that case, can you pull open that drawer please?" Tamarra nodded to the nightstand that Paige was standing next to.

"This top drawer?" Paige asked as she bent to open the drawer. Tamarra nodded and Paige opened the drawer.

"There should be a document right there on top somewhere."

Paige fumbled around in the drawer a little bit.

"You'll know what I'm talking about when you see it," Tamarra remarked.

Paige was a bit confused at first, but then she knew instantly what Tamarra was referring to when she saw a document drafted to look as if it was an official court document. Paige paused, stared at it for a moment, and then slowly pulled it out of the drawer. She looked at Tamarra, then back at the document.

Using every ounce of strength she had, Tamarra turned her body toward the other nightstand and reached for the drawer. Paige raced around to the other side of the bed in an attempt to help her.

"Let me help you with that."

"No," Tamarra snapped. "I have to do this." She coughed.

Paige got tired and worked up a sweat herself just watching Tamarra scoot across the bed and open the drawer. It reminded her of the times she'd taught Adele or Norma to do something that they were having a hard time achieving. She'd wanted so badly to help them do it or to do it for them, but she could see their desire to accomplish the task themselves, without her.

Tamarra fiddled around in the drawer until she got her hands on whatever it was she was looking for. She finally pulled her hands out of the drawer, and dangling from her fingers was a pair of scissors. She lay flat on the bed, huffing and puffing, catching her breath. "I didn't have a problem handing you the scissors to cut me off. So it only makes sense that I hand you the scissors to get rid of the document you gave me to cut me off officially."

Paige looked down at the document she had retrieved from Tamarra's nightstand drawer. She remembered it well. It was the document she'd had Rudy draw up for her. It officially documented the fact that Paige was divorcing Tamarra as a friend. Paige looked up and saw that Tamarra was extending the scissors to her. Paige reached for the scissors, touching Tamarra's hand in the process. She took the scissors from Tamarra's hand and then proceeded to cut the document into pieces. Once Paige was all done, she threw the pieces into the trash can next to Tamarra's dresser.

"As far as I'm concerned, it never existed," Paige declared.

Tamarra smiled as she slid her hand forward and then extended it to Paige. "Friends?"

Paige stared at Tamarra's fragile hand as it quivered in the air. She reached out and took Tamarra's hand in hers. She then looked into Tamarra's eyes and said, "Best friends."

"Forever," Tamarra whispered.

Chapter 30

After Paige and Tamarra made their rekindled friendship official, the nurse and the other visitors, minus one, returned to the room. Paige excused herself and stepped out into the hallway to make a call. She had to call Samantha to let her know what was going on.

"Hey, Sam. How's it going?"

"It's going great. The girls and I just got back to my place," Samantha said through the phone receiver. "I thought you guys would be up in the air. Are you at a layover or something?"

Paige exhaled. "There was a slight change in plans. I uh, didn't get on the plane."

"What?" Samantha said, shocked.

"Did you get the girls' book bags?" Paige asked, setting up the story to tell Samantha.

"Yes, a Lorain gave them to me."

"Yeah, well, Lorain used to attend my church. We have mutual friends. Long story short, she shared with me that one of my best friends, who I hadn't been in touch with for years, was dying."

"Oh, no! That's horrible."

Just then Paige heard the doorbell ring. She continued talking with Samantha. "Yes, and she also told me that the doctors didn't think she would make it through the week. So I just couldn't get on that plane, knowing there was a chance she might be gone when I returned."

"I completely get it. But what did everyone else say about canceling the trip?"

"Everyone else went. I'm the only one who stayed behind," Paige said.

"Oh, my."

"But, anyway, I was wondering, since you planned on keeping the girls for a week, anyway . . . I'd really appreciate it if—"

"Say no more," Samantha said before Paige could even finish her sentence. "You spend every moment you can with your dear friend. And if you need anything, anything at all, you just let me know."

Paige let out a sigh of relief. "Thank you so much, Samantha. Girl, I love you so much. You have always been there for me and the girls."

"And I always will be. I love you too. Take care of yourself and check in to keep me informed, and I'll let Mom and Dad know what's going on."

"I will. Thanks again, Sam. Good-bye."

Paige ended her call with Samantha. She'd call the Vanderdales later so that they could hear what was going on from her as well. Right now, she wanted to go back in there and spend more time with Tamarra. Paige put her phone away.

"Paige, honey, is that you?"

Paige turned to see Pastor Margie coming up the steps. "Pastor!" Paige met her pastor at the top landing, and the two embraced in a hug.

"I'm so glad to see you here," Pastor Margie said as she parted from Paige. "I tried to call you."

"I know. I saw where you called me. I had honestly planned on calling you back, because I wanted to let you know what was going on. It's just that I was so busy planning the wedding—"

"Wedding?" Pastor Margie asked.

"Yes, wedding," Paige confirmed. "I'm sorry, Pastor. I did have every intention of telling you about Ryan."

"Ryan?" Pastor Margie had never met Ryan before.

In the past Paige and Ryan had never stayed connected long enough. It was one of those things where you didn't introduce the person you were dating to all your friends and family until you had been dating awhile, were exclusive, and knew you wanted to be together. Well, whenever Ryan and Paige would get to that point, life would happen. Kind of like it was happening now. This time, however, Paige had no intention of excluding Ryan from her life while she dealt with her situation with Tamarra. Once he returned, Paige wanted very much for him to be by her side through all of this. But judging by the way Ryan had turned away from her at the airport, by the words he'd spoken and the way he'd spoken them, Paige wasn't sure she could say he felt the same about her.

"Yes, Ryan," Paige said and then went on to give Pastor Margie a brief history of her and Ryan's relationship, all the way up to their plans to leave on a plane to get married, her not going, and her coming to see about Tamarra instead.

"I know it must have been hard not to get on that plane," Pastor Margie told Paige, "but obedience to the Lord is better than the sacrifice of the flesh."

"Haven't I learned that the hard way?" Paige joked.

Pastor Margie put her arm around Paige. "It's all going to work out. For now, let me go in here and see about Tamarra." She put her arms down to her sides and looked at Paige. "Were you coming or going?"

"I'm heading back in the room," Paige answered. Paige turned, walked the few steps back to Tamarra's room, and entered. "I'm back, and I brought even more company." Pastor Margie stepped into the room.

"Pastor," Tamarra said, glad to see her former pastor. "You came back."

"Didn't I tell you I would?" Pastor Margie smiled. "I'm just praying I'm going to walk through that front door and find you in the kitchen, making some of your famous macaroni and cheese."

Everyone in the room laughed. Macaroni and cheese had always been Tamarra's signature dish.

"Well, unless Unique gets down in that kitchen and burns, it ain't gon' happen." Tamarra laughed.

"A girl can dream, can't she?" Pastor Margie walked over and patted Tamarra on the hand. She nodded and said her hellos to everyone else in the room whom she hadn't already greeted.

Tamarra broke out in a coughing spell.

"Is she okay?" Paige asked, concerned. "She coughs a lot, like she can't catch her breath."

"Yeah, she'll be fine," her mother said as she stood over her daughter, rubbing her head.

The nurse was preparing a needle for some type of injection.

"What's that?" Paige asked.

"Just something to make her comfortable," the nurse answered as she proceeded to find a vein to inject the fluid in. "The doctor said that if she wanted something on a regular basis, we could set up an IV, but Tamarra declined. She's tough." She winked at her patient.

Paige stood to the side, watching. She was clueless as to what was going on with Tamarra's body and why she was worse off than Blake. Blake looked bad, but he wasn't on his deathbed, like Tamarra was. But what they did have in common was that they'd both given up.

"Comfortable how?" Paige asked. "Is it, like, a medicine for the virus? I don't understand." Paige's curiosity was mixed with frustration.

Sensing this, the nurse looked at Tamarra. Her eyes asked for permission to clue Paige in on Tamarra's health status.

Tamarra nodded and said, "She's my best friend. You can tell her everything."

The nurse informed Paige about the different HIV virus strains and explained how Tamarra's had turned into full-blown AIDS. She told her that the virus that had been transmitted to Tamarra was resistant to the drugs the doctors were using to treat Tamarra. Therefore, the drug therapies hadn't worked on Tamarra.

"In all honesty, I probably contributed to the fact that they haven't worked." Tamarra said. "Upon learning that I was HIV positive, I both thought and spoke death over my life. That was it for me, the straw that broke the camel's back. Seems like I'd been fighting ever since I came out of the womb. I didn't want to fight to the grave. Just wanted to go peacefully. So I didn't fight. Never threw one punch at the disease."

The nurse took over. "Yeah, at first she took all the meds prescribed and did everything the doctors were telling her, only to find out it was like taking sugar pills."

Tamarra interjected, "The treatment and doctor visits drained me of every penny I'd earned. I just couldn't do it. I didn't want to do it."

"And I feel so bad that I just picked up to Atlanta and left you hanging," Unique said.

"You didn't know," Tamarra said. "I'd told you only that I was sick, not the severity of it. Besides, there was nothing you could have done."

"I could have taken over the business," Unique said. "I could have—"

Tamarra put her hand up. "We're not going to do coulda, woulda, shouldas. Everything is what it is. No turning back."

On that note, Unique remained silent. She then looked at the clock on Tamarra's nightstand. "I'm supposed to be having dinner with Mom, my little sisters, and my grandmother tonight," Unique said. "I better get ready to head out. But I'll be back afterward."

Paige recalled how Lorain had told her Unique had been sitting up all night with Tamarra.

"Why don't you take a break and enjoy the evening with your family?" Paige suggested. She then looked at Tamarra. "If it's all right with my best friend, I'm going to go home, pack a bag, and then come back. It's been a long time since we've had a slumber party."

Tamarra smiled. "Don't forget to stop and get the ice cream." She winked.

"I won't," Paige said.

"Are you sure you're good staying?" Unique asked.

"Positive," Paige assured her. "Go on and spend some time with your family. I'm sure they miss you dearly with you living down South and all."

"Well, okay then." Unique looked at Tamarra. "I guess I'll see you tomorrow, then." She kissed Tamarra on the forehead.

"I'll walk out with you," the other visitor said.

"And I guess I'll go check on that old bear of mine downstairs, to see if he needs anything," Mrs. Evans said.

"Don't worry. I'll be right here by Tamarra's side," the nurse said.

Even though Paige had her luggage packed in the car, the apparel was more appropriate for walks on the beach in the Dominican Republic. Her nighties were for Ryan's eyes only. "I'll be back soon," Paige said as everyone who was leaving headed for the exit.

"Wait," Tamarra called out, then looked directly at Paige when she turned around. "If it's not asking too much, can you do something for me before you go?"

"Sure," Paige said.

"One day I came to visit New Day. I sat in the back, with a large brimmed hat on. I left before service was over. I didn't want to stir up any drama in the church." Tamarra coughed.

"Take your time, baby," Tamarra's mother said to her.

Tamarra took a breath. "You were singing a solo that day. I never cried so hard, listening to you sing. It was the same week I'd found out I was HIV positive. As you sang those words, I felt as if you were speaking on my behalf. So if you don't mind, can you sing it again for me?"

"Right now?" Paige asked. She was hoping to God that Tamarra wasn't asking her to sing at her funeral. Although her death was inevitable, Paige didn't want to think about it in this moment.

Tamarra nodded.

"Which song was it?"

"'Take Me to the King,'" Pastor Margie answered on Tamarra's behalf. She looked at Tamarra and said, "I saw you out there in the congregation that day. By the time I finished preaching, you were gone." She looked at Paige. "It was 'Take Me to the King,'" she repeated.

Paige closed her eyes and stepped back toward Tamarra's bed as she said, "Paige sat on the wall. Paige had a great fall. All the king's horses and all the king's men couldn't put Paige back together again. So take me to the king." There wasn't a dry eye in the room as Paige began to sing the popular Tamela Mann song.

When Paige finished, she used her hand to wipe away the tears that were streaming down Tamarra's face. When Paige had the HIV scare, she'd studied up on the disease. Scientists had not found that it could be transmitted through tears. But right now, the way Paige was feeling, she didn't care if Tamarra had Ebola. She was going to wipe away the tears of the only woman she'd ever called a best friend in her entire adulthood.

Tamarra had prayed for Paige. She'd been a mentor to Paige and someone to look up to when Paige had been newly saved and was trying to stay saved. That was why it had hurt Paige so much when she found out about Tamarra's betrayal. But Paige had gotten over it. She'd moved on, and unfortunately, there had been a plethora of other things waiting to hurt Paige ten times more, but she'd survived. She was still standing.

She looked at Tamarra, and nothing negative they had gone through mattered anymore. Yes, Paige was still standing, and she was going to stand by her friend until Tamarra took her last breath.

Chapter 31

By the time Paige made it back to Tamarra's house, Pastor Margie was gone. The nurse let Paige in because both Mr. and Mrs. Evans were in bed. Paige sat her overnight bag down at the foot of the steps, then headed to the kitchen with the tub of ice cream in hand. She scooped ice cream into a single bowl and retrieved two spoons. She put the tub in the freezer and then headed up the steps, grabbing her overnight bag along the way.

The house was quiet, so Paige tried to be as quiet as she could. She wasn't sure if Tamarra was asleep or not. She opened the door to Tamarra's room a crack. The nurse was standing over Tamarra, checking her vitals. The room was dim; the only light was from the flat-screen television hanging on the wall in front of Tamarra's bed.

Tamarra looked past the nurse and saw Paige as she entered the room. Tamarra smiled.

"I'm back." Paige sat her overnight bag at the door.

The nurse finished up with Tamarra and asked her, "Do you want me to get extra bedding for Paige or something?"

"Oh, no," Paige answered for Tamarra.

Tamarra confirmed Paige's sentiments. "Do you know how many slumber parties we've had right here in this bed?" Tamarra patted the space next to her.

"Well, all right now," the nurse said and smiled. "We can never get too old for a slumber party with our bestie."

"Amen to that," Paige attested.

"Well, if you girls need anything, just let me know. I'm right down the hall," the nurse said. She looked at Tamarra. "I suppose we won't need the monitor on tonight." She pointed at the little white intercom box that was beside the lamp on the nightstand.

"Oh, you can turn that off," Tamarra said. "Girl talk is sacred. You know that, Betty," Tamarra said to her nurse.

Betty gathered a few things and then headed out of the room after telling Paige and Tamarra good night.

Paige stood by the doorway for a moment.

"Well, what's that you got there?" Tamarra asked her.

Paige looked down at the bowl. "Pecan pra-
line, of course," she said, then walked over to
the chair that was next to Tamarra's bed. Before
sitting, Paige said to her friend, "Open wide."

Tamarra played along, opening her mouth as
wide as she could. Paige scooped up a little bit of
the ice cream with the spoon, minus any pecans.
She wasn't sure if Tamarra could chew and
swallow them. She fed the portion to Tamarra,
who inhaled it.

"Girl, when was the last time you had some ice
cream?" Paige asked.

"Child, these folks around here won't give me
anything. They act like I'm dying or something."
Tamarra broke out in a laugh.

Paige didn't find it funny, so she just sat there.

"Come on now, Paige. You gotta laugh to keep
from crying," Tamarra said. "Besides, you know
that was funny."

To appease Tamarra, Paige let out a chuckle.
Then another. Before she knew it, she and
Tamarra were roaring with laughter.

When the laughter finally died down, Tamarra
said, "Thank God Betty doesn't have the intercom on. She'd probably call the crazy house to
come haul me away."

"And me right along with you," Paige said.

Tamarra exhaled. "Now, didn't that laughter feel good?"

Paige nodded and then looked down.

"Sit that bowl down and get on over here," Tamarra said, inviting Paige to climb on the bed.

"Let me go get out of these clothes first," Paige said, looking down at the khaki pants and the Old Navy ribbed Henley she was wearing. "I know how you are about folks wearing street clothes while sitting on your bed." Tamarra used to have a fit when Paige came into Tamarra's room and sat down on the bed in her street clothes.

"Don't be bringing all those outside particles and germs from the public places you been sitting at into my nice clean bed," Tamarra would say.

Tamarra stared at her friend, her eyes pleading for Paige to just come next to her. Even if she had on a winter coat and boots, Tamarra's expression made it clear to Paige that getting on the bed in clothing was now the least of Tamarra's concerns.

Paige sat the bowl of ice cream down and took off her shoes. She then walked around to the empty side of the bed and climbed on it. Paige didn't get under the covers, though. "So what are we watching?" she asked as she looked at the television.

"The only show in the world you don't have to DVR, because you'll find it on any given channel at any hour of the day."

"*Law & Order,*" Paige said.

"You know it," Tamarra said. "Just like old times, indeed."

For the next twenty minutes or so, Tamarra and Paige lay in the bed, watching television. They were exhausted, and it didn't take long for both of them to drift off.

Paige was supposed to be spending the next seven days in paradise. Instead, she would be spending the next seven days cooped up with her friend. A slight smile parted her lips as she slept, and it looked as though there wasn't anywhere else she would rather be.

Early the next morning, Paige awoke to the sound of Betty entering the room to look in on Tamarra.

"Did you two sleep tight?" she whispered, so as not to wake Tamarra, who was still sleeping. Before Paige could even answer, she continued. "You didn't even get into your nightclothes, I see."

Paige looked down at herself and saw that she was still very much fully clothed. "I guess not." She sat up and stretched. "Yesterday was such a busy day. All that ripping and running and packing I did." Just then Paige thought about Ryan. She got out of the bed and walked over to her purse, which was sitting next to her overnight bag.

"Is everything okay?" Betty asked.

"Yes. There's just a phone call I need to make." Paige dug her phone out of her purse. The first thing she did was check it to see if she'd missed any calls from Ryan. The phone was dead. "Darn it," Paige said. "My phone died." She dug through her overnight bag until she retrieved her charger.

While Betty proceeded to check on Tamarra, Paige took her phone, charger, and overnight bag into the bathroom. She plugged the phone into the charger, and the charger into the outlet, and then did her business on the commode. After washing her hands and drying them, Paige turned on her phone, which had just enough juice to come on. While it powered up, she walked over to the linen closet and got a towel and washcloth. She pulled all her toiletries out of her bag and brushed her teeth, doing a thorough job since she hadn't brushed them before going to sleep last night. Her breath was probably so bad, she feared Ryan would smell it through the phone. Once her breath was nice and minty, she grabbed her phone and dialed Ryan's number.

"This number cannot currently receive calls," was the recorded message Paige heard after the first ring. She hung up, remembering that Ryan had suspended his phone service temporarily. The international phone plan offered by his cell phone carrier wasn't worth the price. He wanted to take his phone on the trip in order to take pictures, but he didn't want to risk getting charged for roaming, receiving texts, or anything else, even though he was told by his service provider he could just turn his data off. Still, with the prices they were charging, he didn't want to take the chance of slipping up, so he'd suspended his service.

He planned on getting an international phone once they arrived at their destination so that the boys and his neighbor would be able to reach him. They were all going to share the phone while on vacation, so no one else had gotten any type of international plan on their phone, either. Since they were all going to be together, they figured it made sense. At the time it had. But now that Paige didn't have the number, it seemed like a stupid idea.

"Dang it." She went and flopped down on the toilet lid. Now she'd have to play the waiting game and be patient until Ryan reached out to her. She couldn't recall whether or not they were on the same time zone in the Dominican Republic as she was.

Paige showered and got dressed. The bathroom was filled with the fresh, flowery scent of one of her favorite Bath & Body Works products. By the time she came out of the bathroom, Mr. Evans and Mrs. Evans had joined Betty in Tamarra's room.

"Good morning," Paige said, exiting the bathroom.

"Good morning to you, sweetie." Mrs. Evans walked over and gave Paige a hug.

"How you doing?" Mr. Evans asked Paige.

"Just fine, sir. And yourself?" She looked from Tamarra's father to her mother. "How are both of you?" Paige could not imagine what it must be like to wake up in the morning and not know if your child was alive or not.

"We are just fine," Mrs. Evans said. "It's this one here we're worried about." She nodded toward Tamarra.

"Hey, you," Paige said, then went to give Tamarra a kiss on the forehead.

"Good morning, girl," Tamarra replied. "Hey, did you see who raped and killed that girl on the show last night?"

"I was out like a log, just like you," Paige told her.

"Then I guess we should have DVRed it," Tamarra said, and she and Paige laughed.

"I'm going to go whip up a little something for breakfast," Betty said. "I'll make enough for everybody." She walked to the door. "And I already know, Uncle Russ," she said, looking at Mr. Evans. "Don't burn the bacon."

Everyone laughed but Paige. It had be an inside joke. Betty exited the room.

"That's your niece?" Paige asked Tamarra's father.

"My niece-in-law," he replied. "From my wife's side of the family."

"She's a nurse over in West Virginia," Mrs. Evans said. "As a matter of fact, Unique used to work at the nursing home my niece works at. Ain't that something? I mean, what are the odds of that?"

"Trust me. I know about that whole 'six degrees of separation' thing," Paige said, thinking about Blake being Miss Nettie's son.

"Anyway, when we found out they were sending Tamarra home to . . . for hospice, my sister,

Betty's mother, had her come up," Mrs. Evans said. "And she's doing it out of the kindness of her heart. God bless her soul."

"Even if she was charging us money," Mr. Evans said, chiming in, "there isn't enough money in the world to pay her for what she's doing for us."

"That's such a blessing," Paige said. She looked at Tamarra. "Do you need me to help you get cleaned up or anything?"

"That's okay. My mom helps me," Tamarra said.

"Well, I'm here now," Paige said. "I have someone keeping my kids for me, so I'll at least be here the next six days." Paige looked at Mrs. Evans. "After that she's all yours." She turned back to Tamarra and pointed. "But for now she's all mine."

"You are a good friend, indeed," Mrs. Evans said. "Everything Tamarra has told us about you is true. No wonder you've been her best friend all these years."

"Yeah, no wonder." Paige winked at Tamarra.

"Well then, the mister and I are going to head downstairs while you get her together," Mrs. Evans said to Paige.

"See you in a minute, Mom and Dad," Tamarra said as her parents left the room.

Paige watched the door close behind Tamarra's parents. "It's beautiful to see you interacting with your parents like this."

"There is nothing like the power of forgiveness," Tamarra said.

"Touché." Paige smiled.

Paige knew how hard it was for Tamarra to live with the fact that her parents blamed her for her older brother molesting her when she was a child, abuse that had started when she was just ten years old. It had resulted in Tamarra giving birth to a child she couldn't even look at. When Tamarra had told her parents about her brother having sex with her, they'd protected him. They'd faked a divorce. Mr. Evans had had Tamarra's brother live with him, while Mrs. Evans had raised Tamarra. Once Tamarra and her brother were of age, her parents had reunited, and they'd raised the child Tamarra had given birth to as their own. Tamarra's estranged daughter had ended up dying in a car accident before Tamarra could ever form a relationship with her.

Not only had Tamarra had to deal with the death of her daughter, whom her brother had fathered, but she had had to find the courage to finally forgive her brother. It was kind of like how Paige had forgiven Tamarra. Even though Tamarra forgave her brother, she still had nothing to do with him. No one could really blame her for that one. Forgiving him alone had taken a lot.

Paige walked to the bathroom and opened the door. "Is this your towel and washcloth hanging up in here? The plum-colored ones?"

"Yeah, those are it," Tamarra answered.

Paige ran some water in the sink and poured in some of Tamarra's own Bath & Body Works shower gel. For the next half hour Paige washed Tamarra. She was about ready to call someone for assistance when she realized Tamarra was wearing a grown-up diaper. She decided against it, not wanting to make Tamarra feel embarrassed. So she said a silent prayer and changed her diaper and cleaned every nook, cranny, and crevice of Tamarra's body. She lotioned her up with the lotion that matched the shower gel. She put a fresh nightgown on her. It was a little strenuous at times, but Paige managed.

"You sure you don't want to at least call my mother up here to help?" Tamarra asked her midway through the process. "Sometimes Betty even has to help her."

"No, I got it," was all Paige kept saying. And finally, she did get it. Tamarra was smelling good and feeling fresh, thanks to Paige. Once Paige was finished, she went to sit down, but a few seconds later she heard the sound of a ringing cell phone coming from the bathroom.

"Oh, my phone." She ran into the bathroom to catch the call before it went to voice mail. She didn't even bother wasting time by looking down at the caller ID. "Hello," Paige answered.

"Good morning. How are you?"

The biggest smile ever spread across Paige's entire face. She was so relieved. She unplugged her phone from the charger and went and sat down on the toilet lid. "I'm good, now that you've called," Paige said. "Ryan, about how we left things. I'm—"

"Look, I didn't call to get all into that right now," Ryan said, cutting her off. "Your mom and dad wanted to call and talk to you."

Before Paige could say anything, the phone had been passed to her parents.

"Hey, Daddy's baby girl," Paige heard her father say through the phone. "Your mother is standing right here with me, with her ear to the phone."

"Hey, Daddy. Hey, Mom." Paige chuckled at the fact that her parents had no idea they could put the phone on speaker. But she liked picturing them side by side, talking to her on the phone. "How is it there?"

"It would be much better if you were here," Mrs. Robinson said. "But I have to tell you that it's beautiful!"

"Just gorgeous. We didn't think anything would top our trip to Puerto Rico, but this is awesome," Mr. Robinson said.

"How's Tamarra?" Mrs. Robinson asked, her voice now more melancholy.

"Hanging in there," Paige replied.

"Well, let her know that we are all concerned," Mrs. Robinson said.

"Look at all that food!" Paige could hear her father exclaim in the background. She could hear other voices too. It sounded like Ryan and his parents.

"What a feast," her mother said into the phone. "We're down in the resort restaurant. Honey, you should see this spread."

"Well, I wish I was there to see it, Ma," Paige said sadly. "But you guys go ahead and eat. Put Ry—"

"Okay, honey," Mrs. Robinson said, cutting Paige off. "We'll talk to you later."

The phone went dead in Paige's ear. She looked down at the phone. It hurt her feelings that the only reason why Ryan had called was that her parents had asked him to. It was her parents who had wanted to check in with Paige, not him.

She probably would have never even heard his voice if her parents had their own cell phone and knew how to use one. The last thing Paige was going to do was sit in that bathroom and have a pity party, not with her best friend fighting for her life on the other side of the door.

Paige stood up, but before going back out there with Tamarra, she figured she would call the Vanderdales and tell them everything that was going on. She dialed Mrs. Vanderdale's cell phone. Mrs. Vanderdale picked up on the second ring.

"Paige, honey," Mrs. Vanderdale said, "I was going to give you until this afternoon, and then I was going to call you. What in the world is going on? Sam said you didn't go to the Dominican. Something about a sick friend."

"Yes, that's right. I'm still here in Ohio." Paige gave Mrs. Vanderdale the short version of why she didn't get on the plane.

"Well, whatever is meant to be is meant to be. I'm going to be praying for your friend, and your and Ryan's relationship."

"Thank you, Naomi. I appreciate that."

"The girls came over for breakfast. Do you want to speak to them?"

Paige lit up. "Yes, let me speak to the little divas please."

"Okay. Hold on."

A few seconds later Paige could hear Mrs. Vanderdale put the phone on speaker.

"Hi, Mommy," the girls sang in unison.

"Hi, babies," Paige said. "You guys having fun?"

"Yeah. Are you?" Adele said.

"Well, yeah." Paige wasn't quite sure what to say to the girls. She thought for a second and then decided not to mention to them that she hadn't gone out of the country.

"Me and Norma decided you don't have to bring us back a souvenir, since you are bringing us back a daddy," Adele said. "Right, Norma?"

"Right!" Norma confirmed. "Ryan will be our daddy when he gets back. He won't be our real daddy."

"Our real daddy is Norman," Adele said. "But we're gonna have a new daddy."

"We're going to have a new daddy," the girls sang in unison.

"Girls, tell your mommy good-bye," Paige heard Mrs. Vanderdale say in the background.

Mrs. Vanderdale to the rescue, Paige thought.

"Bye, Mommy. We love you!" the girls chorused.

"Bye. I love you guys too," Paige said.

Mrs. Vanderdale took the phone off speaker.

There was a few seconds of silence. "What are you going to tell them? Have you talked to Ryan? Are you guys just going to go ahead and get married when he gets back?"

Mrs. Vanderdale's questions were hitting Paige like a tornado. "I don't know. I don't know anything right now."

"Okay, well, I won't hold you. I'm so glad you called."

"Thank you, and thank you again for helping Sam with the girls."

"These are my grandbabies. That's what grandmothers are for. You take care of yourself, and take care of your friend."

"I will. Talk to you soon." Paige ended the call.

She flopped back down on the toilet lid, not quite ready to leave the pity party, after all. Hearing her girls' words frolic through her head about their souvenir being Ryan coming back as their daddy just broke her heart because she had absolutely no idea where she and Ryan stood. "Well, girls . . . ," Paige said aloud, then exhaled. "You just might get that puppy you've been wanting, after all." She had to do something to make up for the fact that they wouldn't have a daddy . . . again.

Chapter 32

Paige had now spent three nights at Tamarra's and hadn't talked to Ryan since that one time he'd phoned her for her parents. She'd called the phone once, and his mother and father, who, unlike her parents, managed to do the basics on a cell phone, had answered. They'd just happened to have the phone in their room. They assured Paige, though, that they would let Ryan know she'd called to check in.

Ryan's silence truly saddened her heart, but what saddened Paige's heart even more was the fact that Tamarra seemed to be having more and more coughing spells. She was less talkative and hadn't even wanted to get washed up this morning. It was a fight for Betty to even change her diaper. Tamarra complained of pain. Whatever Betty had been giving her to make her comfortable was obviously no longer working. In spite of getting into a tiff with her mother, Tamarra opted to no longer take it.

Over the past couple days Paige had lain in bed with Tamarra and had told her all that had gone on in her life right up to not boarding that plane. When Tamarra learned of the sacrifice Paige had made for her, she'd gone into a coughing and crying spell. During their many conversations Tamarra had reiterated to Paige that she had never really put on her boxing gloves to fight this HIV turned AIDS thing. And Paige hated to admit it, but as she looked in Tamarra's eyes now as she sat by her bedside, she saw absolutely no fight at all.

"Hey, girl," Unique said to Tamarra as she entered the room. She looked at Paige and Tamarra's mother, who were also in the room. She then greeted them. Unique noticed that she got a head nod and a smile, but no one really spoke. Immediately, the heavy spirit invading the room took over Unique's being too. She instantly went into a slump. "She feeling any better since last night?" Unique asked Mrs. Evans. When Unique had left Tamarra's bedside last evening, Tamarra had been vomiting.

Mrs. Evans shook her head. Tamarra just lay there. Her eyes were closed, but she wasn't asleep.

Paige had her head down. She didn't want anyone to see the tears that were building up in her eyes.

Just then someone else entered the room. Mrs. Evans stood. "Hello, Pastor." She walked over and greeted with a hug the gentleman who had just arrived, carrying a Bible. She then turned to Paige. "Paige, this is the pastor of Tamarra's church. Reverend Fields."

"Pleased to meet you, Reverend Fields." Paige went to stand.

"Oh, no need to get up," Reverend Fields said, using his hand to signal to Paige to stay seated. He looked at Unique. "Nice to see you again."

"You too, Reverend," Unique said in a dry voice. The energy in the room was just so low.

"Well, I came to give my sister a word of encouragement," Reverend Fields said, looking at Tamarra and smiling. "If you ladies don't mind, I'd like to read a scripture and then pray."

"Oh, we don't mind at all," Mrs. Evans said.

Granted permission, the reverend opened his Bible and read from the Old Testament. After that he went into prayer. With each word he said, a powerful energy shot through the atmosphere in the room.

"Glory!" Mrs. Evans shouted. "Ooh, I'm sorry," she said, apologizing. She wasn't sure whether nowadays it was against protocol to make a sound if the man of God was speaking. She hadn't visited a church in some time.

"It's okay," Reverend Fields assured her. "I know you said you don't really go to church a lot, but when the spirit hits, it don't care about whether or not you go to church every Sunday. All it cares about is that you know God. That you love God. That you know Jesus. That you love Jesus. That you believe the Holy Spirit is your comforter. That God, Jesus, and the Holy Spirit are one and the same. That Jesus died on the cross for the remission of our sins and that He rose and is at the right hand of the throne. Do you believe?"

"Yes, my God, I believe," Mrs. Evans said, tears falling from her eyes. She was still standing. Her hands were clasped together, and she was bouncing her body slightly.

Reverend Fields began speaking to Tamarra. "And I need you to believe, Miss Tamarra, that the battle is not yours. That the war has already been won, and that you have the victory. The Bible says that in the end you win!" Reverend Fields said, his prayer turning into full-blown preaching. He went to Tamarra's bedside. Even though Tamarra didn't open her eyes once, she was awake. Reverend Fields knew his words were penetrating her soul. He could tell when her bottom lip trembled a couple times.

"Jesus loves us in spite of us," Reverend Fields continued. "Tamarra, Jesus loves you in spite of you. No matter what you think about yourself. No matter what others think about you. No matter what you've done in your past. No matter who saw you do it. You are a child of the King. You are welcomed in His Kingdom. His *casa es su casa*. So when you close your eyes for the last time, when you take your last breath, know within your heart that you are going home."

Tamarra began to nod her belief.

"Daughter, fear not this thing called death, because you are going home!" Reverend Fields shouted.

Finally, Tamarra opened her eyes and streams of tears, which had been trapped beneath her lids, ran down her face. She moved her mouth, but nothing came out. She even tried to move her body, but she didn't have any strength.

It was so evident to Tamarra's supporters in the room that she wished only that she could get up out of that bed and praise God. Seeing that desire and wanting to fulfill it for her best friend, Paige stood up out of her chair, walked over to her friend, and began praising God for Tamarra. She allowed the Holy Ghost to order the steps of her feet as she danced a praiseful dance.

Within seconds, Unique was standing by Tamarra's bedside as well. She too began to call out the name of Jesus on behalf of her former boss and friend. Before she knew it, her feet were stomping and dancing in praise as well. Next, Mrs. Evans began to praise on her daughter's behalf. And so all the women in the room stood in the gap for their sister, friend, and daughter and did what she didn't have the strength to do, which was stand to her feet and praise the Lord.

Tears streamed down Tamarra's face as she watched the women she loved intercede on her behalf. They were, indeed, the women she loved. And clearly, the women loved her as well. With friends like these, the enemy didn't stand a chance at taking her soul.

"My sincere condolences to you."

All day visitors had been coming and going from Tamarra's house, reciting such sentiments.

During the night, hours after the women had praised up a storm at Tamarra's bedside, Tamarra had closed her eyes for the final time. When Paige had woken up next to Tamarra that next morning, like she had the past six mornings, she had looked over at Tamarra. In her spirit she'd known her friend was not just sleeping but had gone on to be with the Lord. Paige had kissed Tamarra on the cheek and had held her lifeless body for a couple minutes before she had summoned anyone. She'd used that time to whisper in her friend's ear and tell her how much she loved her and what an honor it had been to spend those last days with her. Before Paige had left the room, she'd turned around in the doorway, looked at Tamarra, and said, "And on the seventh day, she rested."

Paige had remained at the house to support Mr. and Mrs. Evans during the aftermath of the loss of their daughter. Friends and church members had been coming and going. The food, cards, and flowers they brought were starting to pile up. Paige, Betty, and Unique helped organize everything and kept visitors company if the Evans were having a moment where they just wanted to be alone and grieve.

Paige had planned on meeting Ryan and their parents at the airport. Their flight landed in one hour, but she just didn't feel like it was a good time to leave the Evans. Besides, Ryan had gone an entire week, with the exception of that one time, without talking to Paige. She couldn't imagine he'd miss her at the airport. In addition to that, she'd come this far in being there for Tamarra, and there was no need for her to bail now.

"Paige, dear, I can't thank you enough for all you've done this past week," Mrs. Evans said after she pulled Paige to the side. "You truly are a good friend."

All Paige could do was nod. She honestly didn't feel as though she'd been a good friend to Tamarra. For the past week she'd been by Tamarra's bedside, but where was she when Tamarra found out she'd tested positive for the deadly disease?

"I know you loved Tamarra just as much as we did, and the service is going to be hard, but can I trouble you by asking that you sing at Tamarra's funeral?" Mrs. Evans broke down in tears. "I really don't know who else to ask, and I know how much she loves that one song you sang."

Paige took Mrs. Evans in her arms and held her. "It's okay. Everything is going to be all right. And of course I'm going to sing at my best friend's funeral. I wouldn't have it any other way."

"Thank you." Mrs. Evans sniffed.

Paige smiled. It truly felt like an honor to be asked to be a part of the service.

"I think I'm going to go lie down for a spell. I hate to keep running off and leaving you with all these folks."

"Please don't apologize. This is what I'm here for," Paige said. "You go on and get you some rest. I'll receive the guests."

"Thank you, baby." She went to walk away but then stopped to say something else to Paige. "We're going to the funeral home tomorrow to finalize things for the funeral since it's in two days. You think you might—"

Paige held her hand up to stop Mrs. Evans's words. "Say no more. I'm there."

Mrs. Evans smiled, wiped a tear, and then walked away. Paige watched with complete sadness at the older woman walk away with her head hung low.

Lord, give me strength, Paige said to herself, because God knows, she needed it. She still had to make it through the funeral and face Ryan eventually . . . and her daughters. She didn't need just strength. She needed a miracle.

Chapter 33

"And now we'll have a song from Tamarra's best friend, Paige Vanderdale."

As Paige stood from the first pew of Tamarra's church, she regretted telling Tamarra's mother that she would sing at the funeral. Paige had been crying nonstop ever since she'd walked into the church for the viewing of the body at nine o'clock this morning. Only two days had passed since Tamarra's death. She had thought she'd be all cried out by the time she was called upon to sing today. It was now 10:30 a.m., just a half hour into the actual funeral service.

Paige's legs wobbled as she made the short trek to the altar. She had no idea where she would get the strength to just stand there, let alone belt out a song.

"Come on, Paige," she heard someone say. She recognize the voice as belonging to Pastor Margie. She was sitting up in the pulpit, along with three other pastors, one being Pastor Fields, of course.

When Paige reached the podium, she looked out at those in the sanctuary. It was practically full. Paige didn't recognize most of the people. She figured they were probably members of the church, as well as clients Tamarra had worked for over the years. But on the second pew on the right, she recognized a string of faces. Lorain, Unique, Eleanor, Deborah, Helen, and even Mother Doreen were present. Zelda was there. She too was a former member of New Day. Like Tamarra, Zelda was in the food service business. She worked at a restaurant in Malvonia that everyone frequented.

Then, of course, Tamarra was present: she lay there as peacefully as ever, looking like an angel from above in her casket. All the New Day Divas were present in one room. Paige couldn't remember the last time that had happened. Paige smiled when she even spotted Nita, the woman in charge of the New Day Janitorial Ministry as well as the SWATC Ministry, which stood for Sheltered Women and Their Children. It was a ministry that was born when Nita, a domestic violence survivor, noticed signs of abuse in Paige and reached out to help her deal with her abusive relationship with Blake.

It was like a gust of wind, a fresh wind, swept through the place. It carried in the strength Paige would need to soar proudly before everyone like an eagle. And that feeling brought a sudden change for Paige. Originally, she was going to sing the song Tamarra loved for her to sing, the one by Tamela Mann. But now she wanted to sing one that would express how she truly felt about her dear friend. And at the same time it would be a message to her friends who were still among the living. It was too late for her to share this with Tamarra, but she wouldn't wait another second to share how she felt with the ones who had been named her church family.

Before taking the final step that would place her behind the microphone, she walked over to the pianist, who was going to play "Take Me to the King" for her. She whispered something in the woman's ear. The woman nodded and then Paige walked over back toward the microphone.

"Good morning," Paige greeted everyone through the microphone. She didn't wait for a reply, knowing that for most, it felt like anything but a good morning. "I was asked by the family to sing today at my best friend's funeral. I told them yes, but just a few seconds ago I didn't know if I'd have the strength to stand here and do so. I had to remind myself that I can do all things through Christ, who strengthens me."

"Amen," was called out throughout the sanctuary.

"But for years," Paige continued, "when I felt weak, like I didn't have the strength to do something, I would lie down and do nothing. I would cut everyone in my life off and just wallow in my own misery. I would even turn my face from God. But He never turned His face from me."

"That's right," someone called out.

"Sadly, though," Paige said, "I even turned away from my friends. From the people who loved me." She looked at Tamarra, lying in the casket. She looked back at the audience. "Any hurt and pain I was feeling, I clung to it. And no matter who had caused me the hurt and pain, I held on to the just cause of why I shouldn't allow them to be a part of my life or why I wouldn't be a part of theirs." Once again Paige looked down at Tamarra. "Tamarra was one of those people." Paige's voice cracked, and her eyes filled with tears.

"It's all right," someone said, encouraging Paige to continue.

Paige closed her eyes and gathered her composure. She then opened her eyes and gazed at the audience. "I look out here today, and I see so many people who love Tamarra. Tamarra used to say that when I hurt, she hurt. She might have been able to feel my pain, but today, looking out here at all of you, I feel the love you have for her."

Paige's eyes fell on where her parents were sitting. She'd seen them earlier, when they'd come up front to view the body and give the family their condolences. She was about to continue to roam the sanctuary with her eyes, but then her eyes froze . . . on Ryan. He hadn't been with her parents earlier, but now he was sitting with them. Her heart began doing somersaults. This was just all the added support she needed to get through these next few minutes.

Her eyes smiled at him. She hadn't seen him or talked to him since their return from the Dominican Republic. She'd been busy with Tamarra's family as they made funeral arrangements. Her intentions were to help get the family through this, and then Ryan would have all her time. She hadn't wanted to try to talk to him before the funeral, knowing she didn't have a solid block of time to dedicate to him without interruption. But she had vowed to herself, and she would vow to Ryan if he gave her a chance, that their life together would be uninterrupted from this point on. Anything she went through in life would be with him by her side . . . and vice versa.

"So as I prepare to sing this song," Paige continued, "it actually goes out to Tamarra and each and every one of you."

Paige took a deep breath and then exhaled. She closed her eyes and said a silent prayer. She opened her eyes and then looked at the pianist. The two made eye contact, and Paige gave her a nod. When the pianist hit the first few keys, almost everyone in the room recognized the popular Bette Midler song. After Paige sang the first line of "Wind Beneath My Wings," there were gasps and tears flowing from almost everyone in the sanctuary.

Paige sang that song from her gut, from the bottom of her heart. "Thank you, thank you. Thank God for you . . ." she sang. Paige was so overcome by emotion and in tears that she couldn't even get out the last five words of the song. So everyone in the sanctuary finished for her by saying, "The wind beneath my wings."

Paige slumped over and began to wail. A couple of the pastors got up to tend to her. By that time, Ryan had made it out of his seat, down the aisle, and up to the altar and had wrapped Paige in his arms. He escorted a weeping Paige away from the altar as the pianist continued to play the instrumental part of the song.

Instead of taking Paige back to her seat on the pew, Ryan escorted her outside the sanctuary. "You okay?" he asked her. "Come on. Let's go have a seat."

He walked her over to an area that looked more like a Starbucks than a church. There were coffeepots, tea, hot chocolate, and mugs with the church name and logo imprinted on them. There were tables and chairs. Ryan pulled out a chair for Paige to sit on. He turned another chair to face her and sat down in front of her. Paige was hunched over, in tears. Ryan rubbed her back with his hand. "It's okay. Baby, it's going to be okay. Everything is going to be okay."

Paige sniffed and then looked up. "Is it? Everything? Is it going to be okay with us?"

Ryan looked into the eyes of the woman he loved. They were red and swollen. He didn't reply.

"Is it, Ryan? Are we okay? Do you understand that I had to do this? I had to make this decision. If I had gotten on the plane, when I returned, Tamarra would have been . . ." She broke down in tears again. "I would have never been able to live with that, Ryan." Paige shook her head as she cried. "I love you so much. I want nothing more than to be Mrs. Coleman right now, but—"

"Then why don't you?" Ryan said, cutting Paige off.

Paige was confused. "Why don't I what?"

"Why don't you become Mrs. Coleman right now? I mean, it's not like we don't have the license," Ryan said. "It's still outside in my car from the day we picked it up downtown."

"Even though we didn't need it."

"Even though we thought we wouldn't need it. But it looks like we will, after all. That is, if you still want to marry me."

Paige jumped up. "If I still want to marry you? Heck, yeah, I still want to marry you. It was whether or not you wanted to marry me that I was worried about. I mean, you didn't call me but that one time when you were out of the country. I didn't hear from you when you got back."

"I knew you needed to focus on Tamarra and her family," Ryan said. "It wasn't the right time for us to try to discuss the matter," he reasoned. "I'm a selfish man when it comes to my wife. But we are all trumped by God. If I don't know anything else about you, I am one hundred percent certain that you are a woman of God. I know that He is the only man who will ever come before me. You had to be obedient, and like you said, had you not . . ." Ryan just shook his head. "Anyway, you did what you were called to do. You were where you were supposed to be." He took Paige's hands in his. "And now we are where we are supposed to be. Finally."

"Finally," Paige agreed.

"So does that mean you are still going to marry me?" Ryan asked Paige.

"Abso-freakin'-lutely!" Paige exclaimed and then threw her hands around Ryan's neck. "And I don't want to wait another day, either."

Ryan pulled away from Paige and looked her in the eye. "So what are you saying?"

Paige raised an eyebrow. "I can show you better than I can tell you."

"Pastor Fields, I know this might sound crazy," Paige said, unable to keep the tears from streaming down her face. "But I would like it if Ryan and I, along with two witnesses, could go back to your office and exchange our wedding vows. And I know this is your church, but Pastor Margie is my pastor, and I'd like for her to officiate the ceremony."

"Paige?" Pastor Margie was a little dumbfounded as she stood next to Pastor Fields out in the church vestibule. The service had ended. Tamarra was being cremated, in keeping with her last will and testament and the wishes she'd voiced to her parents, so there was no burial for everyone to go to. Folks were heading to the church cafeteria for the repast.

"Pastor, please don't judge me or think I'm being selfish. But I would love to turn what could possibly be the worst day of my life since the death of Norman into the best day of my life." Paige turned to Ryan, who stood next to her. "Which would entail starting a brand-new life with the love of my life." She placed her hands on Ryan's face. "My soul mate." She kissed his lips. "The love of my life."

"But, Paige, do you realize that in the future you would be celebrating your wedding anniversary on the funeral date of your best friend?" Pastor Margie stated, looking back and forth between Paige and Ryan.

Paige turned to her pastor, excited. "Absolutely, Pastor. That's the whole point of it all. Sometimes God removes people, places, and things from your life in order to make room for other people, places, and things. And it's not always about us. Today I mourn the loss of a best friend. I have to mourn that loss and put it to rest." Paige turned to Ryan again. "But I celebrate the life of a new best friend. I mourn the death of one and celebrate the life of another." Paige had to say it again, it was just so profound.

While Ryan and Paige stared into one another's eyes, Pastor Fields and Pastor Margie stared at each other as well.

"Well, Pastor," Pastor Margie said to Pastor Fields, "this is your church. It's your call."

Pastor Fields looked at Paige and Ryan. "Actually, it's God's church, and it's His call." He looked back at Pastor Margie. "And God is telling me the same thing He's telling you." He nodded toward the couple. "The same thing He's telling them."

Paige and Ryan held each other's hands, as if they were on a sinking ship and were not willing to let go. If one was going down, then so was the other.

"Which is . . . ?" Pastor Margie asked Pastor Fields.

"That if we don't marry these two right here and right now, in the next five minutes, they may end up in sin." Pastor Fields chuckled.

"And I don't want to be responsible for that, that's for sure." Pastor Margie chuckled as well.

Paige turned to both pastors. "Does that mean we have you guys' blessing?" Paige turned to her pastor. "That you'll marry Ryan and me?"

"We have the license in the car," Ryan interjected.

"Well then, go get it," Pastor Fields said.

Ryan took off, heading for the exit door.

"And I'll go get my parents," Paige said. "What about yours?" Paige called to Ryan. "And the kids? My brother? The Vanderdales might want to be here. Even Miss Nettie."

Ryan stopped in his tracks. He looked at Pastor Margie and Pastor Fields with questioning eyes.

"Folks are just now heading down to eat," Pastor Fields said. "Can you guys make some calls and get everyone here within the next hour or so?"

Paige and Ryan looked at each other with anxiety in their eyes. Ryan was the first to answer. "Yes, yes, we can. We'll start making phone calls."

"Fine. Then Pastor Margie and I will head on down to the cafeteria to be with the family," Pastor Fields told them.

Pastor Margie looked intently at Paige. "You sure about this, Paige?"

Paige looked Pastor Margie in the eye. "Pastor Margie, I've never been this sure about anything else in my life."

Pastor Margie smiled. "Very well then. We'll meet you guys up in Pastor Fields's office in what? About an hour?" Pastor Margie turned to Pastor Fields to make sure that was okay with him.

"Actually, I was thinking we should meet in my office with just the bride and groom to be, just for a brief counseling session. Then why not perform the actual ceremony in the sanctuary?" Pastor Fields said. "After all, isn't that where most weddings are held?" He looked at Paige and Ryan. "How does that sound to you guys?"

Ryan replied, "It sounds like God is doing just what He promised."

All Paige could do was shake her head, smile, and say, "Amen to that."

Chapter 34

"I now pronounce you husband and wife," Pastor Margie declared. "You may now lay one on your bride."

Everyone in attendance at the small ceremony chuckled as the groom leaned in and planted a never-ending kiss on the lips of his new bride. Applause sounded throughout the sanctuary.

When the bride and groom parted from their kiss, Paige looked down at Norma and Adele. They were covering their eyes, grossed out by the kissing scene. This made Paige crack up laughing.

Ryan looked over at his boys, who high-fived each other and then their father.

"What a beautiful couple those two make," Mrs. Vanderdale said as Mr. Vanderdale hugged her.

"I'm so happy for them," Samantha said.

"When we called you all up to be here to witness our wedding vows," Paige said, "who knew

that Miss Nettie and Stuart would exchange
vows right after us?"

"An unexpected double wedding ceremony,"
Ryan said. "I guess love is in the air."

"Thank you so much for letting us share the
spotlight with you all," Miss Nettie said as she
and Stuart walked over to them, hand in hand,
after sealing their vows with a kiss.

"This is so special," Paige said.

"Yes. I just wish my son could have been here
to see this," Miss Nettie said, putting her head
down.

It was obvious to Paige that there was something going on that she didn't know about. She
looked at Mrs. Vanderdale with questioning
eyes.

"Miss Nettie's son fell ill a couple days ago,"
Mrs. Vanderdale said. "He's in the hospital."

"I'm sorry to hear that, Miss Nettie," Paige
said. "I'll be sure to pray for him."

Miss Nettie looked up and smiled at Paige.
"Thank you."

Paige nodded. She was truly following scripture. She was praying for her enemies, even
though she really didn't see Blake as an enemy
anymore.

Mother Doreen walked over. "Look at God,"
she said. "Here we all came to gather on such a
sad occasion, and God turned it around for real."

"I know that's right," Deborah said as she approached.

The other friends Paige had been connected with at New Day Temple of Faith all approached. One by one they congratulated Paige and Ryan, as well as Miss Nettie and Stuart.

"Thank you all for being here," Paige said. "I know you didn't come for me, but I'm glad you all ended up being here for me."

"Aw," the women said in unison, and then they all went in for a group hug. And there they stood, near the altar. The New Day Divas, all back together again. And even though Tamarra had gone on to glory, her spirit was there. Smiling down on it all.

Paige could just feel the presence of her friend hovering over her, looking down on her. With all the women hugging in a circle, Paige looked upward to the heavens. She smiled. God loved her so. So much that He'd even given her, her own personal guardian angel, who truly was now the wind beneath her wings.

"That box goes upstairs. First room on the left," Paige instructed one of the movers.

"Yes, ma'am," he replied. Then he walked past Paige, up the walkway, and into the house.

Paige walked down to the FOR SALE sign that had been planted in the middle of Tamarra's yard. She stood by the sign.

"You all right?" Ryan asked as he walked up behind her.

Paige smiled. "I'm better than all right. I'm moving into our new home with my new husband. My new family."

Ryan kissed Paige on the cheek. "I think buying Tamarra's house was a perfect idea."

"Yeah. She worked hard after her divorce to live well and keep a good name. Buying her house gave her family the money to pay off all her debts. She died with a good name and with something she strived to maintain her entire life, which is good credit."

When Paige had suggested to Ryan that they buy Tamarra's house for the full market price instead of negotiating a short sale with the bank, he hadn't even argued with her. It had plenty of room for the family of six. The basement, which ran the full length of the house, provided enough space for Ryan's boys to have their own bedrooms. Paige and Ryan had taken Tamarra's master bedroom, while the girls had taken the other upstairs bedroom, which was a pretty nice size and had its own private bath. That was an amenity the girls were used to. Ryan and Paige had discussed possibly remodeling and adding on to the house.

"Well, I'm glad we could do that for her," Ryan said.

"Funny how everything worked out, isn't it?" Paige asked. "It's amazing what can happen when you're in God's will instead of God's way." And on that note, Paige unhooked the FOR SALE sign and replaced it with a SOLD sign.

Hand in hand, she and Ryan headed back into the house, where just three months ago Paige had ended a chapter in her life and now she was starting a whole new book. And as long as she allowed God to be the author, in the end, she would win.

Readers' Questions

1. Do you like how the author made you think that the novel was perhaps going to be about one thing, for example, the whole skin complexion issue, but it turned out to be about something totally different?
2. With so much going on in the novel, do you feel as though each issue/story line had closure?
3. Do you think as Paige's daughters get older, they are going to question their identity?
4. How do you feel about people who decide not to tell their children who their biological parents are and instead raise them to believe that others are their parents?
5. Miss Nettie felt she owed Paige an apology for the way her son treated her. Do you agree that mothers are to some degree responsible for the way their sons treat women?

6. Paige had to do quite a bit of forgiving in this book. If you were in her shoes, would you have been able to forgive Blake? How about Tamarra?

7. Mrs. Vanderdale wanted Paige to stay single so that she would always feel as though she played the role of her mother-in-law. How do you feel about a woman staying in contact with a past husband's family, even though she has remarried?

8. It took Paige finding out that Tamarra was on her deathbed for her to have a face-to-face with her and rekindle their friendship. Is there anyone you feel as though you might need to have a conversation with to mend things with before it's too late? If so, what is stopping you?

9. Paige had been known to be selfish a time or two. Do you feel it was a selfish act for her to turn the day of Tamarra's funeral into her wedding day?

10. Are there any New Day Diva characters whose full story you would like to know? If so, e-mail the author at enjoywrites@ aol.com to tell her who those characters are and why you would be interested in reading their stories.

11. *When All Is Said and Prayed* is Book 1 of the "Forever Divas" series. Have you read the novels in the "New Day Divas," "The Still Divas," and the "Always Divas" series, or is this your very first book from any Divas series? If you have not read the other books, after finishing this one, are you interested in trying another?

**Joylynn M. Ross is now writing as
BLESSEDselling author
E.N. Joy (Everybody Needs Joy)**

BLESSEDselling author E.N. Joy is the writer behind the five-book series "New Day Divas," the three-book series "Still Divas," the three-book series "Always Divas," and the forthcoming three-book series "Forever Divas," which have been coined "Soap Operas in Print." She is an *Essence* magazine best-selling author and has written secular books under the names Joylynn M. Jossel and JOY.

After thirteen years as a paralegal in the insurance industry, E.N. Joy finally divorced her career and married her mistress and her passion: writing. In 2000 she formed her own publishing company, where she self-published her books until landing a book deal with a major publisher. Her company has published *New York Times* and *Essence* magazine best-selling authors in the "Sinner Series." In 2004 E.N. Joy branched out into the business of literary consulting, providing one-on-one consultations and other literary services, such as ghostwriting, editing, professional read-throughs, and write behinds. Her clients include first-time authors, *Essence* magazine best-selling authors, *New York Times* best-selling authors, and entertainers. This award-winning author has also been sharing her literary expertise on conference panels in her hometown of Columbus, Ohio, as well as in cities across the country.

Not forsaking her love of poetry, E.N. Joy's latest poetic project is an ebook of poetry entitled *Flower in My Hair*. "But my spirit has moved in another direction," she says. Needless to say, she no longer pens street lit. (Two of her titles, *If I Ruled the World* and *Dollar Bill*, made the *Essence* magazine bestsellers' list. *Dollar Bill* was mentioned in *Newsweek* and has been translated into Japanese.) She no longer writes erotica or adult contemporary fiction, either (*An All Night Man,* a collection of novellas to which she and three other authors, including *New York Times* best-selling author Brenda Jackson, contributed, earned the Borders Best-Selling African American Romance Award.)

You can find this author's children's book *The Secret Olivia Told Me,* written under the name N. Joy, in bookstores now. *The Secret Olivia Told Me* received a Coretta Scott King Honor from the American Library Association. The book was also acquired by Scholastic Books and has sold over one hundred thousand copies. E.N. Joy has also penned a tween/young adult ebook entitled *Operation Get Rid of Mom's New Boyfriend* and a children's fairy-tale ebook entitled *Sabella and the Castle Belonging to the Troll.* Elementary and middle school children have fallen in love with reading and creative writing as a result of the readings and workshops E.N. Joy instructs in schools nationwide.

E.N. Joy is the acquisitions editor for Urban Christian, an imprint of Urban Books, the titles of which are distributed by Kensington Publishing Corporation. In addition, she is the artistic developer for a young girls' group called DJHK Gurls. She pens original songs, drama skits, and monologues for the group that deal with issues that affect today's youth, such as bullying.

You can visit BLESSEDselling author E.N. Joy at www.enjoywrites.com, or e-mail enjoywrites@aol.com.

Keep up with the Divas by liking the New Day Divas Fan Page on Facebook.

UC HIS GLORY BOOK CLUB

www.uchisglorybookclub.net

UC His Glory Book Club is the spirit-inspired brainchild of Joylynn Ross, an author and the acquisitions editor at Urban Christian, and Kendra Norman-Bellamy, an author for Urban Christian. It is an online book club that hosts authors of Urban Christian. We welcome as members all men and women who have a passion for reading Christian-based fiction.

UC His Glory Book Club pledges its commitment to providing support, positive feedback, encouragement, and a forum whereby members can openly discuss and review the literary works of Urban Christian authors.

There is no membership fee associated with UC His Glory Book Club; however, we do ask that you support the authors by purchasing their works, encouraging them, providing book reviews, and of course, offering your prayers. We also ask that you respect our beliefs and follow the guidelines of the book club. We hope to receive your valuable input, opinions, and reviews that build up, rather than tear down, our authors.

What We Believe:

—We believe that Jesus is the Christ, Son of the Living God.

—We believe that the Bible is the true, living Word of God.

—We believe that all Urban Christian authors should use their God-given writing abilities to honor God and to share the message of the written word that God has given to each of them uniquely.

—We believe in supporting Urban Christian authors in their literary endeavors by reading their titles, purchasing them, and sharing them with our online community.

—We believe that everything we do in our literary arena should be done in a manner that will lead to God being glorified and honored.

We look forward to online fellowship with you.

Please visit us often at:
www.uchisglorybookclub.net

Many Blessing to You!
Shelia E. Lipsey,
President, UC His Glory Book Club